Togail Bruidne DDerga = The Destruction of DDerga's Hostel

TOGAIL

BRUIDNE DÁ DERGA

THE DESTRUCTION OF DÁ DERGA'S HOSTEL

EDITED WITH TRANSLATION AND GLOSSARIAL INDEX

BY WHITLEY STOKES, D. C. L.

Foreign associate of the Institute of France.
Fellow of the British Academy for promoting historical, philosophical
and philological Studies.

PARIS (2ᵉ)
LIBRAIRIE ÉMILE BOUILLON, ÉDITEUR
67, RUE RICHELIEU, AU PREMIER
—
1902

La littérature épique de l'Irlande est la plus considérable et une des plus curieuses qui existent en Europe. Elle est restée complètement inédite jusqu'à la seconde moitié du xixe siècle. C'est en 1853 qu'a paru le premier texte épique irlandais qui ait vu le jour ; il fut édité par un des membres de l'*Ossianic Society*.

De l'année 1853 date le tome Ier de la collection publiée par cette compagnie On y trouve la « bataille de Gabra » *Cath Gabhra,* texte irlandais et traduction anglaise par Nicolas O'Kearney. Deux ans après a paru le tome II contenant « La fête de la maison de Conan de Cenn-Sleibe », *Feis tighe Chonain Chinn Shleibhe,* copiée et traduite en anglais par le même Nicolas O'Kearney. Dans le tome III de la même collection, 1857, M. Standish Hayes O'Grady a donné le texte et la traduction de « La poursuite de Diarmaid et Grainne, » *Toruigheacht Dhiarmuda agus Ghrainne.* Le tome V, 1860, contient « La promenade de la lourde compagnie, » *Imtheacht na tromdhaime* reproduite et mise en anglais par Connellan.

A l'année 1855, date du tome II de l'*Ossianic Society,* remonte la première publication d'Eugène O'Curry. Cette année il fit imprimer pour la *Celtic Society* deux textes irlandais avec traduction anglaise: « Bataille de Magh Leana, » *Cath Muighe Léana*, et « Cour faite à Moméra, » *Tochmarc Momera*. Puis en 1858 il inséra dans le tome Ier, p. 370-392, de l'*Atlantis*, le texte irlandais et la traduction de la première partie du morceau intitulé *Serig-lige Conculain ocus oen-ét Emire*, « Maladie qui alita Cuchulain et unique jalousie d'Emer ». Il termina cette édition en 1859 dans le tome II de l'*Atlantis*, p. 98-124. En 1862, l'année de sa mort, il donna au même recueil, t. III, p. 398-421, le *Longas mac n-Uisleand*, « Exil des fils d'Usnech, » qui fut suivie d'une œuvre posthume, *Oidhe chloinne Lir*, « Mort violente des enfants de Ler, » et *Aoidhe chloinne Turreann*, « Mort violente des enfants de Turenn, » t. IV, p. 114-227 (1863).

Dans un célèbre ouvrage d'O'Curry, *Lectures on the manuscript Materials of ancient Irish History*, 1861, réimprimé en 1878, on trouve de nombreuses analyses de textes épiques irlandais, considérés par lui comme historiques. La mort l'enleva avant qu'il eût publié la suite de ses leçons qui ne parut qu'en 1873.

D'autres savants irlandais marchèrent sur les traces d'O'Curry. En 1870, on vit paraître dans les *Proceedings of the Royal Irish Academy, Irish mss. Series*, Vol I, Part I, p 134-183, les deux morceaux intitulés *Tain bó Fraich*, « Enlèvement des vaches de Fraech, » et *Tochmarch Bec-fola*, « Cour faite à la femme au petit douaire », textes irlandais et traductions anglaise, publiés le premier morceau par J. O'Beirne Crowe, le second par Brian O'Looney O'Beirne Crowe, qui avait plus de bonne volonté que de science et de tenue, donna en 1871 au *Journal of the royal historical and archaeological Association of Ireland* le *Siabur carpait Conculainn*, « Fantôme du char de Cûchu- « lainn, » texte irlandais et traduction anglaise.

Un homme fort supérieur à lui fut William M. Hennessy

qui en septembre 1873 inséra au *Frasers Magazine* la traduction de la « Vision de Mac Conglinne; » à la même époque il donnait à la *Revue Celtique,* t. II, p. 86-93, le texte et la traduction de *Fotha catha Cnucha,* « Cause de la bataille de Cunucha ».

Il devait en 1889 publier pour la *Royal Irish Academy* dans *Todd Lectures series,* vol I, p. 2-58, *Mesca Ulad,* « Ivresse des guerriers d'Ulster ». C'est la révision d'un cours fait pendant l'année scolaire 1882-1883; la préface est datée de mars 1884.

Mais déjà étaient entrés en scène deux plus forts jouteurs que lui, MM Whitley Stokes et Ernst Windisch.

Dès 1876 M. Whitley Stokes avait donné à la *Revue Celtique,* t III, p. 175-185, un récit abrégé du « Meurtre de Cùchulainn » avec de nombreux extraits du texte irlandais qui est intitulé *Aided Conculainn.* De M. Whitley Stokes le même périodique a publié le texte irlandais avec traduction anglaise des morceaux suivants en 1887, « Le siège de Howth, » *Talland Etair* (t. VIII, p 47-64), en 1888, « Le voyage de Snedgus et de Mac Riagla, » *Imrum Snedgussa ocus Mic Riagla* (t IX, p. 14-25), et « Le voyage du bateau de Mael Duin, » *Immram curaig Mailduin* (t. IX, p 447-493); en 1891 « La [seconde] bataille de Moytura, » *Cath Maige Turedh* (t. XII, p. 52-130); en 1892 la légende de l'impôt appelé Boroma (t. XIII, p. 32-124) et « La bataille de Mag Mucrime, » *Cath Maige Mucrime* (t XIII, p: 426-474, cf. t XIV, p 95); en 1893, « Le voyage de la barque des Hui Corra, » *Iomramh churaig Huag Corra,* t. XIV, p 22-69, « Le meurtre de Goll, fils de Carbad et celui de Garb de Glenn Rige, » *Aided Guill maic Carbada ocus aided Gairb Glenne Rige* (t. XIV, p. 396-449); en 1900 « Le château de Dà Choca, » *Bruiden Dá Choca* (t. XXI, p. 388-402).

Les « *Irische Texte,* deuxième série, deuxième livraison, 1887, contenaient « Le meurtre des fils d'Usnech, » *Aided mac n-Uisnig*, avec traduction anglaise par le même savant qui dans la troisième série en 1891 a donné « Les aventures de Cormac dans la terre de promesse, » *Echtra Cormaic i tir Tairngiri*.

Dans la *Zeitschrift für Celtische Philologie*, t. III, p. 1-14, M. Whitley Stokes a inséré en 1899 « La destruction de Dind Rig, » *Orgain Dind Rig*.

C'est en 1879 qu'ont paru les premiers textes épiques irlandais publiés par M. Ernst Windisch « Les aventures de Condle « le Bossu, fils de Cond aux cent combats ou valant seul cent « guerriers, » *Echtra Condla Chaim maic Chuind Chetchathaig*, et « La cause de la bataille de Cnucha, » *Fotha catha Cnucha*, qui ont été imprimés à la fin de sa *Kurzgefasste irische Grammatik*, p. 118-123. Ce volume a été suivi en 1880 par le tome Ier des *Irische Texte*, dont les pages 59-145 et 197-311 sont occupées par des textes épiques irlandais. « L'exil des fils d'Usnech », *Longes mac n-Usnig*, « L'histoire du cochon de Mac Dà Thô, » *Scél mucci Mic Dá Thó*, « La cour faite à Etain, » *Tochmarc Etaine*, « La maladie qui alita Cûchulainn, » *Serglige Conculainn*; « Le festin de Bricriu, » *Fled Bricrend*. Le texte irlandais de ces documents n'est pas accompagné de traductions, mais un glossaire qui termine la *Kurzgefasste irische Grammatik*, un dictionnaire considérable placé à la fin du tome Ier des *Irische Texte* mettent le lecteur en état de traduire lui-même les récits irlandais contenus dans les deux volumes.

Dans les tomes suivants des *Irische Texte* M. Windisch a reproduit et traduit en allemand les monuments épiques irlandais dont voici les titres : « Festin de Bricriu et bannissement des fils de Dul Dermat, » *Fled Bricrend ocus Loinges Mac n-Dul Dermait*, « Enlèvement des vaches de Dartaid, » *Táin bó Dartada*; « Enlèvement des vaches de Flidais, » *Táin bó Flidais*; « Enlèvement des vaches de Regamon, » *Táin bó Regamain*;

« Enlèvement des vaches de Regamna, » *Táin bó Regamna*, seconde série, deuxième livraison, 1887; « De la génération des deux gardiens de cochons, » *De cophur in dá muccida*, troisième série, 1re livraison, 1891, « Cour faite à Ferb, » *Tochmarc Ferbe*, troisième série, 2e livraison, 1897

Les *Irische Texte* n'ont pas suffi à l'activité de M. Windisch qui a donné aux comptes rendus de la classe de philosophie et d'histoire de l'Académie royale de Saxe, *Genemain Aeda Slane*, « Naissance d'Aed Slane, » et *Noinden Ulad*, « Les guerriers d'Ulster en mal d'enfant » ou « La neuvaine des Ulates, » 1884.

L'émulation attira des concurrents à MM. Windisch et Whitley Stokes. Nous citerons en premier lieu M Kuno Meyer. Il a donné au tome V de la *Revue Celtique*, 1883-1885, « Les exploits de Find enfant, » *Macgnimartha Finn*, au tome VI du même périodique, 1883-1885, « La conception de Conchobar, » *Coimpert Conchobuir*, au tome X, 1889, « Les aventures de Nera, » *Echtra Nerai*, au tome XI, 1890, « La cachette de la colline de Howth, » *Uath beinne Etair*, et la plus ancienne rédaction de « La cour faite à Emer, » *Tochmarc Emire*; au tome XIII, 1892, « l'histoire de Baile aux douces paroles, » *Scél Baili binnberlaig*, et « Ronan tuant son fils, » *Fingal Ronain*; au tome XIV, 1893, deux courtes histoires concernant Finn et « Le marché de l'homme fort, » *Cennadh ind ruanado*, donnant la fin du *Fled Bricrend*, publié en 1880 d'après deux manuscrits incomplets par M Windisch dans le tome I des *Irische Texte*. Dès 1892, M. Kuno Meyer avait fait paraître en un volume le texte irlandais et la traduction anglaise de « La vision de Mac Conglinne, » *Aislinge Meic Conglinne*, dont Hennessy n'avait donné que la traduction. C'est de l'année 1895 que date le livre intitulé *The Voyage of Bran son of Febal to the Land of the Living* publié en collaboration par MM. Kuno Meyer et Alfred Nutt, où M. Kuno

Meyer a fait imprimer le texte irlandais et la traduction anglaise des pièces suivantes. « Voyage maritime de Bran fils de Febal et ses aventures, » *Imram Brain, maic Febail, ocus a echtra*; « Conception de Mongân, » *Compert Mongáin*, « Histoire où l'on raconte que Mongân était Find Mac Cumail et comment fut tué Fothad Airgdech, » *Scél asa m-berar co m-bad hé Find mac Cumail Mongán ocus ani dia fil ailed Fothaid Airgdig*, « Une histoire sur Mongân, *Scél Mongáin*, « Cause de la folie de Mongân, » *Tucait baile Mongáin*, Conception de Mongân et amour de Dub Lacha pour Mongân, » *Compert Mongáin ocus serc Duibe Lacha do Mongán*. En 1897 le même auteur a inséré dans le tome Ier de la *Zeitschrift für celtische Philologie*, deux récits irlandais concernant Find, l'un qu'il intitule Find et Grainne, l'autre consistant en deux fragments relatifs à la mort du héros irlandais.

En 1892 on avait vu reparaître M. Standish Hayes O'Grady, dont la *Silva Gadelica* en deux volumes in-8, l'un de textes irlandais, l'autre de traductions anglaises, contient un trop grand nombre de morceaux épiques pour que nous en donnions ici la nomenclature

La même année le père Edmund Hogan avait donné dans *Todd Lectures Series IV* le texte irlandais et la traduction anglaise de « La bataille de Ross na Rig sur Boyne, » *Cath Ruis na Rig for Bóinn*

En 1898, Miss Eleanor Hull a publié chez David Nutt, le recueil de traductions anglaises qu'elle a intitulé · *Cuchullin Saga*, et 1899 est la date des deux premiers volumes édités par l'*Irish Text* Society, dont le deuxième contient « Le festin de Bricriu »

En 1901, M Rudolf Thurneysen a fait paraître ses *Sagen*

aus dem alten Irland, traductions allemandes de quatorze morceaux épiques irlandais.

Déjà la *Zeitschrift für vergleichende Sprachforschung,* t. XXVIII, 1887, avait publié l'analyse par M. H. Zimmer de six pièces importantes dont deux inédites, les deux plus considérables de la littérature épique irlandaise Táin bó Cúalngi, « Enlèvement des vaches de Cooley, » p. 442-475, et *Orgain* ou *Togail bruidne Dá Derga,* « Destruction du château de Dá Derga, » p. 556-563. Les résumer, en sautant à pieds joints sur les passages difficiles, était plus aisé que de les éditer et de les traduire en entier.

Hennessy avait entrepris la publication de ces deux documents et n'avait pu aboutir[1]. M. E. Windisch fait imprimer le texte et la traduction du premier, qui paraîtra prochainement, et nous sommes heureux d'offrir aux érudits le texte et la traduction anglaise du second, dus à la plume savante de M. Whitley Stokes et extraits du t. XXII de la *Revue Celtique* où sa bienveillance l'a inséré.

H D'A DE J.

---

1 Hennessy est mort le 13 janvier 1889, à l'âge de 60 ans

THE DESTRUCTION OF DÁ DERGA'S HOSTEL

This ancient tale, apart from its pathos and beauty, deserves attention from the facts that it turns on the primeval belief in the ruin wrought by the violation of tabus, that it contains some evidence of the survival of totemism[1], and that it has suggested the noblest English poem ever written by an Irishman[2]. The following edition is based on eight vellum copies, all more or less imperfect. They are as follows

1. LU. The *Lebor na hUidre* or Book of the Dun, a MS. of the end of the eleventh or beginning of the twelfth century, in the library of the Royal Irish Academy Here the beginning of the tale is lost — the first words of it being *. airiut. Nate em,* § 21 infra, p. 83ᵃ of the facsimile, Dublin, 1870.

2. YBL. The Yellow Book of Lecan, a MS. mostly of the fifteenth century, in the library of Trinity College, Dublin, formerly marked H. 2. 16, but now (according to Dr Abbott's catalogue) 1318. The tale here begins at p. 91, and ends on p 104, of the photolithograph published in 1896. It omits the descriptions of many members of Conaire's retinue, which are contained in LU p 93 et seq Though YBL is much later in date than LU. it preserves some Old-Irish forms which have been modernised in the elder copy.

3 YBL² In YBL. are two pages (432, 433) which contain the beginning of our tale in a later hand and corrupt spelling.

---

[1] Nettlau, Rev Celt., XII, 253, and see Salomon Reinach, Rev Celt, XXI, 287.
[2] *Conary,* by the late Sir Samuel Ferguson

This fragment commences with the words *Bui righ aonn ui airegda for Eriinn*, and ends with · *doberlt sidhe .u iii. cumala*, § 8 infra It will here be denoted by YBL².

4. H. This codex, of various dates and handwritings, is also in the library of Trinity College, Dublin It was formerly marked H 2. 17, but is now numbered 1319. It contains three fragments of our tale in a hand, I think, of the fifteenth century. The first begins (p. 477) imperfectly with the words *fosnardm rigrall Temrach Amra, n-amro, ol ind slogh*, § 15 infra, and ends *Cia feras an failler*, § 39 infra The second fragment begins *Atchiusar tet, ol sisr, conach ernabor caer na carnar diot*, § 62, infra, and ends *gala mathgamna 7 brothor leoman*, § 92 infra. The third fragment begins *Ro bor tarum ina collud in maethoclach*, § 101 infra, and ends imperfectly with: *imarresi 7il ni bo*, § 111 For a loan of this MS. I am indebted to the Board of Trinity College

5. F The Book of Fermoy This fifteenth century vellum, now in the library of the Royal Irish Academy, contains in pp 213-216 two fragments of our tale The first begins imperfectly with *rarum inna codluth in moetorclach*, § 101 infra. The second begins (p 214), with *Adcomnarc and nonbor ind imdar*, § 216 infra, and ends imperfectly (p 216) with *oencoss 7 uenlaim 7 mucc*, § 136 infra

6 S. The Stowe MS 992 (now marked D 4. 2) is kept in the library of the Royal Irish Academy. K. Meyer, Rev Celt , VI, 173, 190, XI, 435-436, says that it was written at Frankford, King's Co in 1300 This excellent MS contains three fragments of our tale The first (fo. 85¹-90¹²) extends from the beginning (*Bar ri amrai airegda*, etc) to the end of § 111 infra. The second from § 126 to the second line of § 133 (*o gabars trebad ni ro)* The third from *a ben, ar sa, in cuil* etc § 161 infra, to the colophon *Comd é cath na maidne ar Brindin Da Berg* conice sin FINIT.

7 Eg Egerton 1782, a MS. in the British Museum, described in M d'Arbois de Jubainville's *Essai d'un Catalogue*,

p. XXVI, XXVII. The copy of our tale contained in this MS may be said to belong to a second recension, which was preceded by three foretales *(remscéla)*, viz *Tesbaid Étaine ingine Ailella, Tromdam Echach Aireman* and *Aisnéis Side Maic ind Óc do Mider Breg Leith in a síd* (LU 99ª 13, Eg 120ᵇ 1). It commences (f 118ª), with an account of Eochaid's recapture of his wife Étáin from the elfking Mider of Brí Léith[1]. This incident, according to the second recension, caused the vendetta between the elves and Eochaid's descendants, which resulted in the cruel death of his great-grandson Conaire. Then (fo. 118ᵇ 2) we have the marriage of Cormac « the man of three gifts » to Eochaid's daughter, called, like her mother, Étáin. With his desertion of Étáin because she bore daughters only, Eg. begins to agree almost verbatim with YBL and St. (§ 4 infra), and from fo. 120ᵇ 1 (. *orut Naicem, oll seisium*) with LU. (§ 21 infra) But Eg contains many additions and variants, which are mentioned in Nettlau's able articles on our tale, or in the footnotes and appendix to the present edition On the other hand, it has lost three leaves, one corresponding with LU p 88ª 26, another with LU from 88ᵇ 7, and a third with LU p 93, l 4—95ª 5.

8. Eg [1]. Egerton 92, another MS in the British Museum written in 1453 (Rev Celt, XI, 436) This contains (f. 18) two fragments of our tale, the first extending from the beginning to l. 3 of § 54 *(Tá céin, for Ingcel)*, the second from *iarna rathugud. Teit corrainc*, § 72, to the end of the description of Conaire, § 100.

So much has been already written about the *Bruden Dá Derga* that it is here necessary only to give a list of the chief notices of the subject.

Rorannad Heriu iarsin. hi cóic, iar n-arcain *Conare Mór maic Etarsceoil hi mBrudin Dá Derga*, *Thereafter Ireland was divided into five, after the destruction of Conaire the Great, son of Etarscél, in the Hostel of Dá Derga*, Annals of Tigernach, Rev Celt., XVI, 405

---

1. See the Dindsenchas of Raith Essa, LL 163ª

Togail Bruidne Da Berga[1] (ut alii aiunt, sed certe falluntur) for Conaire Mór *The sack of Dá Derga's Hostel, on Conaire the Great, as some say, but they are surely wrong*, Ibid., p. 411.

(According to the former entry the Destruction took place soon after the battle of Actium, B C 31. According to the latter, the date was A D 43 or thereabouts)

Ar bátar fri hErenn cen smacht rig forro fri re un mbliadan iar ndith Conaire i mBruidin Dá Derca, LU. 46^a 7-9, *for the men of Ireland had no king's authority upon them for the space of seven years after the death of Conaire in Dá Derga's Hostel.*

Orgain Bruidne úi Dergæ, LU 99^1 12 (slicht Libair Dromma snechta)

Et Togail Bruidne úi Dergga, list of the *primscéoil*, LL 189^b last line

No Togail Bruidne dá Derga, Rawl. B 512, fo 109^b 2, and Harl. 5280, fo 47

Togail Tigi Nechtain *ocus* Bruidne Da Derg *ocus* Da Choc. Harl 432, fo 3^b 2, printed in *Ancient Laws*, I, 46

Gilla Coemáin's chronological poems, LL. 129^1 37-40, 131^a 20, 21.

The dindsenchas of Benn Etair, LL 195^a of Ráith Esa, LL 163^a of Ráith Cnámrossa, Rev Celt, XV, 333

The Annals of the Four Masters, A M 5160.

O'Curry, *MS Materials of Irish History*, pp. 258-259

— *Manners and Customs*, I, 20, 72, 74, 219, 306, 335, 350, 355, 370, 379, 382, 383, 390, 431, 433, 447, 462, 463, III, 136-151 (with thirty extracts, all, save two, inaccurate), 165, 183, 184, 189, 190 (with four extracts, all inaccurate), 367 368

d'Arbois de Jubainville, *Essai d'un Catalogue*, 180-181

Zimmer, Zeitschr. f. vergl Sprachforschung, XXVIII, 554-585

---

[1] Here *Berga* (i e *Bherga*) is a corruption of *Derga* (i. e *Dherga*) as *Iubhal* « Jew » of *Iudhal*, etc The gen sg *dá* in *Bruiden dá Derga, dá Choca, dá Reo* (nom sg *Dau*, Trip Life 350, l 30, LL 319^c 17) may stand for *Dáu*, and be cognate, perhaps, with Lat *Dāvus*, a common name for a slave in Plautus and Terence Cf the names of which the first element is *gille, mael, mug*, Rhys, *Celtic Britain*, 259

Zimmer, Zeitschr. f deutsches Alterthum, XXXV, 13.
Nettlau, *Rev. Celt*, XII, 229, 444, XIII, 252; XIV, 137.

In the present edition the version in the Yellow Book of Lecan has been followed as far as the first five words of § 21. Thence to the end the version in Lebor na hUidre has been taken as basis. Letters and words omitted by the scribe are supplied in square brackets All various readings of any importance are given in the footnotes The Appendix contains various illustrative passages, which owing to their length, could not be printed at the bottom of the pages. The Glossarial Index will, I trust, be found a useful supplement to Prof Windisch's Worterbuch The translation must be regarded as merely tentative — so many are the ἅπαξ λεγόμενα in the Irish text, so obvious the corruptions, which I, at least, am unable to cure

W. S

INCIPIT TOGAIL BRUIDNE DA DERGA
(H 2 16, col. 716, facs 91ᵃ)

1. Bui ri amra airegda for Erinn, Eochaid Feidleach a ainm Doluid¹ feacht*us* n-ann dar Aenach mBreg Leith, *co*n*a*ccai in mnai for ur in tobair, 7 cir chuirrél² argit *co* n-ec*o*r de or acthe³ oc folcud al-luing argit, 7 ceithri heoin oir fui*r*ri, 7 gleorgemai beccai di charrmogul chorcrai hi forlleascuib⁴ na luingi Brat cas corcra, foloi⁵ chain aicthe⁶ Dualldai airgdidi ecoirside, [milech] de or oibinniu isi[n] bratt Lene leburchulpatach, is⁷ i chotut[s]lemon dei shittu uainide fo de*r*ginliud oir impi. Tuagmila ingantai di or 7 airget⁸ for a bruindi[b] 7

---

1. Toluid St
2. sic Ir Texte, I, 119 cir chuirrel YBL St. cir coréil YBL²
3. acce St
4. forflescaib St
5. folói St. folói YBL²
6. aicce St aice, aicæ YBL²
7. os St
8. d'or 7 d'argat YBL²

a formnaib 7 a guallib isind lene di cach leith. Taitned¹ fria in grian cobba foderg² dona feraib taidleach ind oir frisin ngrein asin t[s]ittu uain[i]di. Da trilis n-orbuidi for a cind. fige ceithri ndual ceachtar nde, 7 mell for rind cach duail Ba cosmail leo dath ind foilt sin fri barr n ailestair hi samrad, *nó* fri dergór iar ndenam a datha.

Beginneth the Destruction of Dá Derga's Hostel.

1 *There was a famous and noble king over Erin, named Eochaid Feidlech Once upon a time he came over the fairgreen of Bri Leith³, and he saw at the edge of a well a woman with a bright comb of silver adorned with gold, washing in a silver basin wherein were four golden birds and little, bright gems of purple carbuncle in the rims of the basin. A mantle she had, curly and purple, a beautiful cloak, and in the mantle silvery fringes arranged, and a brooch of fairest gold A kirtle she wore, long, hooded, hard-smooth, of green silk, with red embroidery of gold Marvellous clasps of gold and silver in the kirtle on her breasts and her shoulders and spaulds on every side The sun kept shining upon her, so that the glistening of the gold against the sun from the green silk was manifest to men On her head were two golden-yellow tresses, in each of which was a plait of four locks, with a bead at the point of each lock. The hue of that hair seemed to them like the flower of the iris in summer, or like red gold after the burnishing thereof*

2. IS and bui oc taithbiuch a fuilt dia folcud, 7 a da laim tria derc⁴ a sedlaig immach Batar gilithir sneachta n-óenaidche⁵ na di doit, 7 batar maethchoiri, 7 batar dergithir sian slebe⁶ na da gruad nglanailli⁷. Badar duibithir druimne daeil na da malach⁷. Batar inand 7 frais⁸ do nemannaib a deta ina

1 Taithmidh YBL²
2 corbo aiderg St gumba oiderg, YBL²
3 Midir's elfmound, west of Ardagh in the co Longford See the dindsenchas, Rev Celt , XVI, 78
4 tre deirc YBL²
5 noenaichde YBL naonhoidhche YBL² n-oenoidch Ir Texte, I, 119·
6 sión slebe St YBL²
7 *Om* St gruaid YBL²
8 leg frass munn 7 fras, YBL²

cind. Bat*ar* glasithir bug*h*a na di shuil. Bat*ar* d*e*rgithi*r* par-
taing¹ na beoil. Bat*ar* forarda mine maethgela na da gualaind.
Bat*ar* gelglana sithfota na mera. Bat*ar* fota na lama. Ba gilithir uan tuindi in taeb seṅg fota tlaith min maeth am*al* olaind.
Bat*ar* teithblaithi sleamongeala na di sliasait. Bat*ar* cruind-
bega caladgela na di² glun. Bat*ar* gerrgela indildirgi na de²
lurgain. Bat*ar* coirdirgi iaraildi³ na da⁴ shail. Cid riagail focerta forsna traigthib sin⁵ is ing m'adchotad egoir⁶ n-indib,
acht cia-tormaisead feoil na fortche foraib. Solusruidiud inn
esce⁷ ina saeragaid, urthocbail uailli ina minmailgib, ruithen
suirghe ceachtar a da rigrosc⁸. Tibri ainiusa ceachtar a da gruad,
*co n-*amlud indtibsen do ballaib bithchorcra *co n*deirgi fola laig,
7 araill eile co sol*us* gili sneachta. Bocmaerdachd banamail ina
glor, cem⁹ fosud n-inmalla¹⁰ acci, tochim rignaidi le¹¹. Ba si
tra as caemeam 7 as aildeam 7 as coram atconnarcadar¹² suili
doine de mnáib domain. Ba doig leo bed a sidaib di. Ba fria
asbreth « cruth cách co hEtain », « caem cach co hEtain¹³ ».

2. *There she was, undoing her hair to wash it, with her arms
out through the sleeve-holes of her smock. White as the snow of one
night were the two hands, soft and even, and red as foxglove were
the two clear-beautiful cheeks. Dark as the back of a stag-beetle the
two eyebrows. Like a shower of pearls were the teeth in her head.
Blue as a hyacinth were the eyes. Red as rowan-berries the lips.
Very high, smooth and soft-white the shoulders. Clear-white and
lengthy the fingers. Long were the hands. White as the foam of a
wave was the flank, slender, long, tender, smooth, soft as wool.*

1. partaic St.
2. da St.
3. iarslaidi St.
4. di St.
5. sic YBL². *Om.* YBL.
6. ma cor ní ecoir St. mát cottat egoir YBL².
7. Solusruided mi*n*ce St.
8. Tibhra St.
9. ccim St.
10. imínmalla St.
11. YBL² omits this and the two preceding sentences.
12. atcondcatar St. attcondcattar YBL².
13. Cf. *cossin n-óin* .i. *co Crist* (gl. usque ad unum), Wb. 2ª 21 (ad Rom., III, 12).

Polished and warm, sleek and white (were) the two thighs Round and small, hard and white the two knees Short and white and rulestraight the two shins. Justly straight, ... beautiful the two heels If a measure were put on the feet it would hardly have found them unequal, unless the flesh of the coverings should grow upon them The bright radiance of the moon was in her noble face: the loftiness of pride in her smooth eyebrows. the light of wooing in each of her regal eyes A dimple of delight in each of her cheeks, with an amlud [1] *(?) in them (at one time) of purple spots with redness of a calf's blood, and at another with the bright lustre of snow. Soft womanly dignity in her voice; a step steady and slow she had · a queenly gait was hers Verily, of the world's women 'twas she was the dearest and loveliest and justest that the eyes of men had ever beheld. It seemed to them (king Eochaid and his followers) that she was from the elfmounds. Of her was said . « Shapely are all till (compared with) Étáin », « Dear are all till (compared with) Étáin. »*

3. Gabais saint in ri[g] n-impe focetoir, 7 daraide [2] fer dia muindt*ir* riam di[s]a] hastud fo*r*acind Imchomarcair in ri scela di, 7 asbe*rt* fria ina sloindiud « Inum biasa uair coibligi lat? » ol Eochaid.

Is *ed* doroachtmar fo*r*t foesam sunn [3], or si

C*es*t, can deit 7 can dolud [4]? ol Eochaid

Ni *ansa*, ol si Etain missi, ingen Etain ri eochraidi a sidaib. Atusa sund fichit mblia*dan* o ro génar [5] i sid. Fir in tside, et*er* rigu 7 chaemu, oc*um* chuindchid, 7 ni etas fo*r*m [6] fobithin rot-car*usa* [7 tucus] seirc le*l*bhan o ba tualaing [7] labartha ar th' airscelaib 7 t'am*us*, 7 nit-acca riam, 7 atot-gen [8] foc*é*toir ar do thuarascbail, is tu doroacht [9] iar*um*

---

1 The late W M Hennessy rendered this word by « dappling ».
2 rola Ir T, I, 120 dorruide, St dorathte YBL[2]
3 Dorochtamar ci ad boisam sunn, St doro*ich*tamar a boisam sunn YBL[2]
4 dolund, YBL doluidh YBL[2] dollot, Ir Texte, I, 120 dolluid, St
5 genair, YBL YBL[2] St genar, I T, I, 120
6 ni hetus huaim fess ri fer dib, I T, I, 120
7 rotcha*rusa* seirc lelbain obsa tualang St roca*rusa* searc lealu*i* opsa tualaing, YBL[2]
8 atotathgén, I T, I, 120
9 doruachtamar I T, I, 120

Ni ba taig[1] drochcarad hi cein dait em, ol Eochaid. Rotbia [YBL. col. 717, p. 91ᵇ] failte, 7 leicfider cach bean do mnaib airiut, 7 is acut t'aen*ur* biasa cein bas miad lat[2].

Mo thinnscra coir dam, or si, 7 mo riar iar suidhiu.

Rot-bia, ol Eochaid.

Doberthar *secht* cumala di.

3. *A longing for her straightway seized the King; so he sent forward a man of his people to detain her. The king asked tidings of her and said, while announcing himself: « Shall I have an hour of dalliance with thee? »*

« 'Tis for that we have come hither under thy safeguard », quoth she.

« Query, whence art thou and whence hast thou come? » says Eochaid.

« Easy to say », quoth she. « Étáin am I, daughter of Etar, king of the cavalcade from the elfmounds. I have been here for twenty years since I was born in an elfmound. The men of the elfmound, both kings and nobles, have been wooing me; but nought was gotten from me, because ever since I was able to speak, I have loved thee and given thee a child's love for the high tales about thee and thy splendour. And though I had never seen thee, I knew thee at once from thy description: it is thou, then, I have reached. »

« No « seeking of an ill friend afar » shall be thine », says Eochaid. « Thou shalt have welcome, and for thee every (other) woman shall be left (by me), and with thee alone will I live so long as thou hast honour ».

« My proper bride-price to me! » she says, « and afterwards my desire. »

« Thou shalt have (both) », says Eochaid.

Seven cumals[3] are given to her[4].

---

1. tochuiriuth, Ir. Texte, I, 120. ní ba taig .i. ni ba sag*id*, YBL². Cf. taigid = to-ṡaigid § 4.
2. an. céin bus miadh latt, YBL².
3. i. e twenty-one cows.
4. The first three paragraphs agree with *Tochmarc Étáine*, §§ 3, 4, 5, as printed in Ir. Texte, I, 119-120.

4 Atbail in rí iarum .i. Eochaid Feidl*ech*.

IAr cind aimsire leicid Cormac (.i. rí Ulad), fear na tri mbuad[a], ingin [n]Ech*dach*, daig ba haimrit *acht* ingen rug do Chorm*a*c iar ndenum in brothchain dobe*r*t¹ a mathair di .i. in bean a sidaib. Is and asbe*r*t si fria a mathair Is cuil a ndaradais dam², bid ingen nos-ber³.

Ni ba bison⁴, ol a mathair, « biaid taigid rig furri.

4 *Then the king, even Eochaid Feidlech, dies (leaving one daughter named, like her mother, Étáin, and wedded to Cormac, king of Ulaid)*

After the end of a time Cormac, king of Ulaid, « the man of the three gifts », forsakes Eochaid's daughter, because she was barren save for one daughter that she had borne to Cormac after the making of the pottage which her mother — the woman from the elfmounds — gave her. Then she said to her mother « Bad is what thou hast given me it will be a daughter that I shall bear »

« That will not be good », says her mother, « a king's pursuit(?) will be on her. »

5 Dob*er* Corm*a*c⁵ iar*u*m arisi a⁶ mnai .i. Etain, 7 ba si a riar side, ingen na mná ro leigead rempe⁷ do marbad. Nisleicide⁸ Cormac dia mathair di[a] altromm. Nos-berait iar*u*m a da mog*a*d-seom dochum chuithi, 7 tibidsi gen gaire friu oca tabairt isin chuithi⁹. Doluid a ng*u*s n-airriu¹⁰ iar*u*m Nosberad il-lías ngamna buachaille nEterscele m*a*ic h*ui* Iair righ

---

1 in brothchain dombert Eg 118ᵇ 2 in brochain dobert, St YBL²
2 Is cuil dorata dam Eg Is cuil doratus dam, St As cuil a ndorat*us* dam, YBL² The *cuil* is gen sg of *col* Strachan compares the phrase *ba meite*
3 nomber Eg nombera St.
4 Ni ba biason Eg nipa son YBL 124 YBL² Ni ba son St
5 Doperr Cormac (i righ Ulad), YBL²
6 an YBL a St
7 ro leiccedh roimpe, YBL²
8 Nir'leig Eg Nisleicide St
9 For the Egerton version of this and the following sentence see Appendix A
10 Doluid a ngus n-airri, St

Temrach, 7 rosn-altar¹ *side* co mbo druinech maith, 7 ni bui i nHerind in*gen* rig bad chaimiu² oldas.

5. Then Cormac weds again his wife, even Étáin, and this was his desire, that the daughter of the woman who had before been abandoned [i. e. his own daughter] should be killed. So Cormac would not leave the girl to her mother to be nursed. Then his two thralls take her to a pit, and she smiles a laughing smile at them as they were putting her into it. Then their (kindly) nature came to them. They carry her into the calfshed of the cowherds of Etirscél, great-grandson of Iar, king of Tara, and they fostered her till she became a good embroideress; and there was not in Ireland a king's daughter dearer than she.

6. Dogni[th] teach fichti forche³ leosum di, cen dor*us* n-ann et*er*, *acht* seinist*er* 7 forleas nama. Airighit did*u* munt*er* Et*er*scele an teach hisin, 7 adar leo ba biadh bui ann lasna buachailli. Luid fear dib *co n*dercachai⁴ forsin forless, *co n*-accai in n-ingin rochaim roalaind isin tig. Adfiadar don rig anisin. Tiagait a munter uadh fochetoir dia breith cen athchomarc [ona buachaillip — Eg.] 7 do sharugud in tigi, ar ba haimrit in ri, 7 dorairngiread do no berad bean mac dó 7 nad festa a cenél⁵.

Asb*ert*⁶ in rí did*u*: Isi in bean sin dorairngiread damsa.

6. A fenced (?) house of wickerwork was made by them (the thralls) for her, without any door, but only a window and a skylight. King Eterscél's folk espy that house and suppose that it was food that the cowherds kept there. But one of them went and looked through the skylight, and he saw in the house the dearest, beautifullest maiden! This is told to the king, and straightway he sends his

---

1. rosnaltatar, St. rosnalltatta*r* YBL².
2. bu caimiu, St.
3. fithi f*orce* St. fithte forcæ YBL². forcho Eg.
5. sic St. *co*nderca YBL. *co*ndercaidi YBL².
4. Et dorairrngertsit a druidhi don righ co mberath ben na finnfaithea cenel mac dond righ, Eg. 119ᵃ 1. 7 dorairrngered dó no berad ben na festa cenel mac do, St. Et dorairngireth dó nob*er*a ben mac dó natt feasta a cinel.
6. Atb*ert*, St.

people to break the house and carry her off without asking the cow herds. For the king was childless, and it had been prophesied to him (by his wizards) that a woman of unknown race would bear him a son

Then said the king « This is the woman that has been prophesied to me ! »

7 INtan didu bui ann dadaig¹ conacca in n-en forsin forless addochum², 7 facaib a enchendaich³ for lar in tigi, 7 luid chuict[h]e⁴, 7 ardagaib⁵, co n-epert som fria : « Dofilter chucut ón rig do choscrad do thige 7 dot bruth chuci ar eigin, 7 bia⁶ torrach uaimsea, 7 bera mac de, 7 ni marba⁷ eonu in mac sin, 7 bid *Conaire* [mac Mese Buachalla] a ainm, ar ba Mes Buachalla a hainm-si dano

7 Now while she was there next morning she saw a Bird on the skylight coming to her, and he leaves his birdskin on the floor of the house, and went to her and captured her⁸, and said : « They are coming to thee from the king to wreck thy house and to bring thee to him perforce. And thou wilt be pregnant by me, and bear a son, and that son must not kill birds⁹ And « Conaire, son of Mess Buachalla » shall be his name, for hers was Mess Buachalla, « the Cowherds' fosterchild » ¹⁰

8 *Ocus* breatha-si¹¹ cosin righ n-iarum, 7 lotar a hoite le, 7 aranai[s]si dond rig¹², 7 dobert side seacht cumala disi 7

---

1   issin aidhqm Eg
2   dar in forles dia dochum, Eg
3   forfacbaid a enchennaig, St
4   chuice, St
5   luith chuici *co nderna coiblige fric*, Eg
6   acht chena atai, Eg
7   nirra marba Eg
8   il la saisit et la posseda
9   cf § 13 This passage indicates the existence in Ireland of totems, and of the rule that the person to whom a totem belongs must not kill the totem-animal see Rev Celt , XII, 243, XXI, 286 n
10 *meas i dalta*, O'Cl
11 ruccuth sí, Eg   bretha si St
12 rohernas in ingiun iarsin dond rich, Eg

.seacht¹ cumala² aili dia haitib. Ocus dognithea³ airig doib⁴
iarsin, comdar reachtaidi⁵ uile, conid de ataat in da Feidlimid
Reachtaidi. Ocus bert-si iarum mac dond rig .i. Conaire mac
Mesi Buachalla. Ocus batar he a tri drindrosci⁶ forsin rig .i.   *wishes*
altrom a maic eter [t]heora aicce⁷ .i. na haiti⁸ rosn-altadar 7
na⁹ Maine Milscothacha, 7 atacomnaicsi fadeisin¹⁰, 7 adbert-si
inti dudrastar¹¹ ni don mac so di feraib Herind dobera dinaib
teoraib trebaib-sea ar chomet in maic¹².

8. *And then she was brought to the king, and with her went her
fosterers, and she was betrothed to the king, and he gave her seven
cumals and to her fosterers seven other cumals. And afterwards
they were made chieftains, so that they all became legitimate, whence
are the two Fedlimthi Rechtaidi. And then she bore a son to the
king, even Conaire son of Mess Buachalla, and these were her
three urgent prayers to the king, to wit, the nursing of her son
among three households (?), that is, the fosterers who had nur-
tured her, and the (two) Honeyworded Mainès, and she herself is
(the third); and she said that such of the men of Erin as should
wish (to do) aught for this boy should give to those three households
for the boy's protection.*

9. Alta iarum samlaid, 7 ro feadadar¹³ fir Herend in mac so
isin laithiu ir-ro genair fochétoir, 7 ro alta in maic aile lesin
.i. Fer le 7 Fer gar 7 Fer rogein, tri maic hui Duind Desa ind
fendeada .i. fear sochraidhi¹⁴ do shochraidi a Muclesi.   *Eg. Mac*

Sochraite   = so + cara

1. .u.iii. YBL².
2. Here ends YBL².
3. dorighnit, Eg.
4. dib St.
5. rechtairi, Eg. rechtaire St.
6. 7 ba hiat a tri drindruisc, St.
7. i teora aicci St.
8. haiti St. haici YBL.
9. na da St.
10. atcomnaic e bodesin St.
11. duthrastar St.
12. coemad in mic St.
13. rochúalatar Eg.
14. sochraid St.

9. So in that wise he was reared, and the men of Erin straightway knew this boy on the day he was born And other boys were fostered with him, to wit, Fer Le and Fer Gar and Fer Rogein, three great-grandsons of Donn Désa the champion, an army-man of the army from Muc-lesi (?)

10. Ro batar *didu* teora buada for *Conaire* 1 buaid cluaisi[1] 7 buaid radairc 7 buaid n-airdmesa, 7 ro muin buaid cach comalta dia tri comaltaib dibsin[2]. *Ocus* nach[3] sere 1 dognithea dosom doteigtis di a cethroi[4]. Citis teora seire dognithi dosom no teigead cach fear dib dia sere Inund eitiud 7 gaiscead [YBL col 718, p. 92ᵃ] 7 dath each doib a ceathrur.

10 Now Conaire possessed three gifts, to wit, the gift of hearing and the gift of eyesight and the gift of judgment, and of those three gifts he taught one to each of his three fosterbrothers. And whatever meal was prepared for him, the four of them would go to it Even though three meals were prepared for him each of them would go to his meal The same raiment and armour and colour of horses had the four

11. Maib in ri iarum .i. Eterscele *Congrenar* tairbfeis[5] la firu Herend .i. no marbtha[6] tarb leo, 7 no ithead oenfear a saith de, 7 no ibead a enbruithi, 7 no chanta or firindi[7] fair ina ligiu Fer atchichead[8] ina chotlad is e bad ri, 7 atbaildis a beoil intan adbeiread gai.

11. Then the king, even Eterscéle, died A bull-feast[9] is gathered(?) by the men of Erin, (in order to determine their future king) that is, a bull used to be killed by them and thereof one man

---

[1] n estechto Eg
[2] 1 buaid roderce la Fer ngair, buaid n-eistechta la Fer rogein, buaid n-airdmiusa la Fer le, Eg 119ᵃ 2
[3] . cach, St
[4] do teigdis a ceathror co caitis, St
[5] . ISinn amsir sin immorro dognithea tarbfeiss, Eg 119ᵇ 1
[6] romarbtha Eg St nomarbad, YBL.
[7] ór firinde, St
[8] IN fer ateichsed, Eg Fer atchiced, St
[9] See as to this *Serglige Conculainn*, Ir Texte, I, 200, 213, whence it appears that the bull was white *(find)*

would eat his fill and drink its broth[1], and a spell of truth was chanted over him in his bed. Whosoever he would see in his sleep would be king, and the sleeper would perish[2] if he uttered a falsehood.

12. Baei[3] Conairi a ceithri cairpthig[4] il-Lifiu occa cluichiu[5], a tri comaltai 7 se baddeisin. Lotar didu a aite chuice[6] co tuidchised[7] don tairbfeis[8]. Atchonnairc fear na tairbfeisi intan sin ina chotlud fer lomnocht[9] indiaid na haidche iar sligi na Temrach 7 a cloch ina thailm.
Ragatsa dadaig, ol se, in far ndegaid.

*12 Four men in chariots were on (the Plain of) Liffey at their game, Conaire himself and his three fosterbrothers. Then his fosterers went to him that he might repair to the bull-feast. The bullfeaster, then in his sleep, at the end of the night beheld a man starknaked, passing along the road of Tara, with a stone in his sling.
« I will go in the morning after you », quoth he*

13 Fanacbasa[10] a chomaltai occa cluichiu, 7 imasai a charpat 7 a arai[d] co mbai oc Ath cliath[11]. Conacae eonu findbreca mora and ecomdighe[12] ar met 7 dath [7 coemi[13]] Imsai[14] ina ndegaidh comdar scitha ind eich No teigtis fot na hurchara[15]

---

1 At Aegira in Achaia the priestess of Earth drank the fresh blood of a bull before she descended into the cave to prophesy, Frazer, *The Golden Bough*, I, 134, citing Pliny H N xxviii-147
2 literally his lips would perish
3 Bui St
4 a cethror cairpdech, Eg
5 chluichiu St
6 altered in YBL to chuige
7 a aiti chuici co tuidched, St
8 7 asbertatar fris ara ndechsad don tarbfeis co Temraig Ragatsa, ar se, limarach dadaig in barndegaid, Eg
9 faenlomnacht, St
10 leg Foracaib seom ? Fanacbat a comaltai oca chluichiu St *they leave him at his game*
11 IS annsin dano ro fhacaib a tri comaltai acoi cluichi, ocus immarsúi seom ina carpat 7 a ara co mbúi i n-Ath chath Amal rombai seom ann, Eg
12 atc ecomtige Eg
13 sic Eg 7 doturemsium St
14 Gabaid Conaire Eg
15 No theigtis fot n-aurchora St

— 16 —

riam 7 ni theigtis ni bud shure¹ Taurbling 7 gaibid a thailm doib asin charbad². Imsui co mbui oc muir ina ndegaid³. Fosraemet⁴ ind eoin forsin tuind Luid-seom chucu co tabart a laim taursiu. Fofacbad⁵ na heoin a n-enchendcha, 7 imda-suat fair co ngaib ocus claidbib. Aincithi fer dib he⁶, 7 atngladastar co n-epert fris Is mise Nemglan ri enlaithi do athar, 7 aigarad dit dibrugud en⁷, ar ni fuil sund neach na pad⁸ dir⁹ dait o a athair¹⁰ no mathair¹⁰. Ni feadarsa, ol seiseam, cosaniu¹¹ sin

Eirg do Themraig innocht, ol se, is coru deit. Ata tairbfeis ann, 7 is tu bas ri de .i. fer lomnacht [ragas Eg] indiaid na haidchi iar sligi[d] di sligthib na Temrach, 7 cloch 7 tailm lais, is e bas ri.

13. *He left his fosterbrothers at their game, and turned his chariot and his charioteer until he was in Dublin. There he saw great, white-speckled birds, of unusual size and colour and beauty. He pursues them until his horses were tired The birds would go a spearcast before him, and would not go any further He alighted, and takes his sling for them out of the chariot. He goes after them until he was at the sea The birds betake themselves on the wave. He went to them and overcame them¹². The birds quit their birdskins, and turn upon him with spears and swords. One of them protects him, and addressed him, saying* « *I am Némglan, king of thy father's birds, and thou hast been forbidden to cast at birds¹³, for here there is no one that should not be dear to thee because of his father or mother.* »

1 better ni bu sía St
2 Tairling Conaire 7 gabaid a tailm 7 gabud for a ndibrucud, Eg
3 ina ndeadaich YBL na ndegaid, Eg
4 Tiagait Eg Fosrumet, St
5 Facbait Eg St
6 7 marbaid seom cenmotha oenfer ro cuinnig anachul fair, « and he kills them (all) save one man who asked quarter of him », Eg 119ᵇ 2
7 et rofóciad duit, ar se, nemdibrucud en, Eg ardograd dit dibrigud en, St
8 nad pa St
9 duall Eg
10 o athair nó a mathair, St.
11 cosinndiu St
12 Cf doberait laim tairis, LL 402ᵇ 31
13 See § 7 supra

— 17 —

 « *Till today* », *says Conaire*, « *I knew not this.* »
 « *Go to Tara tonight* », *says Nemglan*, « *'tis fittest for thee
A bull-feast is there, and through it thou shalt be king. A man
stark-naked, who shall go at the end of the night along one of the
roads of Tara, having a stone and a sling* — *'tis he that shall be
king.* »

14. Luid-seom iarum in-cruth-sa, 7 badar tri rig cacha
sraite dina ceithri sraitib dia tiagad do Temraig oca urnaide-
seom, 7 etach acco do, ar is lomnacht darairngiread a tai-
deachd Conacce[s|som¹ don(b)rout forsa mbatar² a aite, 7 dober-
tatar etach rig do imbi, 7 da[m]bertatar hi carput, 7 fornenaisc
a giallu.

14. *So in this wise Conaire fared forth, and on each of the four
roads whereby men go to Tara there were three kings awaiting
him, and they had raiment for him, since it had been foretold that
he would come stark-naked. Then he was seen from the road on
which his fosterers were, and they put royal raiment about him, and
placed him in a chariot, and he bound his pledges.*

15 Asbertatar aes na Temrach fris: Atar-lind is coll ro
coillead ar tarbfeis 7 ar n-ór firinde, mad³ gilla oc amulchach
tarfas dunn and

 « Ni métu anni sin⁴ », « ol seiseam. « ni hainim ri óc es-
labar mar missi do bith ir-rigi, uair⁵ is cert n-athar 7 seanathar
damsa fonaidm⁶ ngiall Temrach. »

 « Amrae, n-amrae¹ » ol in sluag. Saidit⁷ rigi n-Erenn⁸ imbi.
Ocus asbert-som « Imcaemrosa⁹ do gaethaib corbom gaeth
iodeisin¹⁰. »

1 conaccessom, Eg
2 sic St formatar YBL
3 inad YBL intan Eg 178? inid, St
4 Ni fircán ám anisin, Eg 120²1
5 sic Eg Here YBL is corrupt and unintelligible hi hainim ri oc es-
labar ni misi didu eiside
6. Here H begins
7 saigid YBL St suidit St
8 Sudit iarsin rig, Eg
9 Imcoemrusa St s-fut sg of imcomarcim Dogénsae imcomarcc, Eg
10. badesin St fodeissin Eg

15. *The folk of Tara said to him.* « *It seems to us that our bullfeast and our spell of truth are a failure, if it be only a young, beardless lad that we have visioned therein* »

« *That is of no moment* », *quoth he* « *For a young, generous king like me to be in the kingship is no disgrace, since the binding of Tara's pledges is mine by right of father and grandsire* »

« *Excellent ! excellent !* » *says the host* They set the kingship of Erin upon him *And he said* « *I will enquire of wise men that I myself may be wise* »

16. Asbert inso huile am*al* rommuin do in fer ocon tuind · Is ed asbert¹ fris ·

Biaid airmitiu² fort flaith, 7 bid sameama*il* ind enflaith, 7 bid si do airmitiu³ ¹⁴ do ghes

Ni thuidchis deasceal⁵ Tem*rach* 7 tuaithbiul mBreg

Nir' taifnefiter⁶ lat claenmila Cernai

Ocus nir' echtra cach nomad⁷ n-aidche seach Theamair⁸.

Ocus nir' fæi⁹ i tig as mbi eggna¹⁰ suillsi tenead inmach iar fuineadh ngréne 7 imbi ecnai dammuig¹¹.

Ocus ni tiassa[t]¹² riut tri Derga¹³ do thig Deirg¹⁴

Ocus nir'ragba*i*ter [YBL col 749, p. 92ᵇ] diberg¹⁵ id¹⁶ flaith

---

1 asber YBL St Is ed ispert H
2 airmitniu YBL
3 airmitiu H St airmitniu dogrés, St
4 sic H *om* YBL
5 desil H deisil St desel Eg. leg desiul
6 7 ni rotaifnither H nir tharbnither St Eg
7 nomad aidche St
8 sech Temraig St sech Temraig iarum H
9 foide H 7 niror St
10 asa mbi spre na soillsi tene imach. St
11 di moigh H da muig St
12 tiasat H
13 Deirg H St
14 Cf co tech nDeirg, LL 1952
15 nu fagbaither dibeirg, St
16. it H St

Ocus ni tae dam aenmna *nó* enfir¹ i tech fort iar fuinead ng*r*éne.
Ocus ni ahurrais² augra do da moghud³.

16 *(Then) he uttered all this as he had been taught by the man at the wave, who said this to him « Thy reign will be subject to a restriction, but the bird-reign will be noble, and this shall be thy restriction, i. e thy tabu*

Thou shalt not go righthandwise round Tara and lefthandwise round Bregia

The evil-beasts of Cerna must not be hunted by thee

And thou shalt not go out every ninth night beyond Tara

Thou shalt not sleep in a house from which firelight is manifest outside, after sunset, and in which (light) is manifest from without

And three Reds shall not go before thee to Red's house.

And no rapine shall be wrought in thy reign.

And after sunset a company of one woman or one man shall not enter the house in which thou art

And thou shalt not settle(?) the quarrel of thy two thralls.

17 Ro batar tra deolatchaire⁴ mora inna flaith 1 secht mbarca cach mis⁵ mithemon⁶ do⁷ gabail oc Inbiur Colbtha cacha bliadna, 7 mes co⁸ gluine cach fogmair⁹, 7 imbas for Buais 7 Boind i medon in mis mithemon cacha bliadna, 7 imbet cainchomraic conarru bi¹⁰ neach in n-aile¹¹ inn Erinn fria flaith *Ocus* ba¹² bindithir la cach n-aen guth aroile inn Erinn fria flaith¹³ *ocus* betis teta mennchrot¹⁴ Ni luaiscead

---

1 ni the dam oenfir no aonmna H oenimna St
2. ugrois H aurrais St
3 mogaid St For the variants of Eg see Appendix § 14
4 deolcaire, H deolathchaire, St
5 cacha mis H cacha inis St
6 mithemain, St
7 da Facs do St
8 con YBL where the dot is a punctum delens
9 co gluinep gacha foghamuir H
10 boi H bai St
11 cona rabi nech ac boin Eg cona rubai, St
12 comba H
13 St omits *inn Erin fria flaith*, which seems wrongly repeated from the preceding sentence
14 *Ocus ba binnithir tetae cach n-oenguth no chanad*, Eg

gaeth cair_ͪcech mbó o medon earraich co meadon foghmair. Nir'bo thoirneach ainbt[h]ineach a flaith¹.

17. Now there were in his reign great bounties, to wit, seven ships in every June in every year arriving at Inver Colptha², and oak-mast up to the knees in every autumn, and plenty (of fish) in (the rivers) Bush and Boyne in the June of each year, and such abundance of good will that no one slew another in Erin during his reign. And to every one in Erin his fellow's voice seemed as sweet as the strings of lutes. From mid-spring to mid-autumn no wind disturbed a cow's tail. His reign was neither thunderous nor stormy³.

18. Fodordsat iarum a chomaltai-seom im gabail dana a n-athar 7 a seanathar dib .i. Gat 7 Brat 7 Guin daine⁴ 7 Diberg. Gatsat side na teora gata ar in n-oenfer .i. mucc 7 ag 7 bo cacha bliadna, co n-accaitis ca hindeochad⁵ doberad in ri forru ind, 7 cia domain doairgebad⁶ don rig in gat in[n]a flaith.

18. Now his fosterbrothers murmured at the taking from them of their father's and their grandsire's gifts, namely Theft and Robbery and Slaughter of men and Rapine. They thieved the three thefts from the same man, to wit, a swine and an ox and a cow, every year, that they might see what punishment therefor the king would inflict upon them, and what damage the theft in his reign would cause to the king.

19. Dotheced⁷ didu⁸ cacha bliadna in fer trebar dia chainead⁹ frisin rig, 7 asberead in rí fris: Eirg co n-arlaiter¹⁰ tri

---

1. The entry in the Annals of the Four Masters at A.M. 5160 seems fashioned on this paragraph.
2. The mouth of the river Boyne.
3. As to the influence of a good king on the seasons, see the Rolls edition of the Tripartite Life, p. 507, note.
4. duine H. St.
5. hindechad Eg. H. hinnechad, St.
6. no taircébad Eg.
7. noteged Eg. Teideth H. Do teged St.
8. diu H.
9. ēcáoine Eg. acacine H. accaine St.
10. Eirg 7 accaill, Eg. conairlaither H.

maccu¹ h*ui* Duind desa, it e rota-thúigsead². Fo*l*aimtis a guin³ cacha fechtais no theigead dia rad friu. Ni tind*t*ádh som cosin rig afrisi⁴ arnach ru*i*dead⁵ [Conaire a lott-som. Eg.]

19. Now every year the farmer would come to the king to complain, and the king would say to him. « Go thou and address Donn désa's three great-grandsons, for 'tis they that have taken the beasts: » Whenever he went to speak to them (Donn Désá's descends) they would almost kill him⁶, and he would not return to the king lest Conaire should attend(?)⁷ his hurt.

20. Onni iar*u*m ros-gab miad 7 imtholtu⁸ iat, gabsat⁹ dibe[i]rg co *m*accaib flaithi fer n-Ere*n*n impu. T*r*i *choecait* fear doib. intan badar oc faelad i *c*rich *Co*nnacht occa munud, *con*dad acca¹⁰ muicid¹¹ Maine Milscothaig iat [occa dénam, Eg.] 7 ni*n*-acca¹² riam anisin. Luid for teichead¹³. O rochualatar¹⁴ som lotar ina deagaid¹⁵. Eigthi in muccid, co tanic tuath¹⁶ in da Maine fae, 7 co n-argabait¹⁷ na tri choecait fer *cona forb*a*n*naib, 7 bertair do Themair¹⁸, 7 fogellsat in ri[g] imbi, *co* n-epert-side: « Oircead cach a *m*ac, 7 ainci*ter* mo daltai-seo.

20. Since, then, pride and wilfulness possessed them, they took to marauding, surrounded by the sons of the lords of the men of

---

1. con-arlaiter t*r*i *m*aic St.
2. is siat rod-ucsat Eg. it hé roda tuicset H. it e roda-huicset, St.
3. ṅguin YBL, St. guin H.
4. doridisi Eg. afrithisi H.
5. ro fuided Eg. ruitheth H. cruided, St.
6. Cf. ac folmasi a gona LL. 74ᵃ 19. *folaimtis* 3d pl. 2dy pres. of *folámur* suscipio, tento, (ἐπιχειρέω, Strachan. Deponent, p. 13, note 4).
7. *ruidead* perhaps = ro-fethed (rofuided, *Eg.*)
8. sic St. imtoltu YBL.
9. gabsait St.
10. conacca Eg. *con*faca H. conacad St.
11. muicide St.
12. ni aca St.
13. Luith-sim *for* teiched rompaib, H.
14. Forochualatar YBL. O ro cualo*tar* H. O ro cualatar St.
15. *ocus* luid for teched mara co*n*cathar lotar na degaid, Eg.
16. Eígis in muccaid co tancatar tuatha Eg.
17. co roergabait Eg. conorgabat H. co*n*orgabait St.
18. Themraig St.

*Erin Thrice fifty men had they as pupils when they (the pupils)
were were-wolfing¹ in the province of Connaught, until Maine Milscothach's swineherd saw them, and he had never seen that before.
He went in flight. When they heard him they pursued him. The
swineherd shouted, and the people of the two Maines came to him,
and the thrice fifty men were arrested, along with their auxiliaries,
and taken to Tara. They consulted the king concerning the matter,
and he said: « Let each (father) slay his son, but let my fosterlings
be spared »*

21 Cet, cet¹ or cach, « dogentar [LU 83ª] airiut.
Naté em, ol sesseom ní haurcur² saegail damsa in breth
ron-ucus. Ni crochfaiter ind fir, *acht* eirget senóri leósom cor-
ralat⁵ a ndiberg for firu Alpan

*21 « Leave, leave! » says every one. « it shall be done for
thee »*

*« Nay indeed », quoth he, no³ « cast of life » by me is the doom
I have delivered. The men shall not be hung, but let veterans go
with them that they may wreak their rapine on the men of Alba »*

22 Dogníat⁴ ani-sin. Tíagait ass forsin farrci co comarnec-
tár⁵ fri mac rig Bretan .i. Ingcél Cáech *h*úa *Conmaic*⁶ tri
.l. fer⁷ *cona* senorib léo co comarnectar⁸ forsind fargge
Dogníat cairdes, 7 tiagait la Ingcel cor-rólsat⁹ a ndiberg
lais.

*22 This they do. Thence they put to sea and met the son of the
king of Britain, even Ingcél the One-eyed, grandson of Conmac:
thrice fifty men and their veterans they met upon the sea.*

1 *faola*.*ih* .i. foglaim, O'Cl., but cf. *fri faelad* .i. *i com[e]achtaibh*, Côir
Anmann, Ir. Texte, III, 376
2 hurcro H hurcra St haurchor YBL
3 co ro laat, St corolat YBL
4 Dogenad, St
5 co comairneachtair YBL gurro comruicsit H cor comraigset St
6. mac hui *Conmaicni* YBL Conmaicne St
7 triar fer H triar fer YBL
8 co gur comaicsit H cur' comraigset St co comarneachtair YBL.
9 co rolasat Eg, 120ᵇ 1ᶜ corrolasat YBL corrolasaut H corralasat St

— 23 —

They make an alliance, and go with Ingcél and wrought rapine with him

23. IS í orcain tuc á áin fén dó som Con[id]si adaig and sin ro curthea a mathair 7 a athair¹ 7 a secht² nderbráthir do thig ríg a thúathe. Ortá uli la Ingcél i n-óen aidchi. Dolotar³ trá forsin fairci⁴ anall hi tír n-Erend do chuingid⁵ oirgne fón orguin ro dligestár⁶ Ingcel dib

23. This is the destruction which his own impulse gave him. That was the night that his mother and his father and his seven brothers had been bidden to the house of the king of his district. All of them were destroyed by Ingcel in a single night. Then they (the Irish pirates) put out to sea to the land of Erin to seek a destruction (as payment) for that to which Ingcél had been entitled from them

24. Lánsid⁷ i n-Erind hi flaith⁸ Conaire, acht bói imnesse catha eter da Corpre hi Túathmumain. Dá chomalta dosom íat. Ni bói a córugud co riacht⁹ Conaire. Geiss dosom techt día n-eterglèod riasiu dorostais¹⁰ chuci. Téit iaiom ciarbo geiss dó, 7 dogéni¹¹ sid n-etarro. Anais cóic¹² aidche la cechtar de¹³ geis dosom dano ani-sin

24. In Conaire's reign there was perfect peace in Erin, save that in Thomond there was a joining of battle between the two Car-

1. Isi orcain tuc Ingcel do adaig rocuretha 7 a mathair, 7 a athair 7 a seacht nderbraithri etc YBL Isi immorro argain tuc Ingcél doib i adaig rocuirthea a athair etc Eg IS í orcuin tug Ingcel doip agaid ro cuirthi a mathair etc H Issi orcuin tuc a ain fen dó adaig ro cuirthea a mathair 7 a athair 7 a secht nderbrathir do thig ríg a tuaithe, St
2. sic H ui LU Óm Eg a seacht YBL
3. Tollotar H Tolotar St
4. fairrgi YBL darsin fairgi Eg
5. chuindchid YBL cuinncith H cuindge St
6. ro dlig Eg sin dligistair YBL
7. Lansith H YBL
8. i n-amsir Eg
9. riacht YBL St.
10. doroistis YBL H dorrostais St
11. dorigni Eg dogni YBL H dognid St.
12. ii Eg
13. la ceachtar n-ae dib YBL la cechtar nae H la cechtar de dib St.

— 24 —

bres. *Two fosterbrothers of his were they. And until Conaire came it was impossible to make peace between them. 'Twas a tabu of his to go to separate them before they had repaired to him. He went, however, although (to do so) was one of his tabus, and he made peace between them. He remained five nights with each of the two. That also was a tabu of his.*

25. Iar ngleod in dá ugrai ro bói-seom oc saigid¹ do Themraig¹. IS*ed* gabsait² do Tem*raig*, sech Usnech Midi, *co* n-accatár³ iarsain a n-indred⁴ anair 7 aníar, 7 an[d]es 7 atúaid, 7 *co* n-accatár na buidne⁵ 7 na slúagu⁶ [7 na firu lomnocht;] 7 ropo nem tened tír⁷ Úa Néill imbi⁸.

25. *After settling the two quarrels, he was travelling to Tara. This is (the way) they took to Tara, past Usnech of Meath; and they saw the raiding from east and west, and from south and north, and they saw the warbands and the hosts, and the men stark-naked; and the land of the (southern) O'Neills was a cloud of fire around him.*

26. Cid aní seo? ol *Conaire*. Ni anse, ol a muin*ter*. Ní duachnid⁹ són, is í in cháin [ríg — Eg.] ro mebaid and in*tan* ro gabad for loscod¹⁰ in tíre.
Cest¹¹, cid gébmani¹²? ol *Conaire*.
Saerthúaid, for a muin*ter*.
IS*s ed* ro gabsat iar*um*, deisiul Temra 7 tuaithbiul Breg. Ocus tosessa¹³ lais clóenmíla Cernai. Ní accai cor-ro scáig a tofond.

1. in da ugrai robui oc soigin co Temraig, YBL.
2. ro gabsat St.
3. *conaices* YBL.
4. innindred St. in n-indred ar Maig Breg. Eg.
5. bidbaid St.
6. sluagu moseach 7 na firu lomnacht YBL 93ª. H adds: 7 na fir lombnoc*ht*
7. rop nem tened i tír, St.
8. impo do gach leth, H. ropa neim tened Mag mBreg huli accu. *Ocus* iss iat robatar ann, sluag síde Breg Leth, *ocus* is iat ro tinoil in n-argain, Eg.
9. duaichni St.
10. rogabad ar forloscudh, Eg. rogabad for loscad, YBL.
11. Cesc H.
12. gebmaitne St.
13. ro taibfindthea, Eg. tossesa YBL. dosesa H. St.

IS iat dodróni in smúitchéo ndruidechta sin di*n* bith, siabrai, fo[bithin a]t*ro*[corpait géssi Conaire[1].

26. « *What is this?* » *asked Conaire.* « *Easy to say,* » *his
people answer.* » *Easy to know that the king's law has broken down
therein, since the country has begun to burn.* »
« *Whither shall we betake ourselves?* » *says Conaire.*
« *To the Northeast* », *say his people.*
*So then they went righthandwise round Tara, and left-hand-
wise round Bregia, and the clóenmíla (« evil beasts? ») of Cerna
were hunted by him. But he saw it not till the chase had ended.*

*They that made of the world that smoky mist of magic were
elves, (and they did so) because Conaire's tabus had been violated.*

27. IMmusrala[2] trá in t-ómon mór-sin[3] do Chonaire, con-
nach rabi dóib *conar* dochoistis[4] *acht for* sligi Midlúachra 7
for sligi Cualann[5].

IS *ed* ro gabsat iarom, la hairer n-Erend antuáid.

IS and asbert Conaire *for* slig*id* Cualan*n* : Cid ragma[6] innocht, ol se.

Domm-áir [a rád], a da[ltai] Conaire[7], *for* Mac çecht mac
Snaide teichid[8], cathmílid Conairi maic Etersccoil. Bátar
menciu fir Her*end* oc do chosnom-so cach n-aidche[9] indás bith
deitsiu[10] *for* merogod tige óiged.

27. *Great fear then fell on Conaire because they had no way to*

---

1. is e ri insin loingsige siabrai di*du* din bith, YBL. IS é ri innsin loing-
side siapro din bith. fobith H. Is hé rí insin loi*n*gshide síabrai din bith, St.
2. Imrola St. imu*s*rola YBL.
3. iarsin St. YBL.
4. co*n*ach rabi co*n*air ra soistis St. co*n*ach roba conar dochostis YBL.
5. *Ocus* ro sóeed iarsin cetfaid 7 ros-lín in t-uaman co*n*nach rabi accu conair dotiastais acht dul hi cend sligedh Midluachra 7 for sligid Cualand,
Eg. 120[b] 2 → 121[a] 1.
6. ragmait St.
7. Con*id* a*n*n atb*er*t Conodor *m*ac cecht mac Snaide seched, Eg.
8. Dom*m*áir a rad a Co*n*aire YBL. 98[a]. Domtair, a daltai, a Conaire H.
Dom*m*air a rad, a dalta Co*n*aire, St.
9. *ocat* cosnamsai H. oc do chosnam so cach n-aidchi YBL.
10. beith duitsu YLB.

wend save upon the Road of Midluachair and the Road of Cualu. So they took their way by the coast of Ireland southward.
Then said Conaire on the Road of Cualu: « whither shall we go tonight ? »
« May I succeed in telling thee¹! my fosterling Conaire » says Mac cecht, son of Snade Teiched, the champion of Conaire son of Eterscél. « Oftener have the men of Erin been contending for thee every night than thou hast been wandering about for a guesthouse. »

28. Tothǽet meis fóamsera²! for Conaire. Bói cara damsa isin tír-se, for Conaire, acht ro³, fesmais conair dia thig⁴.
Cia ainm side? for Mac cēcht.
Da Derga di Lagnib, ol Conaire. Ránic cucumsa em, ol Conaire, do chuingid aisceda [formsa — Eg.], 7 ní thuidchid co n-éru. Ránirusa im chét mbó bóthána. Ranirusa im cét muc [LU. 83ᵇ] muccglassa⁵. Ranirusa im chét mbrat cungas⁶ clithetach⁷. Ranirusa im chét ngaisced⁸ ngormdatha ngubae. Ranirusa im deich ndeilci dercá⁹ diorda. Ranirusa im deich ndabcha déolcha deich donnae¹⁰. Ranirusa im deich mogu¹¹. Ranirusa im deich meile. Ranirusa im tri .ix. con n-[a]engel inna slabradaib argdidib. Ranirusa im cét n-ech mbúada hi sedgregaib¹² oss n-eng¹³. Ní ara maithem¹⁴ dó, cia rised¹⁵ beos

1. literally: « may saying it come to me! »
2. Totet meas fo aimseara YBL. Dotaet m̃ fo aimseruip H. Dotoett mes foaimseraib St. do tháod meas tó aimseara .i. téid an breitheamhnas ris an aimsear, O'Clery's Foclóir, s. v. meas. Read: Dothóet mess fóaimseraib
3. co St.
4. dia mbeth ar n-éolas dia thig, Eg.
5. im cét mucclassa, Eg. mucc muccglasa St. muc muicci glasa YBL.
6. cunglas St.
7. clidetach St YBL. Ranirussa im cét mbratt corcarda cumascda clithétcaid cona delgaib dergaib diórdaib, Eg.
8. im cet ngai ngaiscid. Eg.
9. Om. Eg. H. St. YBL.
10. deelcha dedonda, Eg. ndeolchoi ndedonna H. deolcha deich dondnæ, St.
11. mogodu, Eg. moga St.
12. séderggaib, St.
13. necennsa YBL. necendas (no neng), St.
14. ar maithim H. airmitheam St. YBL.
15. Ni dia maithib dó dia tísad, Eg.

Ďoberad anaill Is ingnad¹ mád brónach frimsa innocht [oc riachtain a trebe chuici², YBL.]

28. « *Judgment goes with good times* », says *Conaire* « *I had a friend in this country, if only we knew the way to his house !* » « *What is his name ?* » *asked Mac cecht*

« *Dá Derga of Leinster* », *answered Conaire* « *He came unto me to seek a gift from me, and he did not come with a refusal I gave him a hundred kine of the drove. I gave him a hundred fatted swine. I gave him a hundred mantles made of(?) close cloth I gave him a hundred blue-coloured weapons of battle I gave him ten red, gilded brooches I gave him ten vats .. good and brown. I gave him ten thralls. I gave him ten querns I gave him thrice nine hounds all-white in their silvern chains. I gave him a hundred race-horses in the herds of deer .*³ *There would be no abatement in his case though he should come again. He would give the other thing (make return). It is strange if he is surly to me tonight when reaching his abode* »

29. A mbása⁴ éolach-sa ém dia thig-side, for Mac cecht, is crich a tribe chuci i(n)tsligi forsatai. Téit co téit isa tech⁵, ar is triasin tech ata in tslige Atát *secht* ndorais⁶ isa tech 7 *secht* n-imda⁷ iter cach da dórus, 7 ni fil acht óenchomlaid⁸ n-airi, 7 imsóither in chomla sin fri cach ndorus dia mbí in gáeth⁹.

Lin atái sund ragai hit brói¹⁰ dirmai co tarblais¹¹ for lár in tige. Masu ed no théig¹², tiag-sa co n-árlór¹³ tenid and ar do chind.

1 ing H
2 iar rochtain á trebe cuice H ar riachtain a treibe chuice, St
3 Compare a similar list of gifts in the *Amra Chonroi*
4 am YBL H St
5 ISam colach tra dia tig side, ol Mac cecht, Eg 121ª2 Am colach-sa etc. YBL
6 ndoirsi YBL
7 n-imdatha H n-imdada, St YBL
8 aen comlo H
9 ni fil acht oencomla fris, 7 doberar in comla sin fri cech ndorus imbi in gaeth, Eg
10. ragai it broin YBL St raga it broin H eirg it bróin Eg But O'Cl has *bro* i imad
11. tairlingis, Eg tarblas St
12 noteige. St leg no teig
13 conarlúr St Masa ed no tége tiagsa reomut co n-adúr tenid ar do

29 « *When I was acquainted with his house* », says Mac cecht, « *the road whereon thou art (going) towards him was the boundary of his abode. It continues till it enters his house, for through the house passes the road. There are seven doorways into the house, and seven bedrooms between every two doorways, but there is only one door-valve on it, and that valve is turned to every doorway to which the wind blows* »

« *With all that thou hast here* », (says Conaire), « *thou shalt go in thy great multitude until thou alight in the midst of the house.* »

» *If so be* » (answers Mac cecht), *that thou goest (thither), I go (on) that I may strike fire there ahead of thee* »

30 INtan ro bói Conaire iar sudiu¹ oc ascnam iar slige Chúaland rat[h]aigés² in t/iar marcach³ dochom in tige. Téora léne⁴ dergae impu, 7 tri bruit dergae impu, 7 tri scéith derga foraib, 7 tri gae derga ina lámaib, 7 tri eich *derga* fo a suidib⁵, 7 tri fuilt *derga* foraib. Dergae uile eter chorp 7 folt 7 etgud⁶, eter echu 7 dáine⁷ dáine

30 When Conaire after this was journeying along the Road of Cúalu, he marked before him three horsemen (riding) towards the house Three red frocks had they, and three red mantles three red bucklers they bore, and three red spears were in their hands: three red steeds they bestrode, and three red heads of hair were on them. Red were they all, both body and hair and raiment, both steeds and men.

31 Cia rédes ri͘nd⁸ ⁾ for Conuic Ba geiss damsa in t/iar

cind Sóeis *Conaire* iarsin for sligid Cualann, Eg Maseth no teig tiagsa riut co *n*-atar temith and ardocind, H
  1 INtan diu boi Conaire H INtan bui *Conaire* iar suide, St
  2 rathaigis St rathaiges YBL
  3 Eg *inserts* remi St and YBL riam
  4 leinte Eg lente H lene St
  5 foitlub Eg fouip H fo suidib St
  6 etir fiaclaib 7 foltaib, Eg *cona* fiaclaib 7 foltaib, YBL *cona* fiaclaib 7 a foltaib, H cona fiaclaib 7 foltaib, St
  7 iter each 7 duine, YBL in t-ech 7 duine, St
  8 ruind YBL cia rethess romaind etir? Eg. Ciai ragas ruin? H

ucut do dul reum¹, for *Conaire*, na tri Deirg do thig Deirg.
Cía ragas inna ndiáid co taessat² il-lorg cucumsa³ ?
Ragat-sa inna ndiáid, for Lé fri⁴ flaith⁵ mac *Conaire*.

31. « Who is it that fares before us? » asked *Conaire*. « It was a tabu of mine for those Three to go before me — the three Reds to the house of Red. Who will follow them and tell them to come towards me in my track? »
« I will follow them », says Lé fri flaith, *Conaire*'s son.

32. Téit ina ndiáid iarom for echláscad 7 nisn-árraid⁶. Bói fot n-aurchora⁷ eturro, ach⁸ ni ructh/isom aire-seom, ni rucad som⁹ foraib seom.

Asbert friu nad remthiastais in rig. Nisn-arraid, *acht* ro chachain in tres fer láid dó dar a ais:

Én a maic, mór a scél, scél o brudin¹⁰ belot long lúaichet fer ṅgablach fiangalach¹¹ ndoguir cnéd miscad mór bet bé find for[s]ndestetar deirgindlid¹² áir. Én a maic.

Tiagait úad iarom¹³, atarói an¹⁴ astód¹⁵.

32. He goes after them, lashing his horse, and overtook them not. There was the length of a spearcast between them: but they did not gain upon him and he did not gain upon them.

He told them not to go before the king. He overtook them not; but one of the three men sang a lay to him over his shoulder:

1. remum St. rium YBL.
2. taiset St. taesead YBL.
3. Cia ragas ina ndiaid, ar *Conaire*, 7 abar riu bith diarneis co rabat hi lorg, Eg. Cia ragas 'na ndiaid co tisith al-lorc cugumsa H.
4. fer YBL. St.
5. Lia fer flatha H. Le fear flaith YBL.
6. nistárraid. Eg.
7. n-urchair, Eg. n-urchuir St. na hurchara YBL.
8. acht Eg. nach St. nachamructais-seom YBL. leg. acht ní ructais som.
9. ni ruc som Eg.
10. The rest of this paragraph is obscure to me. For the lection of Eg. see Appendix § 33.
11. fer ṅgablach fiangalach YBL. St. fíangalach LU.
12. forsndestetar deirind lith YBL. forsndesitaur fir H.
13. The rest of this sentence is obscure to me.
14. sic YBL. *om.* LU.
15. Atróia n-astath H. Atroi n-astad, St. ataroi an astod YBL.

« Lo, my son, great the news, news from a hostel ... Lo, my son ! »

They go away from him then : he could not detain them.

33. Anais in mac ar cind in tsluaig. Asbert fria athair a n-asbreth fris. Ní bo ait laiss. Ina ndiáid deit, or Conaire, 7 tairg tri damu 7 tri tinni doib, 7 airet beti¹ im theglochsa ni bia² nech etarru o thenid³ co fraigid.

33. The boy waited for the host. He told his father what was said to him. Conaire liked it not. « After them, thou ! » says Conaire, « and offer them three oxen and three bacon-pigs, and so long as they shall be in my household, no one shall be among them from fire to wall. »

34. Téit iarom ina ndiaid in gilla, 7 toirgid⁴ dóib anisin, 7 nisn-arraid⁵, acht ro chachain in tres fer láid dó dar a ais:

Én, a maic, mór a scél, gerthiut, gorthiut⁶ robruth rig eslabrae⁷, tri doilbtiu fer forsaid⁸ fordáim dám nónbair. Én a maic.

Tintái in mac afrithisi coeragaib in laíd do Chonaire.

34. So the lad goes after them, and offers them that, and overtook them not. But one of the three men sang a lay to him over his shoulder:

« Lo, my son, great the news ! A generous king's great ardour whets thee, burns thee. Through ancient men's enchantments a company of nine⁹ yields. Lo, my son ! »

The boy turns back and repeated the lay to Conaire.

1. mbete YBL.
2. asbia H.
3. then St. o thein co fraig YBL.
4. toirgenn St. tairgenn amal ispert au ri fris 7 nis-tarraid H.
5. nis-tarraid St.
6. gertitt gortit H. gerthuit gorthuit St.
7. oes labra YBL.
8. forsuith H. farsaig YBL.
9. This agrees with the statement infra that nine only fell, including (or around) Conaire.

35. Eirg ina ndíaid¹, for Conaire, 7 toirg dóib sé damu 7 sé tinni² 7 mo fuidell-sa, 7 aisceda³ imbárach, 7 airet beite im' thegluch-sa ni bía [LU 84ᵃ] nech etúrru o thein⁴ co fraig.

Luid in gilla ina ndíaid iarom, 7 nisn-arraid⁵, acht frisgart in tres fer⁶, co n-epert:

Én, a maic, mór in scél, scitha eich imáriadam⁷. imriadam eochu Duind Tetscoraig⁸ a sídib, cíammin bi amin mairb. móra airdi, airdbi sáeguil. sasad fiach, fothad mbran, bresal airlig, airliachtad fáebuir⁹, ferna tulbochtaib¹⁰ trat[h]aib iar fuin. Én a maic.

Tiagait úad iarom.

35 « Go after them », says Conaire, « and offer them six oxen and six bacon-pigs, and my leavings, and gifts tomorrow, and so long as they shall be in my household no one (to be) among them from fire to wall. »

The lad then went after them, and overtook them not; but one of the three men answered and said:

« Lo, my son, great the news. Weary are the steeds we ride. We ride the steeds of Donn Tetscorach(?) from the elfmounds. Though we are alive we are dead. Great are the signs; destruction of life: sating of ravens. feeding of crows¹¹, strife of slaughter. wetting of sword-edge, shields with broken bosses in hours after sundown. Lo, my son! »

Then they go from him.

36. Atchíu ni ro fastáis¹² ná firu, for Conaire

1. Erc ina ndeguith H
2. tindiu YBL
3. aiscidi YBL
4. teneth H tein St then YBL
5. nisraraid LU nistarraid St
6. ro chach[ain] in tres fer laeith H
7. imdarriadam YBL
8. desscoraig YBL. tet sgoraig H detscoraig, St
9. airliachtuith faepur, H airliachtaid faebur, St arliachtait faebair YBL.
10. tuilli ochtaib, St.
11. Cf Fyri vildak | at Frekasteini | hrafna sedhja | á braeum thinum « First would I at Wolfstone sate ravens with thy corpses », H H, 1, 44 cited by Bugge, *Home of the Eddic Poems*, p 210 n
12. ni rus-astais St. nirosastáis LU nirusfastais YBL, where the f is over the line

Ni mé rod-mert[1] ém (.i. ro follaig cen ir techtairecht do denam) .i. or Lé fri[2] flaith[3].

Radis a n-aithesc ndédenach asbertatár fris. Nirptar failte[4] de, 7 batár iarsain na míthaurrússa (.i. drochmenmand) imómna foraib[5].

Rom-gabsatsa mo gessi uili innocht[6], ol *Conaire*, úair óessa (.i. nárfetad)[7] indarbae in triar sin.

36. « *I see that thou hast not detained the men* », *says Conaire*.
« *Indeed it is not I that betrayed it* » (*i. e. endured not to perform the errand*), *says Lé fri flaith*.

He recited the last answer that they gave him. They (Conaire and his retainers) were not blithe thereat: and afterwards evil forebodings (that is, bad spirits) of terror were on them.

« *All my tabus have seized me tonight* », *says Conaire*, « *since those Three (Reds) (are the) banished folks*[8]. »

37. Dochótar ríam dochom in tige cor-ragbaiset[9] a suide isin tig, 7 coro airgiset[10] (.i. cor cengailset) a n-cocho dergae do dorus in tige.

Remthochim na tri nDerg sin isin Brudin.

37. They went forward to the house and took their seats therein, and fastened their red steeds to the door of the house.

That is the Forefaring of the Three Reds in the Bruden (Dá Derga).

---

1. rotmbert H. rodmeirt YBL.
2. fer St.
3. Ni me im*morro* na targaid, ar Le fri flaith mac *Conaire*, Eg. 121ᵇ 2.
4. failtiu St. failti YBL.
5. Batar im*morro* forro na míturrusa immómna, Eg. mithurassa YBL.
6. Romgabsatarsa mo geissi huli 7 mo micélmaini ar tuidecht cucum huli hinocht, ar Conairi, úaro fessa urbaid in tríar sin dochotar ríam, Eg. Rom gabsat mo gesi uili an*ocht*, ol Conaire, uaire aes indarbthai in triar ugat, H. húair roessa indarbæ in triur san, St.
7. This gloss is obscure to me.
8. *oessa = aesa (d.ina)*, LU. 101ᵃ18. They had been banished from the elfmounds, see infra § 136, and for them to precede Conaire was to violate one of his tabus. See § 16.
9. corragabsat St. corrogabaiset YBL.
10. 7 ro araigset H. 7 cor choraigset St.

— 33 —

38. IS ed rogab *Conaire cona* slúagaib do Áth cliath.
IS and dosn-aráid in fer¹ máeldub *cona* óenláim 7 óensúil
7 óenchoiss. Mael gárb fo[r]suidiu². Cía focertá míach dǿ fiad-
ublaib *for* a mulluch³ ní foichred⁴ ubull *for* lár *acht* no giulad
cach ubull díb *for* a finnu⁵. Cía focertá⁶ a srúb ar gésce⁷ im-
matairisfed dóib. Sithremithir cuing n-imechtair⁸ cechtar a
dá lurgan. Méit mulaig *for* gut⁹ cach mell do mellaib a dromma. Gaboll*órg* iarinn¹⁰ inna láim. Muc máel dub dóthi *for* a
muin, 7 sí oc síregim¹¹, 7 ben bélmar már dub dúabais¹² doch-
raid ina diaíd. Cía focherta dano a srúb ar gesce folilsad¹³.
Tacmaicced¹⁴ a bél ichtarach co a glún¹⁵.

38. This is (the way) that Conaire took with his troops, to Dublin.

'*Tis then the man of the black, cropt hair, with his one hand and one eye and one foot*¹⁶, *overtook them. Rough cropt hair upon him. Though a sackful of wild apples were flung on his crown, not an apple would fall on the ground, but each of them would stick on his hair. Though his snout were flung on a branch they would remain together. Long and thick as an outer yoke was each of*

---

1. dosn-árraid araili fer Eg. 121ᵇ 2. dosfarraig in fer, St. dosnarraid in fear YBL.
2. Móel garb dub fair, Eg. Maelgarb *for* suidiu YBL. Mael garb fair side, H.
3. miach fiadhuboll *for* a moil, H.
4. roised, St.
5. Ce rocraithe, miach do fiádublaib ina mullach is tecmaing día rosed ubull díb *for* lár, acht ro leanfad cach ubull díb *for* a inda. Eg. *for* a findiu YBL. *for* a innu St.
6. O focerded Eg. o focerta YBL.
7. gesco folilsath 7, H. gescoc imatairisfead YBL.
8. Ba sithithir cuing n-imechtraid, Eg. sithremir YBL.
9. *for* got YBL. mullaig for gut YBL.
10. Ms. iarirn LU. faraind Eg. iairn YBL. iarnaid St.
11. oc gréchaig 7 oc síréigim, Eg.
12. duaibsech Eg.
13. folinsat, Eg. folælsad St.
14. Teccmainged Eg. Taiccmaiced St.
15. co rucce a glúni, Eg.
16. See infra § 63, and Rev. Celt., XXI, 395, and, as to standing on one foot, Frazer, *The Golden Bough*, 2d ed. II, 32. Was the custom of going with one foot bare and the other shod (ibid., II, 298 n.) allied to this magical practice?

3

— 34 —

two shins. Each of his buttocks was the size of a cheese on a withe. A forked pole of iron black-pointed was in his hand. A swine, black-bristled, singed, was on his back, squealing continually, and a woman big-mouthed, huge, dark, sorry, hideous, was behind him. Though her snout were flung on a branch, the branch would support it. Her lower lip would reach her knee.

39. Tacurethar[1] bedg ar a chend[2], 7 ferais fáilte[3] fris[4].
Fochen dúit, a phopa Conaire[5]! cian rofess do thíchtu sund[6].
Cia feras in fáilte[7]? for Conaire.
Fer Caille co muic duib dúitsiu do th'occomol[8], arná rabi[9] hi toichned (.i. hi troscud) innocht. Is[10] tú rí as dech tánic inn̄ domon. »
Cia ainm do mná? ol Conaire.
Cichuil, ol se.
Nách n-aidche[11] aile bas áil dúib, for Conaire[12], « roborficba? 7 sechnaid innocht duind. »
Nathó, ol in bachlach, ar rot-ficbam[13] co port i mbía innocht, a phopan chain Chonaire!

39. He starts forward to meet Conaire, and made him welcome.
« Welcome to thee, O master Conaire! Long hath thy coming hither been known. »
« Who gives the welcome? » asks Conaire.
« Fer Caille[14] (here), with (his) black swine for thee to con-

---

1. Docuirethar, Eg. Docurethar H. Tathchoirethar YBL. Tacuirither St.
2. chind, Eg.
3. failti YBL.
4. fri Conare, Eg.
5. a mo popa cáin, a Conaire, Eg.
6. Cian cian o rofess do tiachtain sunn, Eg. cian o rofes do techt sonn. H. Cian ro fes do tiachtain sund, St.
7. failti YBL. Here there is a lacuna in H.
8. cona muicc duitseo dot[f]restul, Eg. co muicc duitsiu do thocomul St.
9. rabais, Eg. arnar rabai St. YBL.
10. Uair is, Eg.
11. adaig Eg.
12. Nach n-aidchi n-aile duib, ol Conaire? YBL. Nach inn aidche etc. St.
13. Acc etir ón, ratessemni, Eg.
14. « Man of (the) Wood », Waldmensch? Zimmer, KZ., XXVIII, 558.

sume(?) that thou be not fasting tonight, (for) 'tis thou art the best king that has come into the world ! »

« *What is thy wife's name?* » says Conaire.

« *Cichuil* », he answers.

« *Any other night* », says Conaire, « *that pleases you, I will come to you, — and leave us alone tonight.* »

« *Nay* », say the churl, « *for we will go to thee to the place wherein thou wilt be tonight, O fair little master Conaire!* »

40. Téit iarom dochom in taige[1], 7 a ben bélmar már ina diáid, 7 a mucc máel dub dóithi oc sirégim[2] for a muin. Geiss dosom aní sin[3], 7 bá geis dó díberg do gabáil i n-Erind ina[4] flaith.

40. *So he goes towards the house, with his great, big-mouthed wife behind him, and his swine short-bristled, black, singed, squealing continually, on his back. That was one of Conaire's tabus, and that plunder should be taken in Ireland during his reign was another tabu of his.*

41. Gabtha tra díberg la maccu Duind nDéssa[5], 7 cóic cét[6] fo churp a ndíberge, cenmota 'na raCbí do fosluag léo. [Ba geiss dano do Conaire annisin[7] — Eg.]. Bái laech[8] maith[9] isin tír thúaid. Fén dar crínach based a ainm[10]. IS de ro bói Fén dar crínach fairsium[11], ár is cumma no cinged dar a cho-[LU. 84ᵇ]laind[12] 7 no chessed[13] fén dar crínach. Gabtha díberg dano la suide, 7 *cóic cét* fo churp a ndíbergae a óenur cenmothá fosluag.

1. Dotaet dano reompa, Eg.
2. sirgréchaig, Eg.
3. inni sin YBL.
4. fria St.
5. desa. YBL. The dot in LU. is a punctum delens.
6. míle, Eg.
7. cenmotha fosluag leo ba ges do Conare annisin, YBL.
8. primlaech, St.
9. amra Eg.
10. YBL. *inserts* primloech.
11. dó St. YBL.
12. tara choland YBL. dar comland YBL². tara chomlann St.
13. cinged Eg. digsed St. *no* teiged tar, St. rochinged, YBL.

41 Now plunder was taken by the sons of Donn Désa, and five hundred there were in the body of their marauders, besides what underlings were with them This, too, was a tabu of Conaire's. There was a good warrior in the north country, « Wain over withered sticks », this was his name Why he was so called was because he used to go over his opponent (?) even as a wain would go over withered sticks Now plunder was taken by him, and there were five hundred in the body of their marauders alone, besides underlings

42 Bátár and tarsin fiallach¹ bátár úallchu² .i. secht maic Ailella 7 Medba, 7 « Mane » for cach fir dib, 7 forainm for cach³ Mani i Mani Athremail 7 Mane Máthramail 7 Mane Mingor 7 Mane Mórgor, Mane Andóe⁴ 7 Mane Milscothach, Mane Cotageib uli, 7 Mane As mó-epert Gibtha dibergla suidib Mane Mathramail dano 7 Mane Andóe, cethri fichit déc fo churp a ndibergae Mane Athremail coeca ar trib cétaib⁵ fo churp a ndibergae Mane Milscothach cóic cét fo churp a ndibergae. Mane Cotageib uile secht⁶ cét fo churp a dibergae Mane As mó epert secht cet fo churp a d(i)bergae Cóic cet fo churp dibergae cach fir dib olchenae

42 There was after that a troop of (still) haughtier heroes, namely, the seven sons of Ailill and Medb, each of whom was called « Mané » And each Mané had a nickname, to wit, Mané Fatherlike and Mané Motherlike, and Mané Gentle-pious, Mané Verypious, Mané Unslow, and Mané Honeyworded, Mané Grasp-themall, and Mané the Loquacious Rapine was wrought by them. As to Mané Motherlike and Mané Unslow there were fourteen score in the body of their marauders. Mane Fatherlike had three hundred and fifty Mané Honeyworded had five hundred Mané Grasp-them-all had seven hundred Mané the Loquacious had seven hundred Each of the others had five hundred in the body of his marauders.

1 lucht Lg
2 uallacha YBL uâlchu St
3 cech YBL
4 Annoe YBL
5 l u cccc. YBL caeca ar cccc. St.
6. ui St

43. Bái triar treblaṅd[1] (.i. gusmar) di feraib.[2] Cúaland di
Lagnib .i. tri Ruadcoin Cúaland (in marg. .i. Cithach 7 Clo-
tach 7 Conall a n-anmand). Gabtha diberg dano la suidiu[3], 7
dá fichit deac fó churp a ndibergae, 7 dám dasachtach léo.
Bátár díbergaig trá trian fer n-Erend hi flaith Conaire. Ro[m]bói-
seom[4] do nirt[5] 7 cumachtai a n-innarbai a tír Herend do athchor a ndíbergae allánall, 7 tuidecht dóib dochom a tíre iar
n-athchor a ndíbergae.

43. *There was a valiant trio of the men of Cúalu of Leinster,
namely, the three Red Hounds of Cualu, called Cethach and Clo-
thach and Conall. Now rapine was wrought by them, and twelve
score were in the body of their marauders, and they had a troop of
madmen[6]. In Conaire's reign a third of the men of Ireland were
reavers. He was of (sufficient) strength and power to drive them
out of the land of Erin (so as) to transfer their marauding to the
other side (Great Britain), but after this transfer they returned to
their country.*

44. INtan ráncatár[7] formnae na fairgge, cotregat[8] fri Iṅgcél
Cáech 7 Eiccel 7 Tulchinni, tri maic úi Chonmaid[9] di Bret-
naib, for dremniu[10] na farrce. Fer anmin mór úathmar anaich-
nid in t-Iṅgcél[11]. Óensúil[12] ina chind[13], lethidir[14] damseche,

1. treblaṅg YBL. treblann St.
2. do Huib Briúin, Eg. di Uib Briuin, YBL. St.
3. leo side Eg. la suidib, St.
4. Romboiseom Eg. Robaiseom YBL Romboi som St.
5. niurt St.
6. Suggested by the *berserkir* of the Scandinavians and the *furor berser-cicus*, « when they howled like wild beasts, foamed at the mouth, and gnawed the iron rim of their shields ».
7. ronancatar YBL. conrancatar St.
8. condrecait Eg. cotrecat YBL. St.
9. fri hIngcel Caech 7 Eiccel, fri da mac hui Conmaicne YBL. 94ᵃ 31. f[ri] Incel caech 7 Eicel 7 fri da mac huai Conmaicne, St.
10. druimni St. druimne YBL.
11. fear anmin uathmar St.
12. oentsuil St. oenshuil, YBL.
13. asa étun, Eg. asa étan YBL. asa etan St.
14. lethir St. leithithir YBL.

duibithir degaid¹, 7 tri² máic imlessen inte ·Tri chét déc fo chuirp a dibergae Bátár lia dibergaig fer n-Erend andáti³.

44. When they had reached the shoulder of the sea, they meet Ingcél the One-eyed and Eiccel and Tulchinne, three greatgrandsons of Conmac of Britain, on the raging of the sea. A man ungentle, huge, fearful, uncouth was Ingcel A single eye in his head, as broad as an oxhide, as black as a chafer, with three pupils therein Thirteen hundred were in the body of his marauders The marauders of the men of Erin were more numerous then they.

45. Tiagait⁴ do muirchomruc forsind [f]airrce. « Ná bad ed dognethi⁵, for Ingcél · ná brisid fír fer fornd⁶, dáig abtar⁷ lia andúsa⁸

Noco raga *acht* comlond fo chutrammus fortso, forda[d]⁹ diberga¹⁰ Herend¹¹

Atá ní as ferr dúib, or Ingcel Dénam córai ol atobrarbradsi¹² (i robar-cured) a tir Herend, 7 atoniárbadni¹³ a tir Alban 7 Brettan. Dénam óentaid etinond. Taitsi co nodrolaid¹⁴ for ndibeirg im tir-se, 7 tiago-sa¹⁵ libse *comd*-ralór¹⁶ mo dibeirg inbar tir-si¹⁷. »

1 dethrug YBL
2 sechi, Eg
3 *om* St
4 Lotar iarum, Eg Batar St YBL
5 dognith St YBL Dia ndernaid for comracc, Eg.
6 formsa Eg YBL
7 *abtar* « ye are », iub YBL. St
8 ocus criimad lia missi andáthisi ni rachad *acht* comlond fa comlin, Eg ni raga ach to comland fortso, St
9 fortat YBL St In *fordad* for *fordat*, the *t* has become *d* before the *d* of *diberga* see Kuhn's Zeitschr, XXXVI, 273, and cf *conateeh*[d] *dig*, and *dalemain ata*[d] *dech*, infra
10 dibergaig YBL
11 Eg omits this sentence
12 ol atarrobiadsi LU oltat dobrarbadse YBL ol atdobrarbadse St
13 atoniarbadne YBL atoniarbadhne St, Robar-toibnedsi a tir Herenn 7 ror-taifnedni Eg
14 ticidsi comralaid Eg taitsi *co*natralaid YBL táitsi *co*nathralaid St leg *co*mdrolaid
15 tiagsa Eg YBL tiagatsa St
16 coralor Eg *comd* athralor YBL. *comd* athralur St
17 i far tir, YBL in far tir si, St

45. They go for a sea-encounter on the main. « Ye should not do this », says Ingcél: « do not break the truth of men (fair play) upon us, for ye are more in number than I »

« Nought but a combat on equal terms shall befall thee », say the reavers of Erin.

» There is somewhat better for you », quoth Ingcél « Let us make peace since ye have been cast out of the land of Erin, and we have been cast out of the land of Alba and Britain Let us make an agreement between us Come ye and wreak your rapine in my country, and I will go with you and wreak my rapine in your country »

46 Dogniat¹ in comairle hísin, 7 dobertatár glinni² ind disiu 7 anall It é aitre dobretha do Ingcél ó feraib Herend, .i. Fer gair 7 Gabur³ (no Fer lee) 7 Fer rogain, im orgain bad toguide⁴ do Ingcél i n-Erind 7 orgain bad togaides⁵ do maccaib Duind Dessa i n-Albain 7 i mBretnaib.

46. They follow this counsel, and they gave pledges therefor from this side and from that There are the sureties that were given to Ingcél by the men of Erin, namely, Fer gair and Gabur (or Fer lee) and Fer rogain, for the destruction that Ingcél should choose (to cause) in Ireland and for the destruction that the sons of Donn Dessa should choose in Alba and Britain.

47 Focres⁶ crandchor forro dús cia dib lasa ragtha i tossoch Dothuit dul la Ingcél dochom a thire Lotar iarom co Bretnu, 7 oirgthe athair 7 máthair 7 a secht nderbrathir amal ro ráidsem reond Lotar iarsin dochom nAlban, 7 ortatar a n-orgain and, 7 doathhisat⁷ iar suidi dochom n-Erend⁸.

---

1 Dognither iarum, Eg. Dogmth YBL Dogmther St
2. Argit dano glinni, Eg
3 i Ger 7 Gabol Eg Ger 7 Gabur St
4. ba togaide St fa togaidhi YBL
5 ba togaidi YBL
6 Doronta cranchor leo, Fg Focreasa crandchor forru, YBL.
7 athralsat YBL atralasat iar suidiu St
8. For this and the preceding sentence Eg has only Lotar iarum la hIngcel docum n-Alban ocus ortatar a n-orgain and And so YBL, omitting la hIngcel.

47. *A lot was cast upon them to see with which of them they should go first. It fell that (they) should go with Ingcél to his country. So they made for Britain, and (there) his father and mother and his seven brothers were slain, as we have said before. Thereafter they made for Alba, and there they wrought the destruction, and then they returned to Erin.*

48. IS andsin trá dolluid *Conaire* mac Eterscéili iar Slige Chualand dochom [LU. 85ª] na Brudne.

IS and sin tancatár na díberga¹ co mbatár i n-airiur Breg comarda Étuir forsind farrci².

IS and asbertatár na díbergae³ : Teilcid⁴ sís na séolu, 7 dénaid óenbudin díb forsind farrci arnáchbar-accaister as'tír⁵, 7 etar⁶ nach traigéscaid úaib isa tir, *dús* in fugebmáis 7 tesorcain ar n-enech⁸ fri⁹ Ingeél. Orguin fón orguin dorat dún ¹⁰.

48. *'Tis then, now, that Conaire son of Eterscéle came towards the Hostel along the Road of Cualu.*

'Tis then that the reavers came till they were in the sea off the coast of Bregia overagainst Howth.

Then said the reavers: « Strike the sails, and make one band of you on the sea that ye may not be sighted from land; and let some lightfoot be found from among you to go on shore to see if we could save our honours with Ingcél. A destruction for the destruction he has given us. »

49. Cést, cía ragas dond éistecht¹¹ isa tir ?[Eirged¹²]nech las

---

1. díbergaig, Eg. YBL. 94ᵇ.
2. facomair Beinni Étair immach ar in[í]airgi, Eg. The *comarda* of LU. (= *comardu* YBL. comarddæ, St.) seems a deriv. of *comair*, Cymr. *cyfer*, Corn. *kever*.
3. na díbergae LU. díbercaig, Eg.
4. Lecid St. telcid YBL.
5. arna aiccithir sib do tir, Eg. arnachabhaccastar astir YBL. na faicther sib don tir, St.
6. ethath St. eththar YBL.
7. fagbaimis YBL. faigbimis St.
8. n-enig St. n-ainech YBL.
9. a leth frí, Eg. do, St.
10. i. e. mar an argain dorat dun, St.
11. citseacht YBL.
12. sic Eg. Om. LU. rachta YBL (= rachthai) teged St.

mbeth¹ na trí búada [and, ol Ingcél, Eg] .i. búaid clúaisse²
7 buaid rodairc 7 buaid n-airdmiusa/.

Atá limsa, for Mane Milscothach, buaid cluaisse.

Atá limsa dano, for Mane Andóe, buaid rodeirc 7 airdmiusa.

IS maith a³ dul duib amláid, for na dibercaig, fó(a)n-innas sin⁴.

49. « *Who will go on shore to listen? Let some one go* », *says Ingcél*, « *who should have there the three gifts, namely, gift of hearing, gift of far sight, and gift of judgment.* »

« *I* », *says Mané Honeyworded*, « *have the gift of hearing.* »

« *And I* », *says Mané Unslow*, « *have the gift of far sight and of judgment* »

« *'Tis well for you to go thus⁵*, » *say the reavers* « *good is that wise.* »

50 Tótiagat⁶ nónbor iarom co mbátar for Beind Étair, drís cid roclótís 7 adchetís.

Tá (.i. clostid) chein! for Mane Milscothach.

Cid sin ? for Mani Andói.

Fuaim n-echraide fórig⁷ rocluiniursa⁸.

Atchíu-sa⁹ tría búaid rodeirc, for a chéli

Cést. cid atcí-siu hi suidiu¹⁰ ?

Atchíu-sa and, for se, echrada ána aurarddai ailde agmaia

---

1 lassa mbiad, Eg lasa mbeth YBL lasimbia St
2 n-éistechta, Eg
3 For the force of *a* here cf *inna thcht* « in so going », Wb 11ᵇ22, and *is feri a tuidecht* LU 100ᵃ10 *a tuidecht* Ml The *amlaid* is tautologous YBL omits it
4 fon indus sin YBL IS con iarum duib dul fon indus sin, ar na dibergaig, St
5 literally « it should be gone »
6 luid St Dotiagad YBL
7 Cf fogur carpait forig, « noise of a good king's chariot », Lismore Lives, l 1163
8 itcluinimsi, St
9 Atachiusa YBL Atciusa dano St
10 in nosa St For the last six lines of § 49 and the first seven lines of § 50 Eg 122ᵇ 2 has only Ataat limii a triur, ar meicc Duind Déssa ocus ragmaitne ann Missi lib, ol Ingcel

Luid iarsin Ingcel 7 tri meicc hi Duind Desa cor'gabsat de Sescund hU urbeoil hi tírib Cúaland dond fairese

IS annsin ro airigsetar réim Conairi atúaid cuccu

IS annsin atbert Ingheel ri Fer ngair. Cid eter atchisi ? Comd ann atbert

— 42 —

allmarda, fosenga scitha sceinmnecha, fégi faebordae fem*en*dae.
foréim¹ focrotha morcheltar talman. doriadat² ilardae uscib
indberaib ingantaib.

50. Then nine men *come* go on till they were on the Hill of Howth,
to know what they might hear and see.
« Be still (i. e. hearken) a while ! » says Mané Honey-worded.
« What is that ? » asks Mané Unslow.
« The sound of a good king's cavalcade I hear. »
« By the gift of far sight, I see », quoth his comrade.
« What seest thou here ? »
« I see there », quoth he, « cavalcades splendid, lofty, beautiful,
warlike, foreign, somewhat slender, weary, active, keen, whetted(?),
vehement(?) a good course that shakes a great covering(?) of land.
They fare to many heights, with wondrous waters and invers. »

51. « Citne usci 7 ardae 7 inbera dorriadat ? »
« Ni anse. INdéoin, Cult³, Cuilten⁴. Máfat⁵, Ammat, Iarmáfat, Finne, Goiste⁶, Guistine. Gai glais⁷ úas charptib⁸.
Calga⁹ dét foi|s liastaib. Scéith airgdidi úasa n-ullib¹⁰. Leth-
ruith¹¹ 7 lethgobra. Etaige cech óendatha impu.
« Atchiusa iarsin sain[s]labra sainaithe¹² remib .i. tri cóecait
gabur ndubglas, Itt é cendbeca, corrderga, biruich, baslethain,
bolg[s]róin¹³, bruinnideirg, beólaide, s[o]aitside¹⁴, soga-
báldai¹⁵, crechfobdi, fégi, faebordae, femendae,/cona trib cóec-
taib srían(cruanmaith¹⁶ friu.

1. leg. fó-réim
2. dorriaghat YBL.
3. Colt St.
4. Tulten St. Inneoin colt cuillend semot mafotherm, Eg.
5. Madat St.
6. Findi, Goiste YBL. Finne. Goisce St.
7. glassae Eg. glas YBL.
8. cairpthib scrutaidi Eg.
9. taga St. calca YBL.
10. os uillib St. huas uillib YBL.
11. leithred Eg
12. sainigthe Eg. sainaigthi YBL. sainaigthe St.
13. bolgsroin St. bolcsroin YBL.
14. soastaide Eg. saitside St. YBL.
15. fogabáltaide Eg. sogabaltaige YBL. sogabalta St.
16. co cruan 7 maithni Eg. cruanmaithne YBL. cruanmoethne St.

51. « What are the waters and heights and invers that they traverse? »

« Easy to say: Indéoin, Cult, Cuiltén, Máfat, Ammat, Iarmáfat, Finne, Goiste, Guistine. Gray spears over chariots: ivory-hilted swords on thighs: silvery shields above their elbows. Half red(?) and half white. Garments of every colour about them.

« Thereafter I see before them special cattle specially keen, to wit, thrice fifty dark-gray steeds. Small-headed are they, red-nosed(?), pointed, broad-hoofed, big-nosed, red-chested, fat, easily-stopt[1], easily-yoked, foray-nimble[2], keen, whetted(?), vehement(?), with their thrice fifty bridles of red enamel upon them. »

52. Tongusa[3] a toinges mo thúath, for fer ind rodairc, is slabra[4] (.i. is cethir) nach suthchernai insin. Is i[5] mo airdmius[s]a de, is é Conaire mac Eterscéle, co formnaib[6] fer nErend n-imbi, daróet in sligi[7].

Tiagait for cúlu iarom co n-ecsetár[8] dona díbergaib[9]. Issed inso ro•chúalammár 7 atconnarcmár, ar iat[10].

52. « I swear by what my tribe swears », says the man of the long sight, « these are the cattle of some good lord. This is my judgment thereof: it is Conaire, son of Eterscéle, with multitudes of the men of Erin around him, who has travelled the road. »

Back then they go that they may tell (it) to the reavers. « This », they say, « is what we have heard and seen. »

53. Bátár sochaide, tra, eter siu 7 anall, in tsluaig-se[11] .i.

1. -aitside for -aistidi, part. perf. pass. of -astaim.
2. -fobdi, pl. n. of fobhaid .i. luath nó ésgaid, O'Cl.
3. Tungsa, Eg.
4. marcsluag, Eg.
5. issé, Eg. is e, St. IS hi mo airdmes de, YBL.
6. formna St.
7. do toet chuccund issin sligid, Eg. 122b 2. doret intligi YBL. doret in tsligi St.
8. co ńdecdetar Eg. condecdatar YBL. (leg. conécatar) 7 indisit St.
9. dibergachaib YBL. St.
10. issed so itcualamar 7 atchonncamar, St. adconnarcmar, YBL., omitting ar iat.
11. Batar sochaidi tra iatsom eter allmarchu 7 erendcha. Rob é immorro a lín huli himmalle, Eg. Bai sochaide tra adiu 7 anall in thsluaig, St.

tri cóecait churach 7 cóic míli¹ indib, 7 deich cét in cach míli.
Ro thocaibset² iarom na séolu forsna curchu³, 7 dos-curethar⁴
dochom tíre, co ragbaiset⁵ hi Tracht Fuirbthi.

*53. Of this host, then, there was a multitude, both on this side
and on that, namely, thrice fifty boats, with five thousand in them,
and ten hundred in every thousand⁶. Then they hoisted the sails on
the boats, and steer them thence to shore, till they landed on the
Strand of Fuirbthe.*

54. Intan ro[n]gabsat⁷ na curaig tír, is and rom [LU. 85ᵇ]-
bói⁸ Mac cecht oc béim tened⁹ i mBrudin Dá Dergae. La
fúaim na spréde socressa na tri cóecait curach¹⁰, co mbátár for
formnu na fairrce.
Tá chein¹¹, for Ingcél, samailte latso¹², a Fir rogain?
Ni fetursa, ol Fer rogain, manid Luchdond¹³ cainte fail i
n-Emain Macha dogní in [m]bosórguin-se oc gait a bid aire¹⁴
ar écin, nó grech ind Luchduind¹⁵ [thiar Eg.] hi Temair
Lochrae, nó béim spréde Maic cecht oc átúd tened ria rig n-
Erend airm hi fói¹⁶. Cach spréd tra, 7 cach frass doléiced a
tene¹⁷ for lar no fonaidfide¹⁸ cét lóeg 7 di lethorc tria.

1. ṫṙi .lll. churach 7 .u. míli chét LU. .u. míli Eg.
2. Arrothocaibset St. Read arrocaibset, and cf. arrocbat LL. 249ᵃ2.
3. for na curchaib Eg. for na crundu YBL. ara curachaib St.
4. nos curethar St.
5. rogaibset Eg. rogaibseat YBL. rogabsat St.
6. Hence, and from § 38, it seems that mîle, like the Germanic thúsundi, was originally a vague abstract noun meaning « many hundreds ».
7. rongabsat YBL.
8. robui YBL.
9. is ann bai Mac cecht ic bein teined, St.
10. rascuichset himmach o thír, Eg. na tri choectu curach, YBL.
11. coistid bic, Eg.
12. samaltai lettso, Eg. cid samalta so, St.
13. manib hi Luchtondd, Eg. mane be Luchdon, St.
14. fair St.
15. luchthoind Eg. luchduind YBL. luchtuinn, St.
16. airm hi fuil hinocht. Eg. airm i foi innocht. St.
17. in spréd, YBL.
18. cech frasta [leg. fras tra] immorro doléiced in spréd for lar no fonfaithea, Eg. for lar fonuinfidi cet laeg 7 de lethore, YBL.
Cech fras tra dolleicid in tened do spredaib ar lar, no fui[n]feda cét laeg 7 de letore, St.

Ní thuca and in fer sin (.i. Conaire) innocht, fordat maic
Duind Désa. Is líach a bith [fo dochur namat — Eg.¹].
Ni bu liachu side limsa², for Ingcél, indás ind orcuin do-
ratsa duibse. ba hé mo líthsa co mbad hé docorad³ and⁴.

54. When the boats reached land, then was Mac cecht a-striking
fire in Dá Derga's Hostel. At the sound of the spark the thrice fifty
boats were hurled out, so that they were on the shoulders of the sea.

« Be silent a while! » says Ingcél. « Liken thou that, O Fer
rogain. »

« I know not », answers Fer rogain, « unless it is Luchdonn
the satirist in Emain Macha⁵, who makes this hand-smiting when
his food is taken from him perforce : or the scream of Luchdonn in
Temair Luachra : or Mac cecht's striking a spark, when he kindles
a fire before a king of Erin where he sleeps. Every spark and every
shower which his fire would let fall on the floor would broil a
hundred calves and two half-pigs.

« May God not bring that man (even Conaire) there tonight! »
say Donn Désa's sons. » Sad that he is under the hurt of foes! »

« Meseems », says Ingcél, « it should be no sadder for me than
the destruction I gave you. This were my feast that he (Conaire)
should chance (to come) there. »

55. Tos-cuirethar[a coblach⁶] dochom tíre. A ngloim⁷ ro
lásat na tri *cóecait* curach oc tuidecht hi tir forroc rath⁸
Brudin Dá Dergae⁹, conná rabi gai [na sciath — Eg.] for

---

1. is liach garsecla do, St.
2. ni mo immorro is liach libebsi(!) in sgél sin. andás ropa líach limsa ind orgain doratusa dúibsi i n-Albain, Eg. nirluga ba liach limsa ind argain ortabairsi limsa 7 doratus duib, St. ni bud liacha suidiu limsa, for Ingcel, indas inn orcuin doratsa duibse, YBL.
3. docuired, Eg.
4. Robad he mo lithsa co mbad he nothecmad ann innocht, St.
5. now the Navan fort, two miles west of Armagh.
6. Doscurethar iartain, Eg. Toscuirithir YBL. omitting *a coblach*
7. In gloimm 7 in bresmaidm, Eg.
8. ro crithnaig 7 ro crothastar, Eg.
9. Gabsat dochum thire iarsin co fortren feramail na tri coecait curach, 7 an glom ro lasat na barcu dochom thire ro la in Bruiden uile i cor 7 i crichnagad [leg. crithnugud], St.

alchaing inte, acht ro lásat grith co mbátár for lar in tige uli¹.

55. Their fleet is steered to land. The noise that the thrice fifty vessels made in running ashore shook Dá Derga's Hostel so that no spear nor shield remained on rack therein, but the weapons uttered a cry and fell all on the floor of the house.

56. Samailte lat², a Chonaire, [ar cách, Eg.], cia fúaim so³ ?

Ním-thása a samail *acht* manid talam immid-róe⁴ (.i. ro bris), *nó* manid⁵ in Leuidán timchella⁶ in ndomon adchomaic a erball do thóchur in betha tar a chend⁷, *nó* barc mac Duind Désa ro gab tír. Dirsan náptar hé bátar⁸ and ! Bátár comaltai carthanġcha⁹ dúnd. Bá inmain in fianlag¹⁰ : nisn-áigfimmis¹¹ innocht.

IS and ránic *Conaire* co mbói hi¹² faichthi na Bruidni¹³.

56. « Liken thou that, O Conaire », says every one: « what is this noise ? »

« *I know nothing like it unless it be the earth that has broken, or the Leviathan that surrounds the globe*¹⁴ *and strikes with its tail to overturn the world, or the barque of the sons of Donn Désa that has reached the shore. Alas that it should not be they who are*

---

1. rolaiset armgrith 7 torcratar for lar na Bruidne, Eg. rolaiset grith co mbatar ar lar Bruidne Da Dergæ, St.
2. Samalta letso so, Eg.
3. cid in fuaim atdcúalamar, Eg. Cid so, a Chonaire, ol a muindter, 7 cia samail in fuaimsea? St.
4. ma*n*ib talam dluges ar do, Eg. Nimtha a tshamail, ol Conaire, manip talam ro mebaid, St.
5. ma*n*ib he Eg. manib, St.
6. timcellas Eg. St. timchela YBL.
7. do chor in betha dar cend, Eg. darachenn St.
8. nach fat ata, Eg.
9. carthacha YBL. Batir comalta cartantach, St.
10. fiallach n-isin, Eg. Batar inmain in fiall*ach* ann, St.
11. *-áigsimmis*, LU. *-ágfimis*, Eg. *-aigfimis*, YBL. ni faigfimísní inocht damtis iat, St.
12. ar faigthi na bruidne, St.
13. bruidne YBL.
14. Cf. the Midhgardhsormr, the world-serpent, « whose coils gird round the whole Midgard ». In old Icelandic translations of legends *Leviathan* is rendered by *Midhgardhsormr*, Cleasby-Vigfusson.

— 47 —

there! Beloved fosterbrothers of our own were they! Dear were the champions. We should not have feared them tonight. »
Then came Conaire, so that he was on the green of the Hostel.

57. In tan ro chúala¹ Mac cecht in fothrond², atar lais roptar óic táncatár co a muintir³. La sodain forling⁴ a gaisced dia cobair. Aidblithir léo bid⁵ torandchles tri cét a chluiche oc forláim⁶ a gaiscid⁷. [Ni bái báa di sodain de sin⁸.]

57. When Mac cecht heard the tumultuous noise, it seemed to him that warriors had attacked his people. Thereat he leapt on to his armour to help them. Vast as the thunder-feat of three hundred did they deem his game in leaping to his weapons. Thereof there was no profit.

58. IN barc iarom i mbátar maic Duind [Désa], ba inte bói in caur márthrelmach andiaraid inna braine⁹ na bárce, in léo uathmar andsa, Ingcél Cáech mac úi Conmaic¹⁰. Lethithir damsechi ind óensúil bói asa étun. Secht maic imlesain inte¹¹. Bátar duibithir degaid¹². Méit chori cholbthaige¹³ cechtar a dá glúne¹⁴. Méit chléib búana cechtar a dá dordn¹⁵. Méit mulaig for gut¹⁶ mella a dromma. Sithithir¹⁷ cuing n-úarmedóin¹⁸ cechtar a dá lurgan.

1. ronchuala YBL.
2. foidtrom St. fothroṁ YBL. In LU. this sentence ends § 56, and *Atar lais*, etc. begins § 57.
3. andar laiss ropa bidbaig no ecnámait tancatar dochum a muintire, Eg.
4. gabais St.
5. Indar léo ba, St.
6. a cuiclige oc forlaimm, YBL.
7. cuiclige ic urtócbáil a gaiscid, Eg. a cui[c]lige a[c] gabail a arm, St.
8. Eg. St. and YBL. omit this sentence, which was, perhaps, a marginal remark.
9. imbraine YBL. St.
10. Conmaicne, St. Conmaicni YBL.
11. indi, Eg. imblesan inti, YBL.
12. Ba duibithir déga hi, Eg. 123ᵇ1. Batar dubithir dethaigh, YBL.
13. méit core hi rachad colptach, Eg.
14. glún Eg. glun St. gluine, YBL.
15. adbrond Eg. dornn St.
16. mullaig ar gut St. for gad, YBL.
17. sithir St.
18. n-imechtraid, Eg. n-iarmedoin St.

— 48 —

eg. curad

Gabsat tra [iarsin na .lll. curaig ocus — Eg] na *cóic* míli cét sin, 7 deich cét cacha¹ mili, hi Tracht Fuirbthe².

58. Now in the bow of the ship wherein were Donn (Désa's) sons was the champion, greatly-accoutred, wrathful, the lion hard and awful, Ingcél the One-eyed, great-grandson of Conmac Wide as an oxhide was the single eye protruding from his forehead, with seven pupils therein, which were black as a chafer. Each of his knees as big as a stripper's caldron, each of his two fists was the size of a reaping-basket; his buttocks as big as a cheese on a withe: each of his shins as long as an outer yoke

So after that, the thrice fifty boats, and those five thousands — with ten hundred in every thousand, — landed on the Strand of Furrbthe.

59 Luid tra Conaire cona muintir isin mBrudin, 7 gabais cách a suide³ is'tig, eter gess⁴ 7 nemgess⁵, 7 gabsat [LU. 86ᵃ] na tri Deirg a suide⁵, 7 gabais Fer caille cona muic a s[h]uide.

59 Then Conaire with his people entered the Hostel, and each took his seat within, both tabu and non-tabu. And the three Reds took their seats, and Fer caille with his swine took his seat

'BC fotal bermm
'Cleary fotalsceith
'a guessed long'

60 Tosn-ánic⁶ Da Dergae iarsin⁷, tri lll óclách⁸, 7 fotol-berrad⁹ co clais a dá chúlad for cach fir dib, 7 gerrchocholl co mell a ndá lárac¹⁰ Berdbróca¹¹ brecglassa impu tri lll maglorg¹² ndraigin co fethnib¹³ iarind¹⁴ ina lamaib

— slant

1 in cach YBL St
2 Muirbthen, Eg Furbthen St Fuirbten YBL
3. imdaid Eg shuidi YBL mad St
4 nemgheis YBL
5 suidiu YBL perperam
6 Tostanic YBL
7 IS ann sin immorro dosn-ánic Da Derga, Eg Dothaet Da Derga cucu istech iarum, St
8. tri coecat oclaech a lin St tri caectaib oclach, YBL
9. fothalberrad St fotalbearrad YBL Cf fotal scéith Lec. 55ᵃ 15.
10. gerrcochaill impu co mellaib a larace, Eg 123ᵇ i gerrcochaill conmellaib allaarg impe, St gerrchochaill co mell a da larce YBL
11. berrbroccí YBL Berrbroca St
12 mutlorc Eg Tri I maglorg St tri caecait maglorg, YBL
13. cona fethanaib, Eg co cendaib St co feithnib, YBL
14 iairn YBL St YBL.

mag-, mog- gross great

— 49 —

Fochen¹, a phopa *Conaire*! *for* se. Cid *formna* fer n-Er*end* dothaistis² latt, ros-biad³ failte [fodeisin, Eg.]

60. *Thereafter Dá Derga came to them, with thrice fifty warriors, each of them having a long head of hair to the hollow of his polls, and a short cloak to their buttocks. Speckled-green drawers*⁴ *they wore, and in their hands were thrice fifty great clubs of thorn with bands of iron.*

« *Welcome, O master Conaire!* » *quoth he.* « *Though the bulk of the men of Erin were to come with thee, they themselves would have a welcome.* »

61. IN tan⁵ bátar and conaccatar a[n]n⁶ óenbandscáil do dorus na Brud*ne*⁷, iar fu*n*iud ngréne, oc cuinchid a[.]eicthe issa tech. Sithidir claideb [n]garmnai⁸ cechtar a dá lurgan. Bátár dubithir druim ndáil⁹. Brat riabach rolómar impi ¹⁰. Tacmainged¹¹ a fés ichtarach co[f-]rici a glún. A béoil *for* le[i]th a cind.

61. *When they were there they saw a lone woman coming to the door of the Hostel, after sunset, and seeking to be let in. As long as a weaver's beam was each of her two shins, and they were as dark as the back of a stag-beetle. A greyish, woolly mantle she wore. Her lower hair used to reach as far as her knee. Her lips were on one side of her head.*

62. Totháet co tard¹² a lethgúalaind fri haursaind in taige, oc

1. IS mochen duit, Eg. Phochen YBL. IS ann asb*er*t Da D*er*ga, Focen, St.
2. tisad St.
3. rosmbiadfaindsea YBL. ros-biathfaindsi, St.
4. See Zimmer, KZ., XXX, 84.
5. Am*al*, Eg.
6. inní Eg. co facatar in. YBL.
7. in n-óenmnái cechndiriuch dochum dorais na Br*udne*, Eg.
8. ngarmnai YBL.
9. Ba duibithir dega cech n-alt 7 cech n-ági di, Eg. 7 badir duibith*i*r degaid, St. batar dubithir dethaich, YBL.
10. Araili arait múscaidi breclachtna impi *cona* imlib iarnaidi si imtromm fri imtecht si aduar fri anad étchig fri airechtai a aithi oénbruitt na araite sin, Eg. 123ᵇ1—123ᵇ2.
11. Rasoiched im*morro* Eg. tacmaicead YBL. Ro soiched St.
12. Toet c[o]tarat Eg. Luid co tard, St. totheit co tard YBL.

4

admilliud ind rig 7 na maccóem ro bátár imbi isin tig. Ésseom
fein atarâglastar¹ (.i. ro aicill) astig².

Maith³, a banscal⁴, or Conaire, cid atchí dúnd massat
fissid⁵?

Atchiusa daitsiu⁶, immorro, ol sisi, nocon ternába⁷ ceinn⁸ ná
cárna dít asind áit hi tudchad⁹ acht 'na mbérat¹⁰ éoin ina crobaib.
Nibu dochél célsammár¹¹, a ben, or ésseom¹², ní tú chélas¹³
dún do grés¹⁴. Cia do chomainm-siu. or se, a banscál?¹⁵

Cailb, or sisi.

Ni forcraid anma son¹⁶, ol Conaire.

« Eché (.i. ni dorcha .i. is follus) it ili mo anmand¹⁷
chena¹⁸, [ol si, — YBL.]

« Cade iat-side¹⁹? ol Conaire.

« Ni anse », or si²⁰ : « Samon, Sinand, Seisclend, Sodb,
[Soéglend²¹, Samlocht²² — Eg.] Caill, Coll, Díchóem²³, Dí-
chiúil, Dithim²⁴, Díchuinne, Dichruidne²⁵, Dairne, Dárine,

---

1. sic YBL. leg. ataragládastar? roboi ica accallaim Eg. aicillestar hi, St.
2. asin tig amach 7 asbert fria, St.
3. maith sin YBL..
4. maith sin a ben St. Maith sin a banscal, YBL.
5. cid dái dún? indat fissid? Eg. inda fisid YBL. 7 indat fisid St.
6. duidseo YBL.
7. conach ernaboi H.
8. cern LU. cer̃r YBL. caer H. St. cáer Eg.
9. co na térnaba cáer na carna dít asin tigh hi tai hinocht, Eg. asin taig
hi taudchud YBL. asin tig ataei H. asin tigsa hi tanacais St.
10. amberat H. ina mberat. St. a mbertae YBL.
11. carsam Eg. carsamar St. celsamar YBL.
12. ol seisem YBL.
13. celmainiges, Eg.
14. See Appendix § 61.
15. Cia do chomainmseo, a banscal, ol Conaire? YBL.
16. ni forcrad n-anma son em YBL.
17. Eché it ilimdoi mo anmonnasa H. hé hé, ar sisi, at ili imdha mo an-
mandsa ol sisi, St.
18. Ni forcraid. Nach mó ón em? ol Conaire. Maith aili at ili imda mo
anmandso chena, ol sissi, Eg. 117ᵃ 1.
19. Cit n eisidí, YBL. Cadí iat sen St.
20. ol sisi YBL.
21. Saiglend YBL. Saigled St.
22. sain locht H. samlocht YBL.
23. Dicheni, St.
24. Dichuil. Dichim YBL.
25. Dicruithne Eg. Dicurumae YBL.

Déruaine[1], Égem, Ágam[2], Ethamne, Gním, Cluiche, Cethardam, Níth, Némain[3], Nóennen[4], Badb, Blosc, B[l]oár, Huae. óe Aife la Sruth, Mache, Médé, Mod›

For óen͡choiss 7 óenláim 7 óen͡anáil r[och]achain[6] dóib insin uil[e] o dorus in tige[7].

[Tungsa na dei día n-adraim nad epur ainm dib rit etur gar cían biasa hifus, Eg. 171ª 1—117ª 2]

62. *She came and put one of her shoulders against the doorpost of the house, casting the evil eye*[8] *on the king and the youths who surrounded him in the Hostel. He himself addressed her from within.*

« *Well, O woman* », *says Conaire*, « *if thou art a wizard, what seest thou for us ?* »

« *Truly I see for thee* », *she answers*, « *that neither fell*[9] *nor flesh of thine shall escape from the place into which thou hast come, save what birds will bear away in their claws* »

« *It was not an evil omen we foreboded, O woman* », *saith he* « *it is not thou that always augurs for us. What is thy name, O woman ?* »

« *Cailb* », *she answers.*

« *That is not much of a name* », *says Conaire.*

« *Lo (i e not dark, i. e manifest), many are my names besides* »

« *Which be they ?* » *asks Conaire.*

« *Easy to say* », *quoth she.* « *Samon, Sinand, etc* [10].

On one foot, and (holding up) one hand, and (breathing) one breath she sang all that to them from the door of the house

---

1 Der Uaine St
2 Ag Eg Agam St
3 Nemaind Eg
4 Noenden Eg YBL Noendhen St
5 After *Bloar* Eg has Uae Arhuath Soe arath Srod, Macha Mede, and H has Uath Meiti mod H hUæth Mede Mod YBL
6 rochacham YBL rochan si, St
7 For *o dorus in tige* Eg has 7 filet na hili huili anmand sin ainm dib sein bas maith letsu frecartsa duitsiu cocertsa húatsiu Eg
8 As to the evil eye, in Ireland, see *Irische Texte* IV, 323
9. The *cern, ceir, caer, cáer* of the MSS give no satisfactory meaning Read *cenm,* (gl scamae) Arm 176ᵇ 2, and cf Cymr *cenn,* ON *hinna* « membrane, film »
10 Compare the strings of mystical names in the charm against the child-stealing witch, ed. Gaster, *Folklore*, XI, 133, 145, 149

« *I swear by the gods whom I adore* », (says *Conaire*), « *that I will call thee by none of these names whether I shall be here a long or a short time.* »

63. Cid as áil dait ? ol C*onaire*.
A n-as áil daitsiu da*no*, or sisi.
Is gess damsa, ol C*onaire*, dám óenmná[1] do airitin iar fuin*iud* gréne[2].
Cid gess, or sisi, ní ragsa co ndecha[3] (.i. co ferur *nó* co rucur) mo aigidecht di ráith[4] isind áidchi-se innocht.
Apraid fria, ol Con*aire*, bérthair dam *ocus*[5] tinne di immach, 7 mo fuidell-sa, 7 anad i*m*-magin aile innocht.
Má dothanic[6] ém dond ríg, or sisi, co[na talla fair, Eg.] praind 7 lepaid óenmná inna thig, fogébthar[7] 'na écmais o neoch aile ocá mbía ainech[8], ma ró scáig coible[9] na flatha fil isin Brudin.
« IS feochair[10] in frecra », ol Con*aire*. « Dos-leic[11] ind, cid gess [LU. 86ᵇ] damsa. »
Búi gráin mór foraib iarsin día haccallaim na mná 7 míthauraras[12], acht nad fetatár ca*n* bói dóib[13].

63. « *What dost thou desire?* » *says Conaire.*
« *That which thou, too, desirest* », *she answered.*

1. H inserts: *no* aoin*ṫ*ir.
2. da airithin iar fuin ng*ré*ne YBL.
3. co comailliur Eg. co tomliur St.
4: m'oethoig*ocht* anorcuinich H. m'oigide*cht* latsa doraith, St. m'aididecht diraith, YBL.
5. co H.
6. donanuic H. dodanic YBL.
7. Ma ro scaith [leg. scáich] co*n*na talla fair proinn do aenmnai *no* lepaid bes fogebthar, St. madroscaich YBL. (leg. marodscáig).
8. adetar na aill o nach ailiu oca mbiad ainech YBL. adetar nach aill o nach ailiu oca mbia oinech H.
9. coiplithi, H. enech St. coibl*ide* YBL.
10. fracchair H. frechuir YBL.
11. leicid St. Read *nos-léic*, or (as in Eg.) *nos-léicid*.
12. mithaurassa, YBL. Boi gráin mor foraib iarsin o*cus* míturrusa athli acalma na mna forru, Eg. 117ᵃ 2. Boi grain mór 7 uamain orra tria irlabra na mna, 7 ro thirchan mor do micelmaine, St.
13. H omits this sentence.

— 53 —

« 'Tis à tabu of mine », says Conaire, « to receive the company of one woman after sunset. »

« Though it be a tabu », she replied, « I will not go until my guesting come at once¹ this very night. »

« Tell her », says Conaire, that an ox and a bacon-pig shall be taken out to her, and my leavings: provided that she stays tonight in some other place. »

« If in sooth », she says, « it has befallen the king not to have room in his house for the meal and bed of a solitary woman, they will be gotten apart from him from some one possessing generosity — if the hospitality of the Prince in the Hostel has departed. »

« Savage is the answer! » says Conaire. « Let her in, though it is a tabu of mine. »

Great loathing they felt after that from the woman's converse, and ill-foreboding; but they knew not the cause thereof.

64. Gabsait na diberga iarsin tir, 7 dollotar² co mbátar oc Leccaib cind ṡlébe. Bithobéle³ trá in Bruiden. Is aire asberthea⁴ « bruden » di, ar is cosmail fri béolu fir oc cor bruiden. Nó « bruden » .i. bruth-en .i. en bruthe inte⁵.

64. The reavers afterwards landed, and fared forth till they were at Lecca cinn ṡlébe. Ever open was the Hostel. Why it was called a Bruden was because it resembles the lips of a man blowing(?) a fire(?). Or bruden is from bruth-en, i. e. en « water », bruthe « of flesh » (broth) therein.

65. Bá mór in tene adsuithe⁶ oc Conairiu cach n-aidche⁷, .i. torc caille. Secht ndoraiss ass. Intan doniscide (.i. ro berthi) crand asa thóib ba mét⁸ daig ndáirthaige cach tob no théiged

1. Cf. doraith St. H. Cf. ni dessetar da ráith LL. 96ᵇ2.
2. Gabsat na diberrgaig tir 7 luidset, St.
3. Bith-oebelen St. Bidobela YBL.
4. atberar YBL. St. atperar H.
5. For this § Eg. has only : Lotar immorro na diberga co mbátar oc Leccaib cind sléibe d'indsaigid na Bruidni. The second etymology of bruden does not occur in the other copies, and is certainly an interpolation in LU.
6. See KZ. XXX 99. no atáithea, Eg. atsuide H. atothea St.
7. n-oidchi H. n-aidchi YBL. 95ᵇ22.
8. meit YBL.

asa tháib for cach ndorus¹. Ro bátár secht carpait deac di charptib Conaire fri cach ndorus don taig, 7 ba airecnai (i ba follus) dond aes bátar oc forcsin ² o͞ na longaib in tsoillsi mór sin tria drochu ³ na carpat.

65 *Great was the fire which was kindled by Conaire every night, to wit, a torc caille « Boar of the Wood » Seven outlets it had When a log was cut out of its side every flame that used to come forth at each outlet was as big as the blaze of a (burning) oratory There were seventeen of Conaire's chariots at every door of the house, and by those that were looking from the vessels that great light was clearly seen through the wheels of the chariots*

66 Samailte lat, a Fir rogain ! for Ingcél, cisi suillse mór sucut ⁴ ?

Noconom-thá⁵ a samail, for Fer rogain, acht manib daig⁶ do ríg Ni tuca⁷ dia and innocht in fer sin Is liach a orguin⁸.

Cid ahé (.i. dno) libse a flathius⁹ iful fir sin hi tir Erend ? ol Ingcel.

IS maith a *flathius*, or Fer rogain. Ní thaudchaid¹⁰ nél dar gréin o gabais¹¹ flathius [i. fri ré loc — Eg.] o medón errair co medon fogamair, 7 ni taudchaid¹² banna drúchta di féor

---

1 intan immorro no gluaisthea crand assa thóib, ba meinthir dam ndertaigh cech tobf (sic) no teiged dar cech ndorus de, Eg INtan dusnisgairti crant asa taob ba met doigh ndartigi gach top noteiged for gach ndorus don tig, H ba meit daig ndartaige, St
2 ba forréil do aes na fairesena Eg don aes na deicesin YBL ba hecnai do aes na forcsinoi, H ba haircenæ do æs na deicsin, St
3 droch*ta*, H triaasna drochu YBL tria doichta St
4 cia soillse mór sut Eg cisi saillsi mor suut, St. sug*ut* H
5 Nimtha so H Nimthi St
6 Nochomthasa a shamail mani dug YBL Nochonamthasa a samail acht memb daig, Eg minap doig H
7 nir lairge Eg ni thuctha YBL.
8 ar is mór liach a olec do dénamh, Eg H omits is liach a bith, St is liach YBL
9 Cinnas a flathuusa libsi? Eg cisi turcuita flatha, H cid ahé libsi a flaithiusa St
10 tainic St taudchad YBL thudchaid Eg
11 rogab St.
12 thuirted St

co medón lái, 7 ni fascnann¹ gáeth² chairchech cethrae³ co
nónae, 7 ní forruich⁴ mac tíre [ní — Eg.] ina flaith acht⁵
tárag⁶ firend⁷ cacha indse⁸ o cind bliadna co araile. Ocus
atat secht maic thíre i ngialnai⁹ fri fraigid ina thig-seom fri
comét¹⁰ ind rechta sin, 7 atá cúl-aittiri iarna chúl .i. Mac locc,
7 is he taccair¹¹ tara chend hi tig Conaire. IS ina flaith atát na
tri bairr for Erind .i. barr días 7 barr scoth 7 barr messa¹².
IS ina flaith as chombind la cach fer guth araile¹³ ocus betis téta
mendchrot, ar febas na cána 7 in tsída 7 in cháincomraic fail
sechnon¹⁴ na hErend. Ni thucca dia and innocht in fer sin. Is
líach a orgain¹⁵. [Is cróeb triana bláth — Eg.] Is mucc remi-
thuit¹⁶ mess. Is nóidiu¹⁷ ar aís. Is líach garsecle¹⁸ dó! »

Ba hé mo lith-sa, for Ingcél, coṁbad sé no beth and¹⁹,
7 robad orgain fo araile insin²⁰. Nípu²¹ andsu²² limsa indás²³
mo athair 7 mo mathair 7 mo secht nderbráthir²⁴ 7 ri mo

1. fascnam LU. fascnan YBL., St. fhasgnánn, H. gluaisind, Eg.
2. gaemgaeth YBL.
3. cairchech[i] erboll míl[i] innili, Eg.
4. marbann Eg. foruich YBL. forruich H. (= fo/-ro-lich), furaich St.
5. om. YBL. H.
6. darag Eg. taroigh H. ag St.
7. on chind YBL.
8. indise YBL. hindsi H. innisi St.
9. hi ngíalluigecht Eg. i ngiallus St. a ngiallnoi H. ingiallnai YBL.
10. imcoimet St. coimet YBL.
11. ag tagair H. tacras adal St.
12. In YBL. Eg. H. and St. this sentence follows the next.
13. achele St. araili YBL.
14. sethnu YBL. sechnón Eg. sethnoi H.
15. turbród Eg.
16. remituit, H. remetuit YBL. re tuitim mesa St. ria n-ithi measa H².
17. noedead St.
18. garsecle YBL. H. garsecle Eg., with the c interlined. garsecla St. gair-
seicle H². garséle LU.
19. comad he no tocrad and hinocht Eg. bid hé dochorad and YBL.
combad he no tecmad ann, St.
20. Ba hé mo lit sie, bit he docorad ann. Bá hé orcuin fon ailiu dún H.
Ba argain már á chele hí, St. Ba he orgain fon aile YBL.
21. nipo Eg. ni ba St.
22. ansu YBL. andsa LU. hindsa St.
23. indas YBL. andás LU. oldas St. oldás Eg.
24. nderbraithre St. nderpraithri H.

thuathi doratus-sa duibsi¹ ria tuidecht (i n-athchor) na diberġac²

IS fír, is fír! or in t-áes³ uile ró bátar immalle frisna dibergachu.

66 « *Canst thou say, O Fer rogain, what that great light yonder resembles?* »

« *I cannot liken it to aught* », answers Fer rogain, « *unless it be the fire of a king. May God not bring that man there tonight! 'Tis a pity to destroy him!* »

« *What then deemest thou* », says Ingcél, « *of that man's reign in the land of Erin?* »

« *Good is his reign* », replied Fer rogain. « *Since he assumed the kingship, no cloud has veiled the sun for the space of a day from the middle of spring to the middle of autumn. And not a dewdrop fell from grass till midday, and wind would not touch a beast's tail until nones. And in his reign, from year's end to year's end, no wolf has attacked aught save one bullcalf of each byre, and to maintain this rule there are seven wolves in hostageship at the sidewall in his house, and behind this a further security, even Maclocc, and 'tis he that pleads (for them) in Conaire's house. In Conaire's reign are the three crowns on Erin, namely, crown of corn-ears, and crown of flowers, and crown of oak mast. In his reign, too, each man deems the other's voice as melodious as the strings of lutes, because of the excellence of the law and the peace and the goodwill prevailing throughout Erin. May God not bring that man there tonight! 'Tis sad to destroy him. 'Tis « a branch through its blossom », 'Tis a swine that falls before mast. 'Tis an infant in age. Sad is the shortness of his life!*

« *This was my luck* » says Ingcél, « *that he should be there, and there should be one Destruction for another. It were not more grievous to me than my father and my mother and my seven brothers, and the king of my country, whom I gave up to you before coming on the transfer of the rapine.* »

---

1 ortapausi limbsoi, H
2 ria taidecht inn athchor ndibeirgi YBL 96ᵃ 1 ria taidecht in athcor ndiberge, St ria toigecht ind athchur ndiperge H
3 in t-aes denma Eg in t-aes demna 7, St

« 'Tis true, 'tis true! » say the evildoers who were along with the reavers.

67. Toscurethar[1] bedg na díbergaig a Tracht Fuirbthen[2], 7 doberat cloich cach fir léo do chur chairnd, ar ba sí deochair lasna[3] fianna hi tossuch eter orgain 7 maidm n-imairic. Corthe no chlantais[4] intan ba[5] maidm n-imairic. Card[6] immorro fochertitis[7] intan ba[8] n-orgain [LU. 87ᵃ] Carnd ro láiset[9] iarom intan sin, úaire ba orgain. Hi cianfocus on tig[10] on, ar na forchlótís 7 na haiccitis[11] ón tig[12].

67. The reavers make a start from the Strand of Fuirbthe, and bring a stone for each man to make a cairn; for this was the distinction which at first the Fians made between a « Destruction » and a « Rout ». A pillar-stone they used to plant when there would be a Rout. A cairn, however, they used to make when there would be a Destruction. At this time, then, they made a cairn, for it was a Destruction. Far from the house was this, that they might not be heard or seen therefrom.

68. Ar díb fát[h]aib dorigset a carnd .i. ar ba bés carnd la dibirg, 7 dano co fintaís a n-esbada oc Brudin. Cach óen no thicfad slán úadi no berad a cloich asin charnd, co farctais immorro cloch[a] in lochta no mair[b]fitis occi, conid assin ro fessatár a n-esbada. Conid ed ármit eólaig in tsenchassa conid fer

---

1. Toschuirther YBL. Doscuirether Eg. Tuscuirethar H. Tucatar St. The « na dibergaig » seems to have been a gloss which has crept into the text (Strachan).
2. fuirbthín YBL. fuirbthe Eg.
3. donitis na St. boi lasna H. no bith laisna H².
4. nocertaís St. no clandaitís YBL. no clandaidís H.
5. ba YBL. bad LU.
6. carn YBL. carnn St.
7. focherdaitis YBL. focheirditis Eg. focerdis H. focertais St. focerdatais H².
8. ba YBL. St. Eg. H. bad LU.
9. lasat YBL. St. H. lásat Eg.
10. tráigh Eg.
11. arna forclostis 7 na hacatais, H. arna forcloitis 7 arna haiccitis, St. arna forclostais 7 na aiccitis YBL.
12. arna forcloistís 7 na faicitís on bruidin, Eg.

cach clochi fil hi Carnd leca ro marbait dona dibergaib oc
Brudin. Comd din charnd sin atberar Leca i n-Úib Cellaig¹.

68 For two causes they built their cairn, namely, (first) since
this was a custom in marauding, and, secondly, that they might
find out their losses at the Hostel Every one that would come safe
from it would take his stone from the cairn. thus the stones of those
that were slain would be left, and thence they would know their
losses² And this is what men skilled in story recount, that for every
stone in Carn leca there was one of the reavers killed at the Hostel.
From that cairn Leca in Huí Cellaig is (so) called

69 Atáither toic tened la maccaib Duind desa do brith robaid do Conaire Comd hi sin céttendál robaid dorigned, 7
comd di adainter³ cech tendal robaid cosindiu

IS ed armit fairend aile comnbad i n-aidchi samna no irrthá
orgain Brudne, 7 comd din tendáil út lentar tendal samna o sin
co sudiu, 7 clocha hi temd samna⁴

69. A « boar of a fire » is kindled by the sons of Donn Desa to
give warning to Conaire So that is the first warning-beacon that has
been made (in Erin), and from it to this day every warning-beacon
is kindled

This is what others recount : that it was on the eve of samain
(All-Saints-day) the destruction of the Hostel was wrought, and
that from yonder beacon the beacon of samain is followed from that
to this, and stones (are placed) in the samain-fire.

70 Doronsat⁵ iarom na dibergaig comarli bali in ro lásat⁶
a carnd⁷.

---

1 Cellaib LU
2 Cf the Persian practice described by Procopius, ed Dindorf, pp 97,
98, and see *The Academy* for August 25, 1891, p 134
3 adairter LU
4. YBL, Eg H and St omit §§ 68 and 69, and the verbal forms shew
that these paragraphs are late interpolations.
5 Dogensat YBL Dogensot H gniset St
6 bali iriolsat YBL uaili rolasit H. doronsat St
7 in cardd, Eg

Maith, tra, or Ingcél frisna héolchu, cid as nesam[1] dún sund?

Ni *anse*, Bruden úi Dergae[2] rígbriugad[3] Herend.

Bátár dócho[4] ém fir maithi do saigid a céli[5] don brudin sin innocht[6]. Ba sí comarli na ndíbergach iarom nech [do chor Eg] úadib do déscin[7] dús cinnas ro[m]both and[8].

Cia ragas and do deicsin in tigi?[9] [ol cách[10]]

Cia no ragad, or Ingcél, *acht* mad messi, úair[11] iss mé dliges fiachu.

70. *Then the reavers framed a counsel at the place where they had put the cairn*

« *Well, then* », *says Ingcél to the guides,* « *what is nearest to us here?* »

« *Easy (to say): the Hostel of Hua Derga, chief-hospitaller of Erin* »

« *Good men indeed* » (*says Ingcél*) « *were likely to seek their fellows at that Hostel tonight* »

This, then, was the counsel of the reavers, to send one of them to see how things were there

« *Who will go there to espy the house?* » *says everyone.*

« *Who should go* », *says Ingcél,* « *but I, for 'tis I that am entitled to dues.* »

71. Totheit[12] Ingcél do thoscélad forsin Brudin cosin sech-

---

1 neasom YBL nesa St iss nessam Eg
2 Bruiden hui da Dergae YBL
3 Bruiden Da Derga, rigbruidin rigbrugad, Eg Bruiden húi Derga ribruigen H Bruiden hui Da Dergæ rigbrugaid YBL Bruiden Da Dergæ rigbrugad, St
4 doichi (pl of doich), YBL dochai H Ropud doich lind Eg
5 a chéle YBL
6 Ropud doich dind, ol Ingcél, fit maithi dochum a celi don Brudin sin hinocht, Eg
7 deicsin YBL dechsain na bruidni St desgin na bruidne H
8 cinnas robus isin Bruidin Eg cindus romboth and YBL cinnus romboth innti H cinnus robas innti St
9 don faircse inti Eg do dfecsin na bruidne H
10 ol cauch H
11 huairi YBL uair St H
12. Taet H Tct H² Totheit YBL Do táet Eg Luid St

tmad (*nó cosin tres*) mac imlessan na hóensúla ro bói asa etun do chommus a ruisc isa tech do admilliud ind ríg 7 na maccóem ro bátar immi isin tig, conda-dercacha¹ tría drochu² na carpat.

Ro ráthaiged³ iarom as[in]tig⁴ anall Ingcél. Docuirethar⁵ bedg ón tig⁶ iarná ráthugud.

71. Ingcél went to reconnoitre the Hostel with one of the seven (or one of the three) pupils of the single eye which stood out of his forehead, to fit his eye into the house in order to destroy the king and the youths who were around him therein. And Ingcél saw them through the wheels of the chariots.

Then Ingcél was perceived from the house. He makes a start from it after being perceived.

72. Téit co[r]ránic na díberga bali hi[r]rábatár⁷. Fochress⁸ cach cúaird imm alaile don dibirg⁹ fri éitsecht¹⁰ in scéoil¹¹. Airig na dibergae hi firmedón na cuardae¹². Batár hésidé Fer gér¹³ 7 Fer gel 7 Fer rogel 7 Fer rogain 7 Lomna druth 7 Ingcél Caech. Sesiur¹⁴ i[n]medón na cuardae¹⁵, 7 luid Fer rogain día [f]rithchomarc¹⁶.

72. He went till he reached the reavers in the stead wherein they were. Each circle of them was set around another to hear the tidings — the chiefs of the reavers being in the very centre of the circles.

1. coro dereca Eg. condodercacha H.
2. drochtai H. dorchu St.
3. Rathaiger St. Rathuiger Eg.¹. ratháigeth H.
4. asin tig YBL. St. Eg. asin tigh H.
5. Tacuirethar YBL. Toc[u]redar St. Tocurethar Eg. Tocuretbar Eg.¹.
6. bed[c] de on tig amach St. Eg.¹.
7. i mbatar St. Eg.¹ i rabatar YBL.
8. focreas YBL. Eg.¹ Focerd H.
9. din dibeirg YBL. Isi annsin dorónsat na díbergaich tri círrchaill dib imm Inghél, Eg.
10. heistecht YBL. eithsecht St.
11. dona dibercachtaib frisna hetsichtaip ina scél, H.
12. cuarta YBL. St. cúartoi H. him-medón na trí circhull, Eg.
13. gair St. YBL. H. St. and Eg. omit Fer gér.
14. seisiur doib YBL. seisir doib St.
15. cuarta YBL. St. circeul, Eg.
16. [f]reisnéis, Eg. ritchomorc Eg.¹

*There were Fer gér and Fer gel and Fer rogel and Fer rogain and
Lomna the Buffoon, and Ingcél the One-eyed — six in the centre
of the circles. And Fer rogain went to question Ingcél.*

73. Cinnas sin, a Ingceoil? for[1] Fer rogain.
Cip indas, for Ingcél, is rigda in costud : is [s]lúagda[2] a
sséselbe[3], is flaithemda a fúaim[4], Cia bé, céin co pé[5] rí and,
gébatsa[6] a tech issinni noh-dligim[7]. Dothǽt cor mo diberga[8] de.
Foracaibsemne[9] fri láim daitsiu[10], a Ingcéoil, fordat co-
maltae Conairi[11], Nadh-iurmais[12] orgain co fesmais cia no
beth inni[13].
Cést[14], in dercacha-su a tech[15] co maith, a Ingceoil? for[16]
Fer rogain.
Ro lá mo súil-se lúathchuaird[17] and, 7 gebait[18] im fiachu
amal atá.

73. « *How is that, O Ingcél?* » *asks Fer rogain.*
« *However it be* », *answers Ingcél*, « *royal is the custom(?),
hostful is the tumult : kingly is the noise thereof. Whether a king be*

---

1. uar H.
2. sluagdo H.
3. in shéissilbe Eg. a séselpe H.
4. in toirmm, Eg.
5. bé fo na be, YBL. St. be fo na be, H. be fo nábe Eg.¹ cia beith cinco rab Eg.
6. gebassa YBL. gebasa St. gébatsa Eg. gebotsai H. gebat Eg.¹
7. isin ni notdligim H. is inni dlegmait St. sinni dlegmait Eg.¹ is inui no dligim YBL. is in ní dligim St.
8. dibergi YBL.
9. Faracbaisemne YBL. forfacboigsimne em H. Faracbamarne St. Forachaibsem Eg. Forfacbamairni Eg.¹.
10. deitsiu YBL
11. ar trí comaltai Conaire Eg. fordat comaltai Conaire, YBL.
12. nat n-iúrfamais H. nad n-irmais St. nadniurmais YBL. nad iúrmaiss Eg. nach n-iurmuis Eg.¹
13. nobíad inti, Eg. no ueith innti, H. no beth indti YBL. nobeth indi St.
14. Cesc H. Eg.
15. in ro dercaissiu in tech, Eg.
16. uar H.
17. luathcuairt St. H. Ro lamusa illuathcuairt Eg.¹ lúathchuáirt Eg.
18. gébat Eg. gebotsai H. gebait St. gebat Eg¹.

there or not, *I will take the house for what I have a right to. Thence
my turn of rapine cometh* ¹.

« *We have left it in thy hand, O Ingcél !* » say Conaire's fosterbrothers. « *(But) we should not wreak the Destruction till we
know who may be therein.* »

« *Question, hast thou seen the house well, O Ingcél ?* » asks Fer
rogain

« *Mine eye cast a rapid glance around it, and I will accept it
for my dues as it stands.* »

74. IS deithbǽr duit², a Ingceóil, cid no³ [LU. 87ᵇ] gabtha,
ol Fer rogain. ar n-aiti uli fil and⁴, ardrí Herend, Conaire
mac Eterscéli⁵ Cést, cid atchondarc-su⁶ isind toclu͞i⁷ férnnda
in tige fri enech [in] ríg⁸ isind leith anall ? »

74 « *Thou mayest well accept it, O Ingcél* », saith Fer rogain.
*the fosterfather of us all is there, Erin's overking, Conaire son of
Eterscéle* »

« *Question, what sawest thou in the champion's high seat of the
house, facing the King, on the opposite side ?* »

Imda Chormaic Coindlongas

75 Atchondarc and, ol se, fer gormainech mar rosc nglan
ngléoirda lais deitgen cóir [comard aicci i se mamda né-
manda⁹] aiged fochael forlethan [leiss, Eg] lin-folt find ¹⁰
forordae fair for tí [caim, Eg] choir imbi¹¹, milech airgit inna

---

1 Here Zimmer would (needlessly, I think) amend the Irish, KZ
XXVIII, 566
2 dait YBL om Eg
3 ro YBL
4 ar n-aitire fil and, St ar n-aitine fil ann Eg YBL Eg ¹
5 Etirsceoil YBL Etirsceoil Lg
6 Cesc cit atconnarcisie, H Cest cid atchonarcaissiu YBL cesc cid at
connaccaiss Lg
7 ochlai Eg tochlu YBL St fochloi H fochlai H ² foclai Eg ¹
8 for aghaidh in righ, H ² fri heinech rig din leith anall Eg ¹
9 sic Eg deitgen coir comard comgel, St deitgen coir comart comgel Eg ¹
10 Linfoltt finn fota, Eg linfolt find YBL St Eg ¹ lind folt LU linfolt
finn H H ²
11 foirtchi coir for a bullu H ².

brut. 7 claideb órduird¹ inna láim: scíath co cóicroth² óir fair³: sleg cóicrind⁴ ina láim: cóinso⁵ chóir cháin chorcorda lais, os é amulach⁶, ailmenmnach in fer sin.
Ocus iarsin cía acca and?

The Room of Cormac Condlongas.

75. « I saw there », says Ingcél, « a man of noble countenance, large, with a clear and sparkling eye, an even set of teeth, a face narrow below, broad above. Fair, flaxen, golden hair upon him, and a proper fillet around it. A brooch of silver in his mantle, and in his hand a gold-hilted sword. A shield with five golden circles upon it: a five-barbed javelin in his hand. A visage just, fair, ruddy he hath: he is also beardless. Modest-minded is that man! »
« And after that, whom sawest thou there? »

IMDA NÓI CÉLI CHORMAIC

76. Atconnarc and tríar fer⁷ fris aniar, 7 tríar fris anair, 7 tríar ara⁸ bélaib ind fir chetnai. Atar-let⁹ is óenmathair 7 óenathair dóib [a nonbur — Eg.]. It é comdesa, comchore, comalli, cosmaile uli. Cúlmongae foraib. Bruit úanidi impu uli. Tanaslaide¹⁰ óir inna mbrataib. Cúarscéith chredumae foraib. Slega druimnecha úasaib¹¹. Calg¹² dét il-láim cach fir díb. Óenreb léo uli .i. gabaid¹³ cach fer díb rind a claidib eter a dá mér

---

1. órduirnd, Eg. orduirn YBL. óirduird LU. orduirnn H. St. Eg.¹.
2. cúicriud, Eg. cocroth H.
3. for a muin H.
4. coícrennach, Eg.
5. caínsiu Eg. cóinsi, H. cainso St. caiusi YBL. cuindsi H.². cainsio Eg.¹.
6. amulchach YBL. St. H.². amulcach Eg. H. Eg.¹.
7. YBL. Eg. and H. omit.
8. ar Eg. Eg.¹.
9. andar latso, Eg. 115ᵃ L. Ata lat, YBL. St. Ada-lat H. Eg.¹.
10. Deilgi, Eg. tanasluidhe H. tanaslaidhi YBL. 96ᵇ 2. tanæslaide St. tanaeslaidea Eg.¹.
11. huáistib Eg. huastu YBL. Sleg druimnech huasa, St. sleg druimnech os detcolg Eg.¹..
12. Calgae Eg. calc YBL.
13. gabuis Eg. gaipith H.

7 imda-cuiret immá mér, 7 nodá-sinet¹ na claid*ib* a n-óenur iar sudi². Samailti lat insin, a Fir rogain? or Ing*c*él.

The Room of Cormac's nine comrades.

76. « There I saw three men to the west of Cormac, and three to the east of him, and three in front of the same man. Thou wouldst deem that the nine of them had one mother and one father. They are of the same age, equally goodly, equally beautiful, all alike. Thin rods (?) of gold in their mantles. Bent shields of bronze they bear. Ribbed javelins above them. An ivory-hilted sword in the hand of each. An unique feat they have, to wit, each of them takes his sword's point between his two fingers, and they twirl the swords round their fingers, and the swords afterwards extend themselves by themselves. Liken thou that, O Fer rogain », says Ingcél.

77. Ni an*se* damsa a samail, for Fer rogain. Cormac Con-dlongas³ m*a*c *Con*chobair insin, laech as dech fil iar⁴ cúl scéith hi tír Her*e*nd. IS ailmenmnach in mac⁵ sin. IS fail ní atá-gethar⁶ innocht, is láth gaile ar gaisced. is bri[u]gu ar tre-b[th]achas⁷. IS é⁸ in nonbor ucut fil⁹ immi-scom, na trí Dún-gusa 7 na trí Dóelgusa 7 na trí D[i]angusa¹⁰, nói céli¹¹ Cor-ma*i*c Co*n*longas ma*i*c *Con*chobair. Ni rubutar firu riam¹² ar a ndochur 7 ni ros-anachtatar ríam ar a sochur¹³. IS maith in

---

1. imdosinet St. nádosinead YBL. nota sinit H. *no* do sinet Eg.¹.
2. intan lecaitt huaidib, Eg. iar suidiu, St. YBL. H.
3. Conloing*es* St. conloingesu Eg.
4. for Eg.
5. fer YBL. St. Eg. H. Eg.¹.
6. isfail madagetar innocht YBL. mad goeth. innocht Eg. is fael mado-getar indo*cht* H. is fáil madagethar inocht, St. is fail madogethar innoct. Eg.¹.
7. trebtachas Eg. trebtach*us* St. trebthochus YBL. trebthach*us* H. treab-tachus Eg.¹.
8. iat dano Eg. is iat a nonbor Eg.¹.
9. fuil*et* H.
10. na tri dóelg*u*sa 7 na t*r*i díangusa 7 tri ángusa Eg. na trí Dungusa 7 na trí Dulg*u*sa 7 na tri Dang*u*sai, Eg.¹.
11. coemchéli Eg.
12. ni rubatar riam firu, YBL. ni rubatar firu riam St. rupa*ta*r H. rubad*ur* H.². rubutar Eg.¹.
13. *Om.* Eg.

láech fail etorru i. Cormac Condlong*as*¹. Tongu a toi*nges* mo thúath², totháetsat *nói* ndeichenbuir la Cormac inna chét-chumsclui, 7 totháetsat *nói* ndechenbair lá muint*ir*, cenmothá fer cech airm dóib 7 fer cech fir dib, 7 roindfid³ Cormac com-gnim fri cach n-óenfer ar dor*us* na Bruidne, 7 máidfid⁴ búaid ríg *nó* rigdamnae *nó* airig díb*er*g*ae*, 7 immaricfa clúd do [féin, Eg] cid crechtach⁵ a muinter uli⁶

77. « *Easy*», *says Fer rogain*, « *for me to liken them. It is Conchobar's son, Cormac Condlongas, the best hero behind a shield in the land of Erin Of modest mind is that boy! Evil is what he dreads tonight7 He is a champion of valour for feats of arms. he is an hospitaller for householding These are yon nine who surround him, the three Dringusses, and the three Doelgusses, and the three Dangusses, the nine comrades of Cormac Conlongas, son of Conchobar. They have never slain men on account of their misery, and they never spared them on account of their prosperity Good is the hero who is among them, even Cormac Condlongas. I swear what my tribe swears*⁸, *nine times ten will fall by Cormac in his first onset, and nine times ten will fall by his people, besides a man for each of their weapons, and a man for each of themselves. And Cormac will share prowess with any man before the Hostel, and he will boast of victory over a king or crownprince or noble of the reavers; and he himself will chance to escape, though all his people be wounded* ».

78. Mairg iuras in n-orgain-sa¹ for Lomna drúth, cid adáig⁹

---

1 *Om* Eg. Conloinges St
2 a toingend mo thuatha YBL a tong mo thuath, St Eg
3 raindfid YBL Eg roindfi St. roinnfi H roindfiu Eg
4. muirfid Eg mundfid St maidfid YBL maoithfi H
5 cithat crechtnaigthe H cid crechtaigthi YBL
6 Eg omits a muinter uli
7 Cf § 105
8 i e his tribal god, or, perhaps, his tribal totem « The Baperi are commonly called Banoku, they of the porcupine Their great oath is that of *ka noku* « by the porcupine », because the majority of them *sing*, to use the consecrated phrase, intimating that they feast, worship or revere that animal », *Folklore*, XII, 32
9. fodaig Eg daig YBL H daig St.

ind óenfir sin, Cormac Condlongas mac Concobair. Tongusa a toinges¹ mo thúath², for³ Lomna [Druth — Eg.] mac Duind Désa, mad messi conísed mo chomarli⁴ ní aidlébthai⁵ ind orgun cid dáig⁶ ind óenfir sin nammá, 7 ar a léchet⁷ 7 ar a febas ind láich.

78. « *Woe to him who shall wreak this Destruction!* » *says Lomna Drúth,* « *even because of that one man, Cormac Condlongas, son of Conchobar.* « *I swear what my tribe swears* », *says Lomna son of Donn Désa,* « *if I could fulfil my counsel, the Destruction would not be attempted were it only because of that one man, and because of the hero's beauty⁸ and goodness!* »

79. Ni chumthi⁹ [a tarmesce — Eg.], for Ingcél: néla fémid¹⁰ dofortecat¹¹. Fir ṅgér ṅgúasfes¹² da ṅgrúad ṅgabair gébthair fris, la lugi Fir rogain ruidfes. Ro gab do guth maidm fortsu, a Lomnae, ol Ingcél: at drochlaech-su 7 rot etar-sa¹³. Néla fémid dofortecat.

A[t] mbia basa lecht bas briscem lurgu mais for traig¹⁴ maitne [LU. 88ᵃ] do thig duind matin moch imbárach.

Assu éc ernbais ar thromsluaigthig¹⁵ coddet co teinnet co dered mbetha.

1. Tung a toing, Eg. Tongusa a toing Eg.¹.
2. thuatha YBL.
3. uar St. H. ol Eg. or Eg.¹.
4. condrissed in comarli, Eg.
5. aidlipther H. aidlebthai St. haidlebthai Eg.¹.
6. fodaig, Eg.
7. lóechdacht Eg. leichet YBL. 96ᵇ 28. lecet H. leicet Eg.¹.
8. ara lechet .i. ara caimi LU. 20ᵃ 29.
9. cumci YBL. 96ᵇ 29. Eg.¹. cuimci Eg. comci H. cumchi St.
10. feimmid YBL. femdith H. feimmid St. feimig Eg.
11. dotecat St. dothecat YBL. dotegat H. dot(ec)ut Eg.¹.
12. nguanfeas St. nguaisfeas YBL. nguaisfis H. nguainfes Eg.¹.
13. rotetatar YBL. St. rotfetatar H
14. Atmbia bas lechtoi bus brisgim lurcoi manaisi fri traig, H. Atmbia basa lecht bas brisce lurcu mais for traig, St. Atmbia basi lecht bas brisceam lurcu manais for traig YBL. Atmbia basalecht brisgem lurgu mas for traig, H². Atmbia bassa lect bas b(riscem) lurcu mais for traig, Eg.¹.
15. tro sluaigthib St. tromsluaigib Eg.¹. Asse cermmais ar tromsluaig tic H.².

Ní aisnébat sin na senchaid[i]¹ dul damsa ónd org*ain*, co-
rom-mé² nosn-órr³. »

79. « *It is not feasible to prevent it* », *says Ingcél:* « *clouds
of weakness come to you. A keen ordeal which will endanger two
cheeks of a goat will be opposed by the oath of Fer rogain, who will
run. Thy voice, O Lomna* », *says Ingcel,* « *hath taken breaking
upon thee: thou art a worthless warrior, and I know thee. Clouds
of weakness come to you.*

. . . .

to a lord's house early tomorrow morning.
Easier ... death on a heavy-host-house ... to the world's end.
*Neither old men nor historians shall declare that I quitted the
Destruction, until I shall wreak it.* »

80. Na haithb*er* ar n-einech⁴, a Ingc*eoi*l, for Gér ⁊ Gab*ur*
⁊ Fer rog*ain*. Iurthar ind org*un* mani má in talam fúe⁵, co-
nonro-marbtharni⁶ uli occi.
Ango⁷ dano, is deithb*er* daitsiu, a Ingc*eoi*l, for Lomna⁸ mac
Duind Desa. Ni daitsiu a dom*ai*ne na orgne⁹. Béra cend rig
ala-thúathe lat hartbe¹⁰ alaile, ⁊ toernae¹¹ as do thriur derbra-
thar assind org*ui*n .i. Ingcél ⁊ Écell ⁊ Dartaid na dibergae.

80. « *Reproach not our honour, O Ingcél* », *say Gér and Gabur
and Fer rogain.* « *The Destruction shall be wrought unless the earth
break under it, until all of us are slain thereby.* »

---

1. ni faisnebot sin nait sencha*dei*, H. ni aisnebet sin na seanchaid YBL.
ni aisnebat sin naid senchaid Eg.¹.
2. from *co-rop mé*
3. gurumme nosnoirr Eg.¹. For the various readings of Eg. see Appendix § 78.
4. Na ben aithb*er* ar ar n-enech, Eg. H.². na aidb*er* ar n-ainech YBL. St.
5. midroe St. Eg.¹. mani maide in talam Eg.
6. cononrobarbtharni LU. co*n*onrommarbtharni YBL. St. nocorom-martharsa Eg. co*n*onromarb*tharn*e H. co*n*onromarbtarni Eg.¹.
7. Is gó, Eg. Angoi H.
8. Lonnæ druth YBL.
9. Ni duitseo a doirthi*us* nó dom*ai*ni inna airgni sea hinocht, Eg. ni duidsiu a dom*ai*ne na hoir*ene* YBL. ni daitsiu a a dom*ai*ne na hoirgne St.
10. la airtbi YBL. lat artbe Eg. lat aitbe St. lat airbiu Eg.¹.
11. doérnaba Eg. taerna YBL. toerna St. to erno Eg.¹. doernabó, H.

« *Truly, then, thou hast reason, O Ingcél* », says Lomna Drúth son of Donn Désa. « *Not to thee is the loss caused by the Destruction. Thou wilt carry off the head of the king of a foreign country, with thy slaughter of another; and thou and thy brothers (will) escape from the Destruction, even Ingcél and Écell and the Yearling of the Rapine.* »

81. IS ansu damsa im*morro*, *for* Lom*n*a drúth. Mairg damsa ria cách, mairg iar cách! Is[1] mo chendsa cetna[2] imc[h]oicert[h]ár and in[n]ocht iarsind uair[3] et*er* fertsib carp*at* áit[4] i comraicfét diabolnámait[5] .i. focicherthar insin Bruidin[6] co fá thri 7 dofoicherthar[7] eisse[8] co fáthri. Mairg no thet[9], mairg lasa tiagár[10], mairg cos' tíagar! It[t]roich[11] no thíagat, it [t]róich c*u*ssa tíagat[12]!

Ni fil nád ró damsa, ol Ingchel, in*i*d[13] mo mathar 7 mo athar 7 mo *secht* nderbrathar[14] [7 ri mo thuaithe — H.] ortabair-si limsa. ni fail ní nád fóel*u*sa o sin inond[15].

Cid finbarc totes*s*ed treu[16], ol Gér 7 Gab*ur* 7 Fer rogain, iúrt[h]ar lat ind orgain innocht.

Mairg dos-béra[17] fó lamaib námat », *for* Lomna. *Ocus* cia acca and iarsin?

1. IS hé Eg.
2. ceto- H. céta St , .c. YBL.
3. cétab*er*tar and iarnuáir Eg. ceta imchoichertthar YBL. ceta imcoichertar Eg.[1]. imchoicerthar St.
4. *fer*stip carpot airm H.
5. diabol namat LU. diabolnamaid YBL. 96[b] 49. na diabulnámait Eg.
6. isin mbruidin YBL. St. Eg.[1]. lafithir isin inBruidin Eg.
7. cuirfithir Eg. no foicerthar St. Eg.[1].
8. esti YBL. H. eisi St. eisti Eg, *esti* H.
9. theit YBL. teit St. Eg.[1]. teít 7, Eg.
10. tiagthar YBL. tíaghar Eg.
11. troich H. troig YBL.
12. IS troich téit, is troich cos' tíagar Eg. (i)troich teit itroig cusa tiagar YBL. cossa tiagar St. g*u*sa tiag*ur* H.[2]. c*u*sa (ti)ag*a*ir Eg.[1].
13. hi n-inad. Eg. indi St. inid YBL. iniit Eg.[1].
14. nderbraithir YBL. nderbrath*air* St.
15. Ni fail ní nad fóel*u*sa osin himach cid mór a domain duinne na airgni, Eg.
16. doteis*ed* tre*t*u (?) YBL. túesad treothu, Eg. treot, H. toteis*sed* treut St. Eg.[1].
17. Iss mairg dalta díles deirberidi dob*er*a fo lámaib a námat n-allmarach, Eg. mairc dob*er*a fa lamu nam*u*tt, Eg.[1].

81. « Harder, however, it is for me », says Lomna Drúth « woe is me before every one ! woe is me after every one ! 'Tis my head that will be first tossed about there tonight after an hour among the chariot-shafts, where devilish foes will meet It will be flung into the Hostel thrice, and thrice will it be flung forth Woe (to him) that comes ! woe (to him) with whom one goes ! woe (to him) to whom one goes ! Wretches are they that go ! wretches are they to whom they go ! »

« There is nothing that will come to me », says Ingcél, « in place of my mother and my father and my seven brothers, and the king of my district, whom ye destroyed with me There is nothing that I shall not endure henceforward »

« Though a .. should go through them », say Gér and Gabur and Fer rogain, « the Destruction will be wrought by thee tonight »

« Woe (to him) who shall put them under the hands of foes ! » says Lomna. « And whom sawest thou afterwards ? »

IMDA NA CRUTHNECH INSO

82 Atconnarc and imdae 7 tríar [adbolmór, Eg] indi, tri donnfir mora, tri crunnd-berrtha foraib, it he [coiri — Eg] comlebra for cul 7 étun ¹ tri geri-chochaill dubae impu co ulmi ² céinndi ³ fota for [s]na cochlaib. Tri claidib duba dimóra léo, 7 téora dubboccóti úasaib, 7 téora dubslega lethanglassa uassaib. Remithir ⁴ imbri cairi crand cachae dib Samailte lat sin, a Fir rogain

The Room of the Picts, this.

82. « I saw another room there, with a huge trio in it three brown, big men : three round heads of hair on them, even, equally long at nape and forehead Three short black cowls about them (reaching) to their elbows long hoods were on the cowls Three black, huge swords they had, and three black shields they bore, with three

1 Here there is a lacuna in Eg down to § 97
2 ulnib YBL huilind St huillm H
3 7 cendidi YBL 7 cennide H
4. reimir, St Eg ¹ remitir YBL reimithir H

dark broad-green javelins above them. Thick as the spit of a caldron was the shaft of each. Liken thou that, O Fer rogain! »

83. IS andsa damsa a samail. Nis-fet*u*rsa[1] i n-Her*ind* in triar sin, *acht* manid hé in triar ucut di[2] Cruithentúaith dodeochatár *for* longais asa tír co*n*da-fil[3] hi tegloch *Conairi*. It é a n-anmand : Dubloinges m*a*c Trebúait 7 Trebuáit m*a*c húi Lonsce[4] 7 Curnach m*a*c úi Fáich[5]. Tri láich ata dech gaibthe[6] gaisced la Cruthentúaith in triar sin. Dofáethsat[7] *nói* ndechenbor léo ina chétch*u*msclíu, 7 dofaeth fer cech airm léo[8] cenmotha a fer fessin, 7 *con*raindfet comgnim fri cach triar[9] isin Bru*din*, 7 maidfit[10] buáid ríg[11] *nó* airig diberg[e], 7 immaricfa élód dóib iarsin cid at crechtaig[12]. Mairg iuras in n-orgain cid daig in trir sin namma! »

Tong*u* do dia tong*es* mo th*u*ath, mad mo chomarle dognethe and ní iurtha[13] ind org*ain*, for Lomna Dr*ú*th.

Ní c*u*mcaid[14], *for* Ingcél : néla femid dof*o*rtecat[15]. Fir ngér [n]gúasfes 7r[l.][16]. O*cus* cia acca and iarsin ?

83. « Hard it is for me (to find) their like. I know not in Erin that trio, unless it be yon trio of Pictland, who went into exile from their country, and are (now) in Conaire's household. These are

1. ni fetar St. Eg.[1]. ni fedursa YBL. ni fhetarsa H.
2. manid iat in triar út do St. minad iatt in triar ucud di H.
3. condofilet H. co*n*dofil Eg.[1].
4. Loingsigh, H. Loinsce, St.
5. Fiaich YBL. H. St. Eg.[1].
6. A Middle-Irish corruption of *gaibte*, pres. ind. relative plural of *gabim*. See Strachan, CZ. II, 488, III, 413.
7. Totaetsot H. dofoethsat Eg.[1].
8. dathæd fer cach airm doib, YBL. dofaeth fer gach airm doib, H. dofoeth fer c*ec*h airm doib Eg.[1].
9. n-oinfer H. Eg.[1]. n-oenfer St.
10. macidfit H.
11. H inserts: no righdamnai, St. no rigdamna, Eg.[1] *no* rigdamnai
12. crechtnaig YBL. *crechtnaig* the H. crechtdnaig, St. cid crechtnaigh Eg.[1].
13. *sic* YBL. St. Eg.[1]. hiurfuithe H. iurfaithe LU.
14. cuimce H. cumgæ, St. c*u*mgai YBL. cuimgaid H.[2]. chumcai Eg.[1].
15. dotecat St. dothecat YBL. dotegat H. dotegait H.[2]. tatecut Eg.[1].
16. ṅguaisfeas 7rl. YBL. fir ṅger ngua(is)fes da ngruad ngabair gebthair fris la luige Fir rogain ruidfes. rogab do guth maidm fortsa, a Lomna, ar Ingcél. at drochlaechsu rotetatar nela femid dotecat 7rl. St. Fír nger nguaisfes etc. H.[2]. fir nger nguainfes etc. Eg.[1].

*their names. Dublonges son of Trebúat, and Trebúat son of Húa-
Lonsce, and Curnach son of Húa Fáich. The three who are best in
Pictland at taking arms are that trio. Nine decads will fall at their
hands in their first encounter, and a man will fall for each of their
weapons, besides one for each of themselves. And they will share
prowess with every trio in the Hostel. They will boast a victory over
a king or a chief of the reavers; and they will afterwards escape
though wounded. Woe to him who shall wreak the Destruction,
though it be only on account of those three ! »*

*Says Lomna Druth. « I swear to God what my tribe swears,
if my counsel were taken, the Destruction would never be wrought. »
« Ye cannot », says Ingcel: « clouds of weakness are coming
to you. A keen ordeal which will endanger, etc. And whom sawest
thou there afterwards? »*

[IMDA NA CUSLENNACH]

84 [LU. 88ᵇ] Atchonnarc and imdai 7 nónbor indi¹ mongae
findbudi foraib, it é comalli² uile. Bruit brechtga³ impu, 7 nói
tinne cetharchóire cumtachtai uasaib Ba leór suillse isind rigthig a cumtach fil forsna tinnib cetharchóirib hísin Samailte⁴
lat, a Fir rogain

Ni anse damsa a samail, for Fer rogain Nónbor cuslennach
insin doroachtátár⁵ co Conaire ar a airscélaib a Sid Breg
It é a n-anmand Bind, Robind, Riarbind, Sibe⁶, Dibe⁷,
Deichrind⁸, Umal, Cumal, Ciallglind⁹ It é cuslennaig ata
dech fil isin domon. Dofoethsat¹⁰ nói [n]deichenbor léo, 7 fer
cech airm, 7 fer cech fir, 7 maidfid cach fer dib¹¹ buaid rig¹² nó

1   inti YBL   innti H   innti H ²
2   comailli YBL   comailliu Eg ¹   comaille comcrotha, H
3   brechachtna H   St breic ligi YBL   brechgdai H ². brechachtai Eg ¹
4   Samail YBL 97¹33
5   dorochtatar St   YBL
6   Nibe H   YBL Ribe St   Ribi Eg ¹
7   Tibe St   Dibi H   Tibi Eg ¹
8   Dechrid St   Deichrid Eg ¹
9   Ciallgrinn YBL   Cialglind St   Eg ¹
10 Dothoetsat St   dothædsad YBL   Totaetsat H   Tothoethsat Eg ¹
11 For 7 fer .   dib H   has   ina cetcuinnsgle 7 maoidfit
12 H inserts   no righdamnai   St   no rigdomnæ, H ². no righdamhna,
Eg ¹ no righdhamhnae

airig díberge, 7 immaricfa elúd dóib[1] iarom asind orgain, ar bid imguin fri scáth[2] imguin friu. Génait 7 ni génaiter[3], úair is a sid[4] dóib. Mairg iúras in n-orgain cid dáig ind nonb*ui*r sin [nammá]!

Ni c*u*mcid[5], for Ingcél. nela fémmid dofortecat. Ocus iarsin cia acca and ? »

The Room of the Pipers.

84. There I beheld a room with nine men in it. Hair fair and yellow was on them : they all are equally beautiful. Mantles speckled with colour they wore, and above them were nine bagpipes, four-tuned[6], ornamented. Enough light in the palace were the ornament on those four-tuned pipes. Liken thou them, O Fer rogain. »

« *Easy for me to liken them* », *says Fer rogain.* « *Those are the nine pipers that came to Conaire out of the Elfmound of Bregia, because of the noble tales about him. These are their names: Bind, Robind, Riarbind, Sibé, Dibé, Deichrind, Umall, Cumal, Ciallglind. They are the best pipers in the world. Nine enneads will fall before them, and a man for each of their weapons, and a man for each of themselves. And each of them will boast a victory over a king or a chief of the reavers. And they will escape from the Destruction; for a conflict with them will be a conflict with a shadow. They will slay, but they will not be slain, for they are out of an elfmound. Woe to him who shall wreak the Destruction, though it be only because of those nine!*

« *Ye cannot* », *says Ingcél.* « *Clouds of weakness come to you* », *etc.* « *And after that, whom sawest thou there?* »

IMDA T*h*SSIG TEGLAIG C*o*NAIRI

85. Atchon*n*arc and imdai 7 óenfer inti. Mael garb[6] for

---

1. H. inserts: cidat crech*t*naig thí
2. sgatho H. scait Eg.[1].
3. genith*er* YBL. genaith*er* Eg.[1] genfaither H.[2].
4. sidhuib H. sidaib St.
5. cumge H. c*u*mgid St. c*u*mcit Eg.[1].
5. This seems to refer to the tuning of the chanter, of the two shorter reed drones, and of the longest drone, four in all.
6. ṅgarb St.

suidiu¹. Cia² focerta miach fiadubull for a máil³ ni fochriched⁴ ubull dib for lár, *acht* no giuglad⁵ *cach* ubull for a finna. A brat rolómar taris isin tig. Cach n-imresain bis isin tig im Ṡuidiu *nó* ligi⁶ is in[n]a réir tiagait⁷ uli. Dofóethsad⁸ snat[h]at isin tig ro cechlastai a totim intan labras béos. Dub*ch*rand mór uaso, cosmail fri mol mulind *cona* sciathaib 7 [a chendraig⁹ 7 a irmtiud¹⁰. Sam*ailte* lat, a Fir ro*gain,* insin.

The Room of Conaire's Majordomo¹¹.

85. « There I saw a room with one man in it. Rough *cropt hair upon him*. *Though a sack of crab-apples should be flung on his head, not one of them would fall on the floor, but every* apple *would stick on his hair*. *His fleecy mantle was over him in the house*. *Every quarrel therein about seat or bed comes to his decision*. *Should a needle drop in the house, its fall would be heard when he speaks. Above him is a huge black tree, like a millshaft, with its paddles and its cap (?) and its spike. Liken thou him, O Fer ro-gain !* »

86. Ni *anse* damsa ón. Tuidle¹² Ul*ad* insin, rechtaire te-glaig Conairi. IS écen aurthuasacht a bre*the*¹³ ind fir sin: fer *connic* suide 7 lige¹⁴ 7 bíad do cháeh¹⁵. IS i a lorg theglaig fail úasa. Feis libsi¹⁶ in fer sin. Tong*u* a to*n*ges¹⁷ mo thúath, bit lia

---

1. sic YBL. suiu St. Eg.¹. suidi LU.
2. o YBL.
3. muil YBL. St. móil H. mhuil Eg.¹.
4. foichread YBL. foicridh H. Eg.¹. foichred St.
5. rogiul*ad* YBL. no giulad H. St. no giugl*ad* Eg.¹.
6. luide [leg. luige] H. ligea Eg.¹.
7. thia*gait* H. tiagat Eg.².
8. Dia faetsad, H. Dia foetsat, St. dia foetsadh Eg.¹.
9. cendairg Eg.¹.
10. irmitiud St.
11. Cf. the Welsh *pen-teilu*.
12. Taidle YBL. 97ᵇ 1 St. Toigli H. Taidlea Eg.¹.
13. brethi YBL. brethri H.
14. luighe H. luigiu Eg.¹.
15. H. adds: isin tig, F.
16. faeth lipsi, H. feth libsi YBL. tæd libsi, St. foed libsi Eg.¹.
17. toingti H. toinges St.

[a] mairb leis na hoirgni¹ andáte² a mbí. Totháethsat³ a thri comlín⁴ lais, 7 dofaeth féin and⁵ Mairg iuras ind orgain⁶, 7 il

Ni cumcid⁷, for Ingcel Nela femid doforlecat. Cia acca and tarsin ?

86 « *Easy for me is this Tuidle of Ulaid is he, the steward of Conaire's household 'T is needful to hearken to the decision of that man, the man that rules seat and bed and food for each 'Tis his household staff that is above him. That man will fight with you I swear what my tribe swears, the dead at the Destruction (slain) by him will be more numerous than the living Thrice his number will fall by him, and he himself will fall there Woe to him who shall wreak the Destruction* ! *etc.*

« Ye cannot », says Ingcél « *Clouds of weakness come upon you What sawest thou there after that ?* »

IMDA MAIC CECHT CATHMILED CONAIRE.

87 Atconnarc and imdae n-aile 7 triar indi tri muil⁸ midrecht⁹ moab¹⁰ dib in mael medonach Múad-blosc bráenach, bairend-choirp¹¹, bánnech, béimnech, balc-buillech¹² benas ar nói cétaib hi cath-c[h]omlond. Crandscíath odor iarndae¹³ fair co mbil chotat¹⁴ condúala forsa¹⁵ talla certchossair cethri ndi ong ndechenbair ndedbol for a tanscíu thairlethair¹⁶. Taul fair fortrend,

1 oirgain, St
2 oldait H andata YBL
3 Dotactsat H totoetsatt Eg ¹
4 chomlond, St YBL
5 7 dothaeth and fodeisin YBL 7 dotaet ann fodesin H 7 totoetad and fadeisin Eg ¹
6 H inserts cit daig ind fir sin
7 chuincait St cumcait Eg ¹
8 móil H
9 midrech St Eg ¹ mirdeacht YBL midrecht H ²
10 moam YBL H Eg ¹ moam St moom H ²
11 Bairennchoir H ²
12 H adds lais
13 iarnaidi St iarn e YBL iarnuidi H iarnaide Eg ¹
14 cothat LU chotut St YBL codat H
15 forsna YBL
16 tarrlethair H thairlethair, St tairletair Eg ¹

— 75 —

fodomain cairi¹ chóir chutrummae cet[h]ri² ndam tollchrúis tolberbud³ im cheth[e]óra⁴ mucca midisi inna midchróes mórthaltu. Atát fria di n-airchind n-airidi di nóe chúicsesschurach cutrummae dingbála tri ndrong ndechenbair⁵ [LU. 89ᵃ] cechtar a dá trénchoblach.

Gai laiss gormrúad glacthomside for a chrund comaccmaic. Ro saig iar fraig for clethi conid fri talmain tairissidar. Foriarnd⁶ fair dubderg, drúchtach. Cethri traigid tromthomsidi⁷ eter a dán(ao)g imfáebair⁸.

Tricha traiged tromthomsidi in[n]a⁹ claidiub glondbéimnech o dubdé[i]s co iarndord¹⁰. Tadbat túidle tentidi forosnac Tech Midchúarda o cléithib co talmandae¹¹.

Trénecosc adchíu¹². [Becc] nach imrala¹³ úathbás oc imcaissiú¹⁴ in trir sin. ni fail ni bas decmaicci¹⁵.

Días máel and sin im fer co folt¹⁶. Dá loch im sliab¹⁷: da sechi¹⁸ im rolaig¹⁹: dá nóine²⁰ lána de delgib sciach for rothchomlai²¹ occaib, 7 is cosmail limsa fri cóelglais²² n-usci²³

1. core cói[r] colbthaige H. choiri YBL. coiria Eg.¹.
2. ceitheorai H. ceithri YBL.
3. thollberbud, St. tollberboth H.
4. cetheora YBL. cctheorai H. teorai Eg.¹.
5. H. adds ndedbar
6. Fail iarn, H. fail iarnn, St. Eg.¹.
7. trethoimsidi YBL. tretoimside St. tretomside Eg.¹.
8. iter a dana ogh imthaebuir YBL. eter a di n-uag des n-imfaebuir H. iter a da naug imfaebair, St. iter a da n-ug imfoebair Eg.¹.
9. ina H. inna St.
10. iarnorn YBL. iarndornn, St. hiarndornn H. hiardornn Eg.¹.
11. talmain St. Eg.¹.
12. tren a ecosc atciu H.
13. Bec nachamraloi H. Becc nach imrala YBL.
14. imchaisin St. H. Eg.¹.
15. decmuccu, St. Eg.¹.
16. fult YBL. St.
17. YBL. 97ᵇ 31 inserts: do drumcla tuindi tulguirmi. And St. da drumchla tuinde tulguirme.
18. sechid St. seichi H.² seichid Eg.¹.
19. Ni uil ni bus decmaici dip indas in dias maeloi sin imon fer co folt. Da loch im ralaig, da sheichid im hsliab H.
20. noi H. nocine Eg.¹. YBL. noei St.
21. for rothcomloi rigthige. H.
22. cloenglais St. caelglais YBL.
23. n-uscide H.

forsa¹ taitni grian 7 a treban² úadi sis, 7 seche i n-ecrus³ iarna chul, 7 turi⁴ rigthaige co ndeilb Ligin móir uassae. Dagere cuinge sesrige a crand fil indi⁵.
Samailte lat sin, a Fir rogain?

The Room of Mac cecht, Conaire's battle-soldier.

87 There I beheld another room with a trio in it, three half-furious⁶ nobles the biggest of them in the middle, very noisy, rock-bodied, angry, smiting, dealing strong blows, who beats nine hundred in battle-conflict A wooden shield, dark, covered with iron, he bears, with a hard rim, (a shield) whereon would fit the proper litter of four troops of ten weaklings on its . . of . leather A boss thereon, the depth of a caldron, fit to cook four oxen, a hollow maw, a great boiling, with four swine in its mid-maw great At his two smooth sides are two five-thwarted boats fit for three parties of ten in each of his two strong fleets.

A spear he hath, blue-red, hand-fitting, on its puissant shaft. It stretches along the wall on the roof and rests on the ground. An iron point upon it, dark-red, dripping Four amply-measured feet between the two points of its edge

Thirty amply-measured feet in his deadly-striking sword from dark point to iron hilt. It shews forth fiery sparks which illumine the Mid-court House from roof to ground

('Tis a) strong countenance that I see A swoon from horror almost befell me while staring at those three There is nothing stranger.

Two bare hills were there by the man with hair. Two loughs by a mountain of the . of a blue-fronted wave. two hides by a tree. Two boats near them full of thorns of a white thorntree on a circular board And there seems to me (somewhat) like a slender stream of water on which the sun is shining, and its trickle down from it, and a hide arranged behind it, and a palace house-post shaped like

---

1 frisi H
2 sreban H St Eg ı treban YBL
3 in incchrus St in inecras Eg ı
4 tauri YBL St tairni Eg ı
5 innter H
6 mid-recht lit « of half-furies »

a great lance above it. A good weight of a plough-yoke is the shaft that is therein. Liken thou that, O Fer rogain!

88. Ni *anse* lim[1] a sam*ail*, [*for* Fer *rogain*. — H. Eg.[1]] Mac cecht mac Snáidi teichid[2] insin, cathmilid *Conaire* maic Eterscéoil. IS maith in láech Mac cecht. Inna thotam[3] chotulta ro bói fáen inna imdai intan at*ch*onnarcaissiu[4]. In dias mael im fer co folt[5] at*c*onnarcsu, it é a dá glún immá chend. In da loch im śliab[6] at*cond*arc[7] [ann, St.] at é a di śúil imma sróin. In di sechi[8] im rolaig[9] at*cond*arc it é a dá n-o immá chend. In dá cóicseis[cur*ach*[10] — YBL.] *for* rothchomlae[11] at*cond*arc at é a dí bróic *for* a sciath[12]. In cóelglais[13] usci[14] at*cond*arc *for*[s]a taitni[15] grian 7 a trebán[16] úadi sís iss é brecht*r*ad[17] a claid*ib* sin[18]. In tseche i n-ecr*us*[19] at*cond*arc fil iarna chúl is í truaill a claid*ib* insin. In turi rigthigi at*cond*arc is í a lágin som sin da*no*, 7 cressaigthi[20] seom in gai sin co comraicet a da n-ind, 7 doléice aurchur a ríada[21] di intan as n-áil dó. Is maith in láech Mac cecht![22]

1. damsoi H. damsa St. Eg.[1].
2. theiched YBL. mac snoidti seichid H. teged St.
3. tothom, St. tatham H. tothum Eg.[1].
4. atcondairccsu, St. atchounnarc siu YBL. atconnarcaise H.
5. fult St.
6. ral*aig* H.
7. adchondarcaisi YBL.
8. seichid St. seicid Eg.[1].
9. shl*iab* H.
10. cuicsescur*ach* H.
11. *for* rothcomloi rigthigi H.
12. H. inserts: in[dá] dromclo tuinne tulguirme at*connarcaise* at iat a da mhalaigh corc cutromoi tarsnoi a gn*use* d*er*gi dathaille.
13. claenglais St. Eg.[1]. chaelglais YBL.
14. uisgithi H.
15. frisi taitne H. *for*sataitne St.
16. sreban H. Eg.[1]. trebain, St.
17. m̃brechtrad St. mbrectradh Eg.[1].
18. insin St. Eg.[1].
19. inn inecras Eg.[1].
20. i. e. *cressaigib* + *i*, literally « brandishes it ». So *cressaigth-e* and *gabth-ai*. In *ní chotl-ai* 7 *ní loingth-e* § 92 infra, the affixed pronoun seems in the nom. sg.
21. a riara St. a riara YBL. 98ᵃ. a riarai H. Eg.[1].
22. YBL. 98ᵃ 3 adds: IN da drumcla thuindi tulguirmi atchondair*cis* and it iat a da malaig choiri chutrumae tarrsnu a gnuisi deirgi dathailli.

88. « *Easy, meseems, to liken him! That is Mac cecht son of Snaide Teichid, the battle-soldier of Conaire son of Eterscél. Good is the hero Mac cecht! Supine he was in his room, in his sleep, when thou beheldest him. The two bare hills which thou sawest by the man with hair, these are his two knees by his head. The two loughs by the mountain which thou sawest, these are his two eyes by his nose. The two hides by a tree which thou sawest, these are his two ears by his head. The two five-thwarted boats on a circular board, which thou sawest, these are his two sandals* [1] *on his shield. The slender stream of water which thou sawest, whereon the sun shines, and its trickle down from it, this is the flickering of his sword. The hide which thou sawest arranged behind him, that is his sword's scabbard. The palace-housepost which thou sawest, that is his lance, and he brandishes this spear till its two ends meet, and he hurls a wilful (?) cast of it when he pleases. Good is the hero, Mac cecht!* »

89. Tothaetsat[2] sé chét ina chetchumschu lais, 7 fer cach airm dó, cenmothá a fer fodessin[3], 7 conrainfi[4] comgnim fri cach n-óenfer isin Brudin, 7 maidfid buaid rig[5] no aurg dibergi ar dorus Brudne. Ocus immárícfa élúd dó cid crechtnaigthe[6]. Ocus intan immárícfa dó[7] tuidecht foraib asin tig[8], bít lir bo[m]mand ega 7 fér for faichthi 7 renna nime for lethchind 7 for lethclocind 7 cáp for n-incindi 7 for cnámradach[9] 7 dáisse do for n-apaigib combrutib[10] laiss iarna scáiliud dó fó na fuithairbi[11].

---

[1] Hence we may suppose that the *bróc* or sandal here referred to was fastened to the foot by five transverse straps or thongs

[2] dotaetsat H Tothactsa[t] St Totocthsat Eg [1]

[3] fesin H fodesin Bg [1]

[4] comroinnfe St

[5] 7 maoithfith búaith rig no rigdamnoi H 7 maidfi buaid rig no rigdamni, St 7 moidfid buaidh rig (no rig)damnai Eg [2]

[6] crecht ich St

[7] 7 intan immiricfa elud cid crechtnaigthe LU

[8] 7 intan imaricfa do tuidecht forub isin tig, YBL 98[1] ro 7 intan imaricfor dó toidecht forub amich asin tigh, H

[9] cnámrethach YBL St H Eg [1] cnambrugha H [2]

[10] combruth ub YBL combruithib St mono mionbruidhtei, H combrum H [2]

[11] fuithribi YBL H [2] futhuirbip H fuithrib St fuitribiu Eg.[1]

89. « Six hundred will fall by him in his first encounter, and a man for each of his weapons, besides a man for himself. And he will share prowess with every one in the Hostel, and he will boast of triumph over a king or chief of the reavers in front of the Hostel. He will chance to escape though wounded. And when he shall chance to come upon you out of the house, as numerous as hailstones, and grass on a green, and stars of heaven will be your cloven heads and skulls, and the clots of your brains, your bones and the heaps of your bowels, crushed by him and scattered throughout the ridges. »

90. Techit¹ iarom dar téora fuithairbi² la crith 7 omon Maic cecht.

Gabsait na haittiri etorro afrisi³ .i. Ger 7 Gabur 7 Fer rogain. Mairg iuras in n-orgain⁴! for Lomna druth. Friscichset for cenna dib.

Ni chumcid⁵, for Ingcél : néla femmid dofortecat⁶.

Ango [LU. 89ᵇ] dano, a Ingceoil, for Lomna mac Duind Désa : ní deit atá a domaine na orgne. Mairg damsa ind orgain, ar bid hé cétchend rosía i mBrudin mo chend-sa.

IS andso⁷ damsa, or Ingcél, is i mo orgain doruided and.

Ango dano, for Ingcél, atm-bía bása lecht bas briscem a[n]d⁸ 7rl⁹. Ocus iarsin cia acca and?

90. Then with trembling and terror of Mac cecht they flee over three ridges.

1. Teichsitt H. Teigsit St. YBL. Teigsid Eg.¹.
2. foithribi YBL. St. futhurbe H. fuitribea Eg.¹.
3. afrit(h)isi YBL. afrithisi H.
4. YBL. adds: cid daig ind oenfir sin. St. adds: cídeg ind oenfir sin. Eg.¹ adds: gid daigh in oenfir sin, Eg ¹. H. adds: cith deg ind oinfhir sin nama 7 ara leceth 7 ara febus.
5. cuimge H. cumcid St. YBL. cumcit Eg.¹.
6. dotecat St. totecut Eg.¹.
7. annsu YBL.
8. bas briscem lurcu mais YBL.
9. ni det domaine na horcne. Mairg 7rl. IS annsai damsai is mo cendsai, is mo cendso ceta-imchocertar ann iarsan uair eter ferstip carpat ait a comruicfit diabulnamait .i. focicertar isin mbrudin co bho tri 7 dofocerthar esti co bo tri, etc. H. and (with trifling variations in spelling) St. and Eg.¹ ut supra.

They took the pledges among them again[1], even Gér and Gabur and Fer rogain.

« *Woe to him that shall wreak the Destruction!* » *says Lomna Drúth* · « *your heads will depart from you* »

« *Ye cannot* », *says Ingcél*. « *clouds of weakness are coming to you* » *etc.*

« *True indeed, O Ingcél* », *says Lomna Drúth son of Donn Désa* « *Not unto thee is the loss caused by the Destruction. Woe is me for the Destruction, for the first head that will reach the Hostel will be mine!* »

« *'Tis harder for me* », *says Ingcél*. « *'tis my destruction that has been . there*

« *Truly then* », *says Ingcél*, « *maybe I shall be the corpse that is frailest there* », *etc*

And afterwards whom sawest thou there? »

Imda trí mac Conaire i Oball 7 Oblín 7 Corpre

91. Atconda*r*c and imdae 7 triar inti 1. trí móethóclaig, 7 trí bruit sirecdai impu. Téora bretnassa órdai inna mbrattaib Téora monga órbudi foraib Intan folongat abairbthiu[2] tacmoing in mong orbudi dóib co braine a n-imdae Inbuid conóebat a rosc[3] conócaib in folt[4] connaich ishiu rind a n-úae[5] Cassithir rethe copad Cóicroth óir[6] 7 caindel rigthige úas cach ae Nach duini fil isin tig artacessi[7] guth 7 gním 7 bréthir. Samailte lat [sin] a Fir rogain [ol Ingcél — H]

The Room of Conaire's three sons, Oball and Oblín and Corpre

91. « *There I beheld a room with a trio in it, to wit, three tender striplings, wearing three silken mantles. In their mantles were three golden brooches. Three golden-yellow manes were on them. When they undergo headcleansing(?) their golden-yellow*

---

1 see § 46 supra, p 47
2 abairbte H abairbtiu H ² Eg ¹ ambairthiu Eg
3 rusco H ruscí Eg ¹ roscc Eg
4 rofolt YBL folit fandclechtach forórdá Eg
5 a n-o H
6 cuic roith n-ou, Eg.¹ u roith óu Eg
7 ardoces H artaceisi YBL Eg ¹ artaireisi Eg

-mane reaches the edge of their haunches When they raise their eye
it raises the hair so that it is not lower than the tips of their ears,
(and it is) as curly as a ram's head (?). A.. of gold and a
palace-flambeau above each of them. Every one who is in the house
spares them, voice and deed and word. Likest thou that, O Fer rogain », says Ingcél.

92. Rochí[1] Fer *rogain* co mbo fliuch a brat for á bélaib[2],
7 ní hétas[3] guth assa chind co trían na haidchi.

A beccu[4], or Fer *rogain*, is deithber dam a ndogniu!
Oball 7 Oblini 7 Corpri Findmór[5], trí maic ríg Herend insin.

Ron-mairg masa fír in scél[6], ordat maic Duind Desa IS
maith in triar fil isind[7] imdái. Gnása ingen macdacht léo,
7 cride bráthar, 7 gala mathgamna, 7 brotha léoman[8], Cach
óen bís ina ngnáis 7 inna lepaid ní chotlai 7 ní loingthe[9] [hi
samai] co cend nomaide, iar scarad fríu asa[10] n-ingnais It mathi
ind óic ina n-áes! Dotháetsat[11] trí dechenbáir la cach n-ai dib
ina cétchumscle[12], 7 fer cech ainm, 7 a trí fir fessin Ocus do-
fáeth in tres fer dibseom and. Mairg turas in n-orgain fóbithin
in triar sin[13] !

Ní cumeid, for Ingcél ; nela fémmid dofortecat, 7c. Ocus cia
acca iarsin ?

92. Fer rogain wept, so that his mantle in front of him became
moist And no voice was gotten out of his head till a third of the
night (had passed)

1 Ro chich St
2 See the *Acallam na Senórach* (Ir Texte, IV), ll 1521, 1952, 2839,
3266, 3379, and cf the Iliad, IX, 570 ὀλοοντο δὲ ἄκροις κόλποι
3 íetas YBL etas H hetus Eg
4 becco YBL becoi H becu St Eg ¹ bechu LU baechu Eg
5 Corpre musc YBL Corpri musc St Coirpre musc St Carpre Muscc Eg
6 Romairg masarscel YBL Ronmairg masa fir a mbith and, Eg
7 isinn YBL isin H St insind LU
8 leomain YBL brotha lonna leoman Eg Here another lacuna in H
9 loingi hi samæ YBL longæ hi samæ St ni longai hi saimea Eg ¹ ni
contuil 7 ni loing for congain cridhe, H ² ni cotail 7 ni loing i same Eg
10 ara YBL St ar ingnais Eg
11 Totoetsat St. Totaetsat Eg ¹ Totaethsat Eg
12 cetcuinschu St Eg ¹ cetcuinscli YBL
13 7 dothoet dias dib and Mairg turas in n-orcum cid fobith na deisi
sin ¹ YBL 98ᵃ 42 7 totoetsat dias dib ann Mairg etc St. Eg ¹

« *O little ones* », says Fer rogain, « *I have good reason for what I do! Those are three sons of the king of Erin: Oball and Oblíne and Corpre Findmor.* »

« *It grieves us if the tale be true* », say the sons of Donn Désa. « *Good is the trio in that room. Manners of ripe maidens have they, and hearts of brothers, and valours of bears, and furies of lions. Whosoever is in their company and in their couch, and parts from them, he sleeps not and eats not at ease till the end of nine days, from lack of their companionship. Good are the youths for their age! Thrice ten will fall by each of them in their first encounter, and a man for each weapon, and three men for themselves. And one of the three will fall there. Because of that trio, woe to him that shall wreak the Destruction!* »

« *Ye cannot* », says Ingcél : « *clouds of weakness are coming to you etc. And whom sawest thou afterwards?* »

Imda na Fomorach

93. Atcondarc and imdae 7 triar inti .i. triar úathmar ane-
targnaid trechend[1].
Tri fothucht fomórach nad ndelb dúine nduinegin
fora ndreich du[a]ichni[2] díulathar
rodafer lond lathrastar
lánchend tri lorg línfiaclach
o urbél co úae[3] rechtaira
[rechtaire] múad[4] muinter cech cétglonnaig
claidib tri slúag selgatar
? roselt ar[5] borg mbúredach[6]
Brudne Da Dergae turchomruc.
Samaille lat [sin,] a Fir rogain.

---

1. trecheann YBL. trecenn Eg.¹. trechenn St. = trecheng, as to which see Fél. Oeng. Sep. 16 and gloss. I leave untranslated the rest of this paragraph, as I understand only a few words of it. In the ms. the nine lines are not divided. All save the fifth end in a trisyllable. For the readings of Eg. see Appendix.
2. duaithni YBL.
3. aua St. Eg.². uoe YBL. This seems to mean that the Fomorians had three rows of teeth extending from mouth to ear.
4. muaid YBL. St. muaidh Eg.¹.
5. ar YBL. roseltar St.
6. brog mburethach, St. Eg.¹. borg mbuireadach YBL.

The Room of the Fomorians.

93. I beheld there a room with a trio in it, to wit, a trio horrible, unheard-of, a triad of champions, etc.

. . . .

Liken thou that, O Fer rogain?

94. Is andsa damsa a samail ón. Ni fetursa di feraib Herend nach di feraib betha, manip é[1] in triar thuc[2] Mac cecht a tirib na Fomóre ar galaib óenfer[3]. Ni frith do Fomórib[4] fer do chomruc fris, co tucc [LU. 90ª] in triar sin úadib, condafil hi tig Conaire hi ngiallnae nar' coillet ith na blicht i nHerind tar a cáin téchta céin bes[5] Conaire hi flaithius[6]. IS deithber cid grain a n-imcuissiu[7]. Tri luirg fiacal[8] o húi díarailiu inna cind[9]. Dam co tinniu iss ed mir (.i. cuit) cach fir dib, 7 is ecna in mír sin doberat inna mbéolo co teit sech a n-imlind sís. Cuimm chnáma (.i. cen alt intib) uli in triar sin. Tongu[10] a toinges mo thúath bit lia a mmairb léo na orgne[11] andáta a mbí. Toth[o]étsat[12] sé cét laech léo inna cetchumscli[13], 7 fer cech airm, 7 a triar fessin, 7 máidfit búaid ríg nó airig díbergi. Ocus ní bá mó nó ó mir nó ó dúrnn nó o lúa[14] mair[b]fes cach fer léo. Dáig ní léicter airm léo isin tig, daire is in n-giallnai[15] fri fraigid atá[a]t[16], arná dernat midénom issin tig. Tongu a tonges

---

1. manid iat St. mainidh iat Eg.¹.
2. Here relativity is expressed by « aspiration » of the *t*. dasfuc Eg.
3. enfir YBL. ar galaid oenfer St.
4. la Fomoiri YBL. Eg.¹. la Fomore St. Eg.
5. tar in cain techtai cen mbes Eg.¹.
6. flaith YBL. rigi, St. richiu Eg.¹.
7. n-imchaiseo YBL. n-imcisiu St. n-imcaissi H.². n-imchaissin Eg.
8. fiaclai YBL. Eg.¹. fiaclai St. d'fiaclaibh H.².
9. ón chlúais co 'raile ina cennaib H.². ónn ó co araile Eg.
10. Toingim St.
11. ond orguin YBL.
12. Totóethsat St. Totoettsat Eg.¹.
13. cétchunscléo, St. cétchuinnscleo Eg.¹.
14. Ocus ni ba mo mir na dorn no lau YBL. 7 ni bá mó mír ina dorn na láu St.
15. giallu YBL. is i ngiallai St.
16. ataat St. YBL. Eg.¹.

mo thúath, dia mbeth¹ gaisced foraib arnonsligfitis co trían².
Mairg iuras in n-orgain fo ndaig! ni comrac fri seguinni³.
Ni chumcid, for Ingcél, 7rl. Ocus iarsin cia acca and?

94. « *'Tis hard for me to liken that (trio), Neither of the men of Erin nor of the men of the world*⁴ *do I know it, unless it be the trio that Mac cecht brought out of the land of the Fomorians by dint of duels. Not one of the Fomorians was found to fight him, so he brought away those three, and they are in Conaire's house as sureties that, while Conaire is reigning, the Fomorians destroy neither corn nor milk in Erin beyond their fair tribute. Well may their aspect be loathly! Three rows of teeth in their heads from one ear to another. An ox with a bacon-pig, this is the ration of each of them, and that ration which they put into their mouths is visible till it comes down past their navels. Bodies of bone (i. e. without a joint in them) all those three have. I swear what my tribe swears, more will be killed by them at the Destruction than those they leave alive. Six hundred warriors will fall by them in their first conflict, and a man for each of their weapons, and one for each of the three themselves. And they will boast a triumph over a king or chief of the reavers. It will not be more than with a bite(?) or a blow or a kick that each of those men will kill, for no arms are allowed them in the house, since they are in « hostageship at the wall » lest they do a misdeed therein. I swear what my tribe swears, if they had armour on them, they would slay us all but a third. Woe to him that shall wreak the Destruction, because it is not a combat against sluggards (?)*

« *Ye cannot* », *says Ingcél etc.* » *And whom sawest thou there after that?* ».

IMDA MUNREMAR (.I. MAIC GERRCIND) 7 BIRDERG MAIC RUAIN 7 MAIL MAIC TELBAIND

95. Atcondarc and imdae 7 triar indi. Tri dondfir móra,

1. Toingim do dia a toinges mo thuatha dia mbeith YBL.
2. Eg.¹ adds :· an tsluaigh
3. seganna YBL. seguinne St. Eg.¹. segunnu Eg.
4. i. e. the Continent of Europe.

tri dondberrtha foraib buind¹ cholbthae remrae léo, remithir² medon fir cach ball dib. tri dondfuilt chassa foraib co remorchind Téora lenna brecderga impu, tri duibscéith co tuagmilib óir, 7 teora slega coicrindni³ úasaib, 7 claideb⁴ dét [illaim YBL.] cach fir dib IS sí reb dogniat dia claid*bib* focherdat⁵ i n-ardae, 7 focherdat⁶ na trualli ina ndiaid, 7 nodasamaigetar⁷ isna trua*llib* riasiu tháirset talmain⁸. Focherdát dano na trualli 7 na claid*biu* ina ndiaid, 7 atethát⁹ na tru[a]*lli* conda-samaige*tar*¹⁰ impu a n-oenur riasiu tairset tal*main* Samailte lat sin, a Fir rogain

The Room of Munremar son of Gerrchenn¹¹ and Buiderg son of Ruan and Mál son of Telband.

95. « *I beheld a room there, with a trio in it. Three brown, big men, with three brown heads of short hair Thick calf-bottoms (ankles?) they had As thick as a man's waist was each of their limbs. Three brown and curled masses of hair upon them, with a thick head. three cloaks, red and speckled, they wore three black shields with clasps(?) of gold, and three five-barbed javelins, and each had in hand an ivory-hilted sword This is the feat they perform with their swords. they throw them high up, and they throw the scabbards after them, and the swords, before reaching the ground, place themselves in the scabbards. Then they throw the scabbards (first), and the swords after them, and the scabbards meet the swords and place themselves round them before they reach the ground Liken thou that, O Fer rogain!* »

96 Ni anse damsa a sam*ail*. Mál mac Telbaind 7 Muinre-

---

1 buinm St buindiu Eg ¹. ate bondcolbthae Eg
2. reimithir Eg remir, St reimir Eg ¹
3 cuicrinde, St cuicrindi YBL Eg ¹
4 colg, St colga Eg cloidib YBL
5 foscerdad St foscerdat YBL foscertat Eg ¹ focertat Eg
6 foscerdat St focertat YBL foscertat Eg ¹
7 nadasamaiget YBL notasamaiget St nodosamaiget Eg rotasamaiget na claid*ib* Eg ¹
8 talam YBL
9 adethat St Eg ¹ atethat YBL
10 com*i*dasamaiget YBL com*i*dsamaiget St conidh samaigit Eg ¹
11 a compound like βραχυκέφαλος

mor mac Gerrcind¹ 7 Birderg mac Rúain². Tri rígdamnae, tri láith gaile, tri láich ata dech íar cúl gascid i n-Herind. Tothaethsat³ cét láech léo ina cétchumscliu, 7 cónroindfet⁴ comgním fri cach n-óenfer isin Brudin, 7 maid*fit* buaid ríg *nó* airig díberge, 7 immáricfa elúd dóib iarom. Nípu orta⁵ ind orgain cid dáig in trír⁶ sin.
  Mair[g] iuras in n-orgain! for Lomnae: ba fer[r] buáid a n-anacail oldás buaid a ngona. Cénmair noda-ansed⁷, mairg noda-géna⁸!
  Ni cumthi⁹, for Ingcél 7r. Ocus cía acca and iarsin? »

  96. « *Easy for me to liken them! Mál son of Telband, and Munremar son of Gerrcenn, and Birderg son of Rúan. Three crown-princes, three champions of valour, three heroes the best behind weapons in Erin! A hundred heroes will fall by them in their first conflict, and they will share prowess with every man in the Hostel, and they will boast of the victory over a king or chief of the reavers, and afterwards they will chance to escape. The Destruction should not be wrought even because of those three.* »
  « *Woe to him that shall wreak the Destruction!* » *says Lomna*. « *Better were the victory of saving them than the victory of slaying them! Happy he who should save them! Woe to him that shall slay them!* »
  « *It is not feasible* » says *Ingcel*, etc. « *And afterwards whom sawest thou?* »

Imda Conaill Chernaig.

  97. Atcondarc and i n-imdae chumtachtae fer as cháinem¹⁰ do laechaib Herend. Brat caschorcra¹¹ imbi. Gilithir snechtae

  1. Gcirrgind YBL. Ergind St. Eirrgind Eg. hEirrcind Eg.¹.
  2. Ruaid YBL. St. Ruáid Eg. Ruaidh Eg.¹.
  3. Tothocth YBL. Totoet St. Eg.¹. Dotoeth Eg.
  4. conaraindfet YBL. conrainfet St.
  5. Nib iurtha YBL. horta St. Eg.¹.
  6. triair St.
  7. no damised St.
  8. nodagena YBL. nodogéna LU. nodogenai Eg.¹.
  9. cuimgi St. cumchi YBL. cumcit Eg.¹.
  10. caímem Eg. caime YBL. cainemh Eg.¹.
  11. corcra YBL. corcrai Eg.¹. cass corcra Eg.

— 87 —

ind-ala grúaid [LU. 90ᵇ] dó, breedergithir sion¹ a ngrúad n-aile². IS glasidir buga ind-ala suil IS dubithir druim³ ndáil in tsúil aile Méit cliab⁴ búana in dosbili find fororda⁵ fil fair Benaid⁶ braini a da imdae (.i a da less) IS cassidir rethe coppad⁷ Cia dóforte⁸ miach di chnoib dergfuiscib⁹ for a mullach¹⁰ ni foichred cnoi dib for lár¹¹ [acht a fossugud¹² ar drolaib 7 ar clechtaib 7 ar claidimib in fuilt sin — Eg] Claudeb órduirn ina láim. Sciath cróderg ro breccad do semmannaib¹³ findruim eter eclannu¹⁴ óir Sleg fota [tromm, Eg] tredruimnech remithir¹⁵ cuing n-imechtraid¹⁶ a crand fil indi¹⁷. Samailte lat sin, a Fir rogain

The Room of Conall Cernach

97 *There I beheld in a decorated room the fairest man of Erin's heroes. He wore a tufted purple cloak. White as snow was one of his cheeks, the other was red and speckled like foxglove Blue as hyacinth was one of his eyes, dark as a stagbeetle's back was the other The bushy head of fair golden hair* ¹⁸ *upon him was as large as a reaping-basket, and it touches the edge of his haunches It is as curly as a ram's head. If a sackful of red-shelled nuts were spilt on the crown of his head, not one of them would fall on the floor, but remain on the hooks and plaits and swordlets of that hair A gold-*

1 sian sleibe St sian slebhiu Eg ¹ sian YBL
2 Giluthir snechta cechtar a da grúad indara fecht, in fecht aih breedergithir sian sleibe, Eg
3 druimmni Eg drumme YBL druimm St druimnea Eg ¹
4 cliab Eg cleib St Eg ¹ leg chleib, as in § 58 or Méitithir chab
5 finnbuidi fororda Eg dosbile find fororda fuilt St
6 co mbenand fri brainee na imdad, Eg
7 coemcoppad Eg copad, St YBL
8 no dortaithea Eg ma dodortte St cia doratt thai Eg ¹
9 donna der[g]fuisci Eg dergfuiscib YBL dergfuiscuib St derefuiscthib Eg ¹
10 a mullach a chinn clechtaig chassbuidi Eg
11 ni rossed cnú dib lar Eg
12 Eg fossudug
13 semandaib YBL St hsemunuib Eg ¹ semmannaib firglana Eg
14 eclanda YBL Eg ¹ (ex anth-clanda ⁵), éclanniu Eg éclannu St
15 remir St remithir YBL 99² ¹ remhir Eg ¹
16 n-imechtair YBL St n-imeetair Eg ¹ n-oill imectraid Eg
17 in crand comthend colgdirech fil inti, Eg a crand fil innti, St
18 literally « the fair golden bush *(dos)* of a great tree *(bile)* »

hilted sword in his hand ; a blood-red shield which has been speckled with rivets of white bronze between plates of gold. A long, heavy, three-ridged spear, as thick as an outer yoke is the shaft that is in it. Liken thou that, O Fer rogain! »

98 Ni anse damsa on a *samail*, ar rofetartar[1] fir Herend an ngein sin[2] Conall Cernach mac Amorgein insin Dorecmaing immale[3] fri *Conaire* ind inbuid-se. IS é charas *Conair*e sech cách, fobith a chosmailiusa fris ar febas a chrotha 7 a delba[4] [is a dénma, Eg.]. IS máith in láech fil and, Conall Cernach IN sciath cróderg sin fil ar a duind[5] ro brecad do semmannaib findruim[6] comid brec, ro nóesiged ainm dó[7] la Ultu .i. in Bricriu Conall Chernaig[8].

Tongu a toinges mo thuath[9], bid imda bróen dérg[fola] tairse innocht ar dorus [na] Brudne. In tsleg druimnech[10] sin fil úasa bid sochaidi forsa ndailfe deoga tonnaid[11] innocht ar dorus [na]Brudne[12] Atá[a]t *secht* ndorus asin[13] tig 7 arricfa[14] Conall Cernach b[e]ith for cach dorus dib, 7 ni bia a thesbaid ar[15] nách dorus[16] Tothaethsat trí cet la Conall ina chétchumsclu[17], cenmotha fer cach airm, 7 a fer fessin, 7 conráinnfi[18] comgnim fri

---

1 Rofetatar Eg rofeatatar YBL rofetatu St rofeatatar Eg¹
2 in fer sin¹ Conall cóem Cernach mac allatt Amargin Eg
3 Darrcemaing immaleith St dorrecmaing immaille Eg¹
4 delbæ YBL dealbae Eg¹
5 ina durnn, Eg ara durn, St, ara druim YBL for a durn Eg¹
6 finddruine St
7 a hainm dano St Eg¹
8 Eg adds Ainm aili di and, Lámtapad Conaill Cernaig ara tricci ocus ara athlaime gabair 7 immirthir in sciath sin Conall Cernaig
9 Toingim a toinges me thuatha YBL
10 fadesin St fadeissin Eg¹ drúchtach Eg
11 tondaig YBL tonnaigh Eg¹ troimcinn tonnaig, Eg tonda H²
12 St adds Da Berga, Eg Da Derga, and Eg¹ Di Dercai
13 isin YBL for St Eg¹
14 Atat in ndorais fortig immaricfa, St Eg¹ Atat in ndorais forsin mbruidin 7 aricfao, Eg
15 as St
16 ni bid tesbaid as cach ndorus YBL ar cech ndorus Eg.
17 cetchunnselco YBL
18. comrainnse St

ca*ch* n-oén isin Bru*din*¹, 7 intan immaricfa tuidecht² dó foraib asin tig³ beit lir bommand ega [7 fer for faithchi 7 renna nimi, Eg. Eg ¹] for lethchind 7 for lethclo*icind*⁴ 7 for cnáma fó déis a claid*ib*, 7 immáricfa élúd dó cid créchtach. Mairg iur*as* in n-orgain fod*áig* ind fir sin namm*á*!⁵

Ni cumgid⁶, for Ingcél. Néla 7r *Ocus* iarsin cia acca ?

98 « *Easy for me to liken him, for the men of Erin know that scion That is Conall Cernach, son of Amorgen He has chanced to be along with Conaire at this time. 'Tis he whom Conaire loves beyond every one, because of his resemblance to him in goodness of form and shape. Goodly is the hero that is there, Conall Cernach!* To that bloodied shield on his fist, which has been speckled with rivets of white bronze, the Ulaid have given a famous name, to wit, the Bricriu *of Conall Cernach.*

[*Another name for it is Conall Cernach's* Lámthapad, *because of the quickness and readiness with which that shield of Conall Cernach is seized and wielded*⁷ — Eg]

I swear what my tribe swears, plenteous will be the rain of red blood over it to-night before the Hostel ! That ridged spear above him, many will there be unto whom to-night, before the Hostel, it will deal drinks of death. Seven doorways there are out of the house, and Conall Cernach will continue to be at each of them, and from no doorway will he be absent Three hundred will fall by Conall in his first conflict, besides a man for each (of his) weapons and one for himself He will share prowess with every one in the Hostel, and when he shall happen to sally upon you from the house, as

---

1 St inserts 7 maidf*id* buaid rig *no* rigdamna *no* airig diber*ge*, and so Eg ¹, with trifling changes
2. elud St Eg ¹
3 Toethsatt ccc la Con*all* ina cetcuindsch ccinmotat a brathbéimend archena, oc*us* primlaech cec*h* airmim di armaib, oc*us* maidfid echt n-ard do nach rig *nó* rigdomna *no* airig diberga, 7 intan doficfa himmach roindfid coingnim fri cech n-oenfer isin Bruidin, Eg
4 After *letheloicind* St has 7 caip far n-inchindi 7 far cnaimrethach, taisi do far n-apaigib combruithib lais iarna scailiud do fona fuithribe Mairg etc So Eg ¹ with trifling changes For the corresponding passage in Eg see Appendix
5 St adds for Lomna Druth, friscichfet [leg -set] far cenda dib
6 c*u*mcid YBL cumcit Eg ¹
7. As to Conall Cernach's *Lámthapad*, see also LL 107ª 3

numerous as hailstones and grass on green and stars of heaven will be your half-heads and cloven skulls, and your bones under the point of his sword. He will succeed in escaping though wounded. Woe to him that shall wreak the Destruction, were it but for this man only! »

« *Ye cannot* », says Ingcél « *Clouds etc
And after that whom sawest thou?* »

IMDA CONAIRE TESSIN

99. Atcondarc and imdae, 7 bá caimiu¹ a cumtach oldáta² imdada in tigi olchena Seolbrat³ n-airgdidi impe, 7 cumtaige isind imdae Atcondarc triar n-inni In dias im[m]echtrach dib, finna dib linaib, *cona* foltaib 7 a [m]brataib⁴, 7 it gilithir snechtae. Rudiud roilaind fo gruad cechtar n-ae Mócthóclach etorro im-medon Bruth 7 gnim tuirech lais 7 comarli senchad⁵ Brat atcomarc imbi, is cubés *ocus*⁶ céo cétamain. Is [s]ain dath 7 écose cacha húari tadbat⁷ fair aildiu cach dath alailiu. Atcondarc roth n-óir isin brut ar a bélaib, adcomaic húa smech có a imlind⁸ IS cosmail fri túidlig⁹ n-óir forloscthi dath a fuilt. Di¹⁰ neoch atcondarc de delbaib betha is í delb as aldem dib Atcondarc a claideb n-órduind¹¹ occo this Ro bói anther¹² láime din claidiub fria truaill anechtair. A n-arther láim¹³ sin fer no bid i n-authiur [nói n-iarthai — Eg] in tigi tís cébad¹⁴ frigit¹⁵

1 caimiu YBL coimiu Eg¹
2 oldaat, Eg oldata YBL St oldaata Eg¹
3 seol YBL St Eg¹
4 mbrataib YBL St mbruta Eg¹
5 hsenchad Eg¹ For the various readings of Eg in ll 1-6 see Appendix § 99
6 cosmail is, Eg coibes 7, YBL cubeis 7, St Eg¹
7 doadobantar Eg
8 Eg adds 10 soich in 10th sin
9 tuidlig Eg tuidlig YBL St tuidligh Eg¹
10 Do YBL
11 n-orduirn, YBL ndorduirn, St n-orduirnn Eg¹ órduirnd Eg
12 fot airther Eg
13 in t-hed láim Eg in t-arther lainn YBL
14 doberat Eg gebad YBL St gebidh Eg¹
15 in frighit YBL in frigit Eg friggit St

scath : reflection

fri foscod in claidib. Is binni[u]¹ bindfogrogod² in claidib oldas³ bindfogur na cuslend n-ordae [LU 91ᵃ] fochanat céol isind rigthig.

The Room of Conaire himself.

99. *There I beheld a room, more beautifully decorated than the other rooms of the house. A silvery curtain around it, and (there were) ornaments in the room. I beheld a trio in it. The outer two of them were, both of them, fair, with their hair and eyelashes, and they are as bright as snow. A very lovely blush on the cheek of each of the twain. A tender lad in the midst between them. The ardour and energy of a king has he, and the counsel of a sage. The mantle I saw around him is even as the mist of Mayday. Diverse are the hue and semblance each moment shewn upon it. Lovelier is each hue than the other. In front of him in the mantle I beheld a wheel of gold which reached from his chin to his navel. The colour of his hair was like the sheen of smelted gold. Of all the world's forms that I beheld, this is the most beautiful. I saw his golden-hilted glaive down beside him. A forearm's length of the sword was outside the scabbard. That forearm, a man down in the front of the house could see a fleshworm by the shadow of the sword! Sweeter is the melodious sounding of the sword than the melodious sound of the golden pipes that accompany music in the palace.»*

100 IS and asbertsa⁴, for Ingcél, ac á déscin⁵ ·

    a. Atchíu flaith n-árd n-airegdae
       asa⁶ bith buillech búredach
g. pl of ro-mess   bruchtas róimse robortae⁷
       rechtbruth cáin-cruth ciallathar

    b. Atchíu clothrig costodach⁸

₴ robart · flut des Meeres

1 bindiu, YBL St binniu Eg
2 findfogrugud Eg binfoghraid St binniograidh Eg¹
3 inda Eg oldás Eg¹
4. adbertsa Eg¹
5 oca deicsi[n] YBL oca déscin Eg oca deicsiu St occa decsin Fg¹
6 os Eg St Eg¹ as YBL
7 romsi robarta Eg roimse robartai YBL roimsi robartai Eg¹
8 costudach Eg costadach YBL Eg¹ costadhach St

cotngaib inna chertraind chóir chomchétbuid [1]
o chrund co fraig fo a suidi[u] [2].

c. A[t]chíu a mind findflatha [3]
conid fri recht ruirech rathordan [4]
ruithen a gnúis[e] comdetae (nó comdéntae) [5].

d. Atchiu a dá [6] ngrúaid [7] ngormgela [8]
conid fri fúamun find fuinechdae
fordath sóerdath [9] snechtaide
di díb súilib sellglassaib
glanmu a rosc robuga [10]
teinniu a chuinscliu [11] cáintocud [12]
iter clethchor [13] ndub ndóelabrat [14].

e. Atchiu [a] ardroth n-imnaisse [15]
imm a chend [coir] cocorse
conid fri fultu frithecnus [16]
fordath n-órda n-ollmaisse
fil úas a berrad buidechas [17].

f. Atchiu a brat nerg [18] n-ildathach
nóitech [19] siric srethchisse

1. comchéthbuid LU. comcétfaid Eg. comcetbuid St. comhcetbuid Eg. [1].
2. fo suidiu, Eg. Eg. [1]. fo suidhiu YBL. fo suidiu St.
3. Atchiu a mind finn flathemon Eg. Atchiu a mind find fl. Eg. [1].
4. rathordain Eg. rathortan Eg. [1].
5. a gnúisi coemdatae Eg. a gnuisi coimdetæ, YBL. a gnuise comdetæ, St. a gnuisi comdetae Eg. [1].
6. nda LU.
7. ngruad YBL. St. ngruad Eg. [1].
8. a da ngrúad ngelcorcra Eg.
9. soerda Eg. fordæ saerdath St.
10. glaini a rosc ruibnige nó robuige Eg. gloiniu a rosc robuidi YBL. glainiu a rosc robuide St. robuidea Eg. [1].
11. chuindsi Eg. chuindscliu YBL. caintocaid Eg [1].
12. chaintucud YBL. cáintoccud Eg.
13. clechtchor St. clechtcor Eg. clectcor Eg. [1].
14. dóel abraitt Eg.
15. a ardroth n-immaisi Eg. artrot n-imnaissi Eg. [1].
16. frithecrus Eg. St. Eg. [1]. frithechrus YBL.
17. fail uas a barr buidechass Eg.
18. nderg YBL. nderg Eg. n-erc St. nderc Eg. [1].
19. nothech YBL. noethech St. noetheach Eg. [1]. noetech Eg.

sluind ar delbthor ndímaisse¹
dind ór aúrderc ail[i]bend²
alathúaith ndronaicdi³

g. Atchíu delg n-and olladbol
de ór uili intlaisse
lassaid⁴ ar lúth lanésci
lainne o chuaird corcorgemmach⁵
caera crethir comraicthe
congaib ar dreich ndendmaisse
eter a dá gelgúalannchor⁶.

h Atchíu⁷ a léine ligdie hnide
comd fri sreband sirechtach⁸
scáthderc sceo deilb ildat[h]aig⁹
ingelt súla¹⁰ sochaide
cot[n]gaib¹¹ ar méit muinenchor¹²
sóerthus ai néim imdenam¹³
ór¹⁴ fri siric srethchisse
o adbrund co urglune¹⁵.

i Atchíu a chlaideb n-orduirn n-intlaisse

1 de sluind ar delbthor ndenmaissi Eg 1 ca 1 sluinn ar delbaetha n-innmaise, St sluind ar delbthar ndimaisi YBL sluind ar dealbthai n-indmaisi Eg 1
2 ailibenn Eg ailbeand YBL dian ór aurderg ailbenn, St dia nor aurderg Eg 1 diannor aundreic ailbeand YBL
3 alatuaithe dronaicde Eg
4 lasfaid Eg lasaid YBL St Eg 1
5 laind a cuaird corrgemmach Eg lainne a cuairt chorcaigemach YBL lainde a cuairt corcaigemach, St lainde a cuaird corcaigemach Eg 1
6 a di gelgualaind chóir LU 91ᵃ22 a da gelgualaind choir St a da gel guallannchór Eg a di gelgualainn choir Eg 1 Cf osa gel gualaudchor LL 72ᵅ 17
7 atcondaic Eg
8 sirrectach Eg Eg 1
9 illathaig Eg illdathaig Eg 1
10 suili YBL suile St Eg 1, súla Eg
11 cotngeib Eg cotagaib St cotgaib YBL Eg 1
12 muinechor Eg muinencor Eg 1
13 imdenum YBL imdenum Eg imdenam Eg 1
14 oir YBL St óir Eg 1 om Eg
15 co urgualaind no co a urglune YBL co aurgluine St Eg 1 co urguailli no co hirgluini Eg

ma findṁch¹ findargit²
aisnéid³ ar cheirr cóicroth
comd fri cruaid n-aurdairc n-aister⁴.

j Atchíu⁵ a scíath n-etrocht n-áilenda
fail úas⁶ drongaib dímes
tréthín di ór oiblech
ar thur⁷ scéo bil banbruth
forosnai lith⁸ lúachet

k. Turi di ór⁹ intlassi
lám ríg fris dess dingabai
fri trieth taile taurgaib¹⁰
comd fri cernu crúadchassa¹¹
tri cét chorac¹² comlána
úasind rurig rathruanaid¹³
fri boidb hi mbrói bertas[a]¹⁴
is[in] Brudin bróntig¹⁵ a[t]chíu.
    Atchíu flaith n-ard.

« 100. « Then », quoth Ingcél, « I said, gazing at him
a   I see a high, stately prince, etc
b   I see a famous king, etc.
c   I see his white prince's diadem, etc

1 intnuch Eg intnich St aintec Lg ¹
2 find argit LU findargait Eg findarcit Eg ¹
3 aisndeith YBL St aisndeich Eg ¹
4 comd fri cernao cruaid casra aisnéid ar cheirnd cóicroith Eg comd fri cruidd n-aurdairc n-aister St comd fri cruaid n-aurrdric n-aister YBL comd fri cuaird n-urdairc n-aister, Eg ¹
5 atcondairc a sciath netrocht n'telendi Eg
6 huasa YBL St St ¹
7 ara thul Eg ara ur YBL ar thaur St ar tuar Eg ¹
8 frisnai hi lith Lg
9 diórda Eg di ór St
10 fri tech tailec taurcabair Eg fri truth taile taurgub YBL fri tneach taile taurgaib St fri tnech taile tiurcub Eg ¹
11 cornu cruadchassa, Eg YBL cernu cruadchassa St cernai cruadcassi Eg ¹ cronu cruidchassa YBL
12 coire córe, Eg coirae comluin YBL coerai comlánai Eg ¹
13 rathrunigh YBL radiunaid St rath ruinaid Lg rathrunnigh Eg ·
14 i mbroe berthasa Eg hi mbru bertas Eg ¹
15 isin bruidin brontaigh Eg isin bruidin brontig, YBL brontaig St mbrontuich Eg ¹

d. *I see his two blue-bright cheeks, etc.*
e. *I see his high wheel . . round his head   which is over his yellow-curly hair.*
f. *I see his mantle red, many-coloured, etc.*
g. *I see therein a huge brooch of gold, etc.*
h. *I see his beautiful linen frock . from ankle to knee-caps*
i. *I see his sword golden-hilted, inlaid, its in scabbard of white silver, etc*
j. *I see his shield bright, chalky, etc* [1].
k. *A tower of inlaid gold, etc*

101 *a* Ro bói iarom [2] in móethóclach ina chotlud [3], 7 a chossa i n-ucht ind-ala fir 7 a chend i n-ucht araile. Doríusaig [4] iarom assa chotlud, 7 at/raracht, 7 ro chachain in laid-se ·
« Gáir Ossair (.i. cu *Conaire*) assir [5] chumall goin gair ooc im-mullach Thuil Gossi [6] gáeth úar tar fáebru [7] eslind adaig do thogail ríg ind adaig-se [8]

b. Cotlais afridise 7 díuchtrais ass, 7 canais in retoiric-se [9]
[LU. 91ᵇ] « Gáir Ossir (.i. messan *Conaire*) ossai [10] chumall cath ro[n]dlom [11] doerad [12] túathe togail [13] Bruidni bióncha fianna fir gúiti. góith [14] imómain. mórchor sleg sáeth écomluind. ascuir tige Temuir fás. forba n-aniuil

---

1 For some unlucky guesswork purporting to be a translation of the whole of this piece, see O'Curry's *Manners and Customs*, III, 142
2 Here F begins, and H recommences with *Robo*ı
3 in macthóglach am/a sin Eg
4 Co ro dusid Eg doriussaig YBL Doriuisind H St Doriuisaidh F
5 osar YBL osair H ossar F
6 im muallach tuil goissi YBL i muallach tuil gaeisi H im-mullach tuil goisi, F immullach thuil goisi St
7 faebur YBL faepm H foebur, F Faebar St
8 Gáir Osair imso Osair caumall goin gair ooc hi mullach thuil geissi gaeth huar tar foebar eislind adaig do togail rig ind adaig seo fessat gul gaire Gair Ossair Eg
9 co clos ni arithise, YBL F Co clos ní afrithisie H Roraid doridisi Eg co clos ni arithissi St
10 osair H Osar Eg
11 rondlom Eg YBL H St F.
12 deorad YBL. doerath F daerath H doerat Eg
13 tail F H YBL Eg. St
14 góite goeth Eg goite goit F. guiti goith YBL goite gaeth H

comgné¹, cáiniud *Conaire*. coll etha. lith ngaland. gáir égem. orgain ríg Herend. carpait hi cucligi². dochraite³ ríg Temrach. [fessa[it] guil gaire. Gáir *Ossair* — Eg.]

c. Asbert in tresfecht⁴.

Domm-árfás⁵ imned., imned siabrai, slúag fáen. fálgud námat. comrac fer for Dothrai. dochraite ríg Temrach. i n-oitid ortae. [fessat guil gáre. Gair *Osar* — Eg.] Samailte let, a Fir *rogain*, cía ro cháchain in laid sin.

101. a. *Now the tender warrior was asleep, with his feet in the lap of one of the two men and his head in the lap of the other. Then he awoke out of his sleep, and arose, and chanted this lay:*

« *The howl of Ossar (Conaire's dog)... cry of warriors on the summit of Tol Géisse; a cold wind over edges perilous: a night to destroy a king is this night.* »

b. *He slept again, and awoke thereout, and sang this rhetoric:*

« *The howl of Ossar (Conaire's lapdog)... a battle he announced: enslavement of a people: sack of the Hostel: mournful are the champions: men wounded: wind of terror: hurling of javelins: trouble of unfair fight: wreck of houses: Tara waste: a foreign heritage: like (is) lamenting Conaire: destruction of corn: feast of arms: cry of screams: destruction of Erin's king: chariots a-tottering: oppression of the king of Tara: lamentations will overcome laughter: Ossar's howl.* »

c. *He said the third time:*

« *Trouble hath been shewn to me: a multitude of elves: a host supine: foes' prostration: a conflict of men on the Dodder⁶: oppression of Tara's king: in youth he was destroyed: lamentations will overcome laughter: Ossar's howl.* »

1. *Om*. Eg. coigne H. F. congne St.
2. a cuicligiu F. hi cuicligi YBL. St. a cuiclidhe H.
3. drochuiti, H. dochruiti F.
4. YBL. 99ᵇ 34 *inserts*: Gair Osair, Osair enmoll combaig anrad oic inn orcain, orcuin iurthar, orta curaid, claentar fir, fadbaidther laith gaili buiread tromthresa toigebthar gairi. *And* H. *inserts*: Gair Ossair, osair comoll, combaid anradh, oic ind orcuin, orcuin iurbar, ortai curaid, claentar fir, faentar fir, fadbuither laith goili, gair in tresoi, tocepthar gair.
5. Domtarfas H. Domarsad YBL. Domtarfas Eg.
6. A small river near Dublin, which is said to have passed through the Bruden.

« Liken thou, O Fer rogain, him who has sung that lay. »

102. *a*. Ni anse damsa a samail, for Fer *rogain*: ní ésce cen ríg¹ ón im*m*orro: is é rí as an*em* 7 as ordnidem 7 as cháinem² 7 as chumachtom³ thánic i ndomon uli⁴. Is hé rí as bláthem 7 as mínem 7 as becda⁵ dodánic⁶ .i. Con*ai*re Mór *mac* Eterscéoil, is é fil and, ardrí Her*e*nd uli⁷. Nicon fil locht and⁸ isind fir sin, e*ter* chruth 7 deilb 7 dechelt, e*ter* méit 7 chórae 7 c[h]utru*m*mae, e(*ter*) rosc 7 folt 7 gili⁹, e*ter* gáis¹⁰ 7 álaig¹¹ 7 erlabrae, e*ter* arm 7 eirriud 7 écosc, e*ter* ani 7 im*m*ud 7 ordan, e*ter* ergnas 7 gaisciud¹² 7 cenél.

b. Már a óitiu ind fir cháldae forbáith¹³ *con*idralá ar gním ngaiscid. Mád día ndersaigther¹⁴ a bruth 7 a gal o beit fianna fer nEr*end* 7 Alban dó ar thig, ní iurthar ind oruin céin bes inni¹⁵. Tothóetsat¹⁶ sé chét la Con*ai*re ríasiu rosia¹⁷ a árm, 7 tothóetsat secht¹⁸ cet lais ina chétch*um*scliu iar saigid¹⁹ a airm.

1. rige Eg. riga YBL. rígho H. rig. St.
2. cáemem Eg. coinem F. chainem YBL.
3. cumachtacha Eg. cum*ach*tachamh F. cumachtachom YBL. St. cumta*ch*tacham H.
4. riam. Ise in mor mállau móerda fri muintir 7 fria cairdiu. IS é im*m*orro in t-agarb écennais fria naimthib [leg. náim*t*ib] 7 echtrannaib i nhuáir catha 7 comlaind, Eg.
5. becdam H. begda F. becdæ YBL.
6. tanic a ndoma*n* riam H. is é d*an*o rí as cendsa 7 as míniu 7 is becme*n*m*n*aigi túraill tal*m*ain, Eg.
7. Eg. *inserts*: Ni fil nach locht *nó* nach anim isind [f]ir sin do neoch is ailbéim aiccenta do ch*u*rp duiniu o bond co a baithiss acht ro dearscaig do ce*ch* deilb duiniu, Eg.
8. Nochanfuil tra locht na anim Eg. Ní fuil loc*h*t isind fir sin H.²
9. oc*us* roscc 7 ingili Eg.
10. gnais H.
11. alaid St.
12. eti*r* érgna oc*us* crôdacht, Eg. iter ergna 7 gaisc*ed* St. iter gnais 7 gaisciud YBL.
13. Mór aicci in fir sin, málla in degduini lenmaigi [leg. lenbaide], Eg.
14. ndersaigt*er* F. YBL. St. n-eirsuigter H. derscaigther LU.
15. inti YBL. innti H. intiu H. Mad andside im*m*orro dia n-éirge a bruth 7 a ferg, cia no beitís fianna Her*enn* ac*us* Alban i mBruidin, 7 seissium a hoenar, nochon-iurfaitís ind argain cein no beth som istigh. Mairg iur*as* ind argain céin bes inti, Eg.
16. Dotuetsat F. Dothoetsat YBL. St. Totaetsat H,
17. rosoa YBL. St. laid F. riachtain H.
18. sé YBL. ui. F. .uiii. Eg. se cet eli H.
19. rochtain Eg. riachta*i*n H. soigid F.

7

Tongu¹ do Dia a toinges² mo thuath, mani gabthar deog de céin co beth³ nách⁴ aile isin tig chenae acht é a óenur, [no gébad som in Bruidin conas-toirsed cobair — Eg.] tanairsed⁵ in fer ó Thuind Chlidna 7 o Thuind Essa Rúaid, sibsi ocon Brudin⁶.

c. Atát⁷ nói ndorais forsin⁸ tig, 7 dofáeth⁹ cét laech lais cech dorais¹⁰, 7 intan ro scáig do chách is'tig airbert a gascid is and fochicher som¹¹ ar gnim n-aithergaid¹², 7 diamairi¹³ dó¹⁴ tuidecht¹⁵ foraib asin tig, bit lir bommand¹⁶ ega 7 fér for fagthi¹⁷ for lethchind 7 for lethchlocind 7 for cnáimred fo fáebur a chlaidib.

d. IS dochu limsa nimmaricfa dó tuidecht asin tig¹⁸. Is inmain laisseom in dias fil imbi isind imdae¹⁹ .i. a dá aiti, Dris 7 Sníthi. Tothóetsat²⁰ tri cóecait láech la cechtar de²¹ i ndorus na Brudne²², 7 ni bá sire traigid²³ úaid ille 7 innond [airm — H.] hi tóetsat.

e. Mairg iuras in n-orgain²⁴ cid dáig na dessi sin 7 na

1. Tuṅgu YBL.
2. tongthi H. toing F.
3. ce ni beth F. ceni beth YBL.
4. nech St.
5. darnársed Eg. tairsed F. St. tanairsed YBL.
6. YBL. omits sibsi etc. H. has : tairsit in fer a Tig Duinn 7 o Tuind Tuaide 7 Clidhna 7 Esa Ruaid.
7. Ata YBL.
8. asin YBL.
9. dothoeth YBL. dotaetsat H. tothoet St. dofoeth Eg.
10. gacha doruis dip H. cach doruis YBL.
11. fodcicher seom YBL. fodcichersom St. H. fotcicher som F.
12. n-aithergaib YBL. St. naithergaib H. n-aitherraig LU.
13. diambarich H. dianmairi St. diammairi F. diamari YBL. for dia n-immari, s. conj. sg. 3 of immaricim.
14. do LU. YBL.
15. tuidecht YBL. thuidecht LU. St. toigecht H.
16. is ann raga som ar gnim n-atheraig a gaiscid, ocus dia tecmad do tuidect foraib ammach asin tigh bat lir bommanna, etc. Eg.
17. H. inserts : 7 rendo nime: St. 7 renna nime : F. 7 rendai nime
18. toidhecht foruib asin tig amach H. tuidecht do isin tig YBL.
19. imdaid Eg.
20. Dofoethsat, Eg. Totaetsat H. Dothoetsad YBL. Tothoetsat F.
21. lasin cechtar nde, H.
22. ar dorus mBruidne H.
23. sirem troig H.
24. ind orcain F. ind orcuin H.

flatha fil etorro [.i.] ardri Here*nd*, Co*n*aire [Mór] mac Eters-
ceóil. Bá¹ líach díbdud na flatha sin, [LU. 92ᵃ] for Lomna
Drúth mac Duind désa ².

f. Ni c*u*mcid, for Ing*cél* : néla femmid dof*or*fecat 7rl.

g. IS deithb*er* duitsiu, a Ing*ceoil*, for Lo*m*na [Druth —
YBL.] m*ac* Dui[n]d D*ésa*. Ni dáit³ atá a domáin na orgne⁴,
ar béra cend rig ala-thuathe lat, 7 doernaba fessin. IS andso
damsa chena, ar bid mé cetaⁱ-ortábthar for Brud*in* ⁶.

h. Ango da*n*o, for Ing*cél*, adfía basa lecht bas briscium⁷, 7r.
Ocus cia acca and iarsin?

102. a. « *Easy for me to liken him* », *says Fer rogain*. « *No
« conflict without a king* » *this. He is the most splendid and noble
and beautiful and mighty king that has come into the whole world.
He is the mildest and gentlest and most perfect king that has come
to it, even Conaire son of Eterscél. 'Tis he that is overking of all
Erin. There is no defect in that man, whether in form or shape or
vesture: whether in size or fitness or proportion, whether in eye or
hair or brightness, whether in wisdom or skill or eloquence, whether
in weapon or dress or appearance, whether in splendour or abundance or dignity, whether in knowledge or valour or kindred.*

b. *Great is the tenderness of the sleepy simple man till he has
chanced on a deed of valour. (But) if his fury and his courage be
awakened when the champions of Erin and Alba are at him in the
house, the Destruction will not be wrought so long as he is therein.
Six hundred will fall by Conaire before he shall attain his arms,
and seven hundred will fall by him in his first conflict after at-
taining his arms. I swear to God what my tribe swears, unless*

---

1. bid H.
2. For the rest of this § H has only: Ni ditsi doma*i*ne na horene. Mairc damsai ria cach [MS. ciach] is mairc iar cach. is mo cennso 7rl. Ag*us* iarsin cia aco ann? St. has: ni deit a domain na horgne. Muithfe búaid ríg *no* rigdamna *no* airig dibergæ. Is annsu damsa im*m*orro, for Lomna Druth. Mairg damsa ria cach, mairg iar cach, ar is mo cenn-sa ceta-imchoicerthar ann iarsind uair (iter fertsib 7rl.) 7 iarsin cia acca and? Sic F.
3. duit Eg. deit St.
4. hoirgne. Néla f. Eg.
5. cena LU.
6. for ar ... Bruidin YBL. has muithfi rl. isansu rl.
7. YBL. 100ᵃ 20 adds: lurga manais

drink be taken from him, though there be no one else in the house, but he alone, he would hold the Hostel until help would reach it which the man would prepare for him from the Wave of Clidna[1] and the Wave of Assaroe[2] (while) ye (are) at the Hostel.

c. Nine doors there are to the house, and at each door a hundred warriors will fall by his hand. And when every one in the house has ceased to ply his weapon, 'tis then he will resort to a deed of arms And if he chance to come upon you out of the house, as numerous as hailstones and grass on a green will be your halves of heads and your cloven skulls and your bones under the edge of his sword.

d. 'Tis my opinion that he will not chance to get out of the house. Dear to him are the two that are with him in the room, his two fosterers, Dris and Snithe Thrice fifty warriors will fall before each of them in front of the Hostel, and not farther that a foot from him, on this side and that, will they (too) fall

e « Woe to him who shall wreak the Destruction, were it only because of that pair and the prince that is between them, the overking of Erin, Conaire son of Eterscél! Sad were the quenching of that reign ! » says Lomna Drúth, son of Donn Désa.

f. « Ye cannot », says Ingcel. « Clouds of weakness are coming to you », etc.

g « Good cause hast thou, O Ingcél », says Lomna son of Donn Désa « Not unto thee is the loss caused by the Destruction. for thou wilt carry off the head of the king of another country, and thyself wilt escape Howbeit 'tis hard for me, for I shall be the first to be slain at the Hostel. »

h. « Alas for me ! » says Ingcél, « peradventure I shall be the frailest corpse, etc

And whom sawest thou afterwards ? »

Imda na Culchometaide

103 « Atcondarc and da fer deac for cliathaib airgdidib immón n-imda sin [in rig — Eg.] immácúaird. Monga findbudi

---

[1] in the bay of Glandore, co Cork, Rev Celt , XV, 438
[2]. at Ballyshannon, co Donegal, Rev. Celt., XVI, 33.

— 101 —

foraib Lente glassa¹ impu. It é comaldi, comchróda², comdelba. Claideb co [n-eltaib — Eg.] dét³ il-laim cach fir dib, 7 nís-teilget⁴ sís eter, acht it é⁵ echlasca⁶ fil [ina lámaib⁷] immon imdúi⁸ sin immácuaird. Samailte let sin, a Fir rogain

co n-dét
Identify

The Room of the Rearguards.

103 There I saw twelve men on silvery hurdles all around that room of the king. Light yellow hair was on them. Blue kilts they wore. Equally beautiful were they, equally hardy, equally shapely. An ivory-hilted sword in each man's hand, and they cast them not down; but it is the horse-rods in their hands that are all round the room Liken thou that, O Fer rogain. »

104 Ní anse damsa ón cométaide rig Temrach andsin⁹. It é a n-anmand tri Luind¹⁰ Liphe, 7 tri Airt Átha cliath, 7 tri Budir Búagnige¹¹ 7 tri Trenfir Chúilne¹² Tongu a toinges mo thúath, bát ili mairb ocço immon mBrudin·¹³, 7 immáricfa élud dóib ass cid at crechtnaigthi Mairg iuras in n-orgain fodéig inna buidn[e] sin. Ocus iarsin cia acca and?

deaf
cit)
occaib

104. Easy for me (to say). The king of Tara's guardsmen are there. These are their names: three Londs of Liffey-plain. three Arts of Áth cliath (Dublin) three Budars of Búagneeh and three Trénfers of Cúilne (Cúilenn?) I swear what my tribe swears, (slain) that many will be the dead by them around the Hostel

---

1 lene glas, YBL leinte glassa Eg
2 chomcrotha YBL conferotha H St Eg
3 condet YBL St condett F co n-imdorn det H
4 ni lécait Eg nis-teilcet YBL St nistelcit H nistelcett, F
5 acht ised YBL
6. echalsca St
7 Sic Eg YBL inna lammaib St ina laim H inna lamha F
8 imdha H
9 cometaidi rig Erenn insin, Eg cometaighe rig Temrach innsin H
10 Luirg, Eg Luin Eg
11 Buaidhnigi Eg Buaidnigh F Buaidneidh YBL Buaidlnighe H Buaidnige St.
12 Cúailcm H Cuilne St Eg
13 Tonga do Dia tongait mo tuath, bid ila mairb na horene, H Tongu 7rl. bit ila a mairb 7rl YBL.

And they will escape from it although they are wounded. Woe to him who shall wreak the Destruction (were it only) because of that band! And afterwards whom sawest thou there? »

Lé fri flaith mac Conaire asa sammail so

105. Atcondarc and mac brecderg i mbrut chorcra, atá oc sirchói¹ isin tig. Bale hi fail in *tricha cét* gabthai cach fer a ucht i n-ucht. Atá iarom 7 catháir glas airgdidi fo a suidiu² *for* lár in tige [*ocus* sé, Eg.] oc sirchói¹. Angó³ *dano* it brónaig a theglach occ a clóistin⁴. Tri fuilt *for*sin mac sin : it é *tri* fuilt ón .i. folt úani⁵ 7 folt corcorda⁶ 7 folt fororda. Nocon fet*ur*sa⁷ indat ilgné dochuirther⁸ in folt fair nó indat [in tri gnée — Eg.] fuilt⁹ failet fair. *Acht* ro fetar ¹⁰ is f[á]il ní adage*thar* innocht¹¹. Atcondarc tri cóectu mac for¹² catháirib argdidib imni, 7 ro bátár .xu. bon-simne¹³ il-láim in maic brecdé[i]rg¹⁴ sin, 7 delg scíath a cind¹⁵ cach¹⁶ simni díb, 7 ro bámárni .xu. feraib¹⁷ 7 ar cóic súili déc dessa do cháechad dó¹⁸, 7 in secht-

---

1. sirchiu YBL. sírchúi St. Eg. sirchói H.
2. cathair glassairgit foe, Eg. cathair glas argidi fo a suidhiu YBL.
3. iñgo YBL. St. F. *Om.* H.
4. Is bronach in teglach ic a cloistin sin, Eg. it bronaich a teglach oc a cluais YBL. At brónaig a teg*lach* oc a cluais H. it bronaig a teglach occa chluais, St. at bronaich... chluaiss, F.
5. uainidi YBL. uainidhe H. huanide Eg. huainide St.
6. buidicorcrai YBL.
7. Ní *con* fetarsai H. Nocho n-etarsa Eg. nochanfet*a*rsa St.
8. docuirith*er* St. dochuirither YBL. docuir*e*thar Eg. H.
9. fo indat tri fuilt YBL. fa andai tri fuilt H. fa inda tri fuilt, St.
10. forrosfetar YBL.
11. is fil ni adagen ... i*n*nocht YBL. Dofuil ni atagere hinocht, Eg. is fael madogetar ano*cht* H. is fil ní mádágethar St. is fil magen innochd F.
12. fo YBL. St.
13. bondsim*m*ni Eg. bonsibne YBL. .u. bocsimni *déc* luac*h*ro H. bocsibne St. bogsibne F.
14. brecc*d*eirg Eg. brec*d*eirg H.
15. scíach i cind sciach YBL. sgiach a cinn, H. scíach hi cind Eg. sciach i cind cec*h* hsibne díbh F.
16. cec*h*a Eg. cac*h*a St. gac*h*a H.
17. sic St. This may be added to Pedersen's list of instrumentals used without possessive pronouns, Celt. Zeitsch., II, 379. ro bamairne .xu. fir, Eg. ro uabmairni .u. fir deg, H. robamarn[i] ar .u. feruibh deacc, F.
18. ro coechastar Eg. do coech*a*d doa F.

mad mac imblesen ro boi im chind-sa do chaechad do¹, ol Ingcél. Samailte let sin, a Fir rogain ?

Lé fri flaith son of Conaire, whose likeness this is.

105. *There I beheld a red-freckled boy in a purple cloak. He is always awaiting in the house. A stead wherein is the (king of a) cantred², whom each man takes from bosom to bosom.* So he is with a blue silvery chair under his seat in the midst of the house, and he always a-waiting. Truly then, sad are his household listening to him ! Three heads of hair on that boy, and these are the three · green hair and purple hair and all-golden hair. I know not whether they are many appearances which the hair receives, or whether they are three kinds of hair which are (naturally) upon him. But I know that evil is the thing he dreads tonight ³ I beheld thrice fifty boys on silvern chairs around him, and there were fifteen bulrushes in the hand of that red-freckled boy, with a thorn at the end of each of the rushes. And we were fifteen men, and our fifteen right eyes were blinded by him, and he blinded one of the seven pupils which was in my head » saith Ingcél. « Hast thou his like, O Fer rogain ? »

106. Ni anse damsa on a samail Ro chi⁴ Fer rogain co tarlaic a déra fola [dara grúaidib⁵ — Eg] Dirsan do¹ ol se, iss ed gein n-im[m]arbaga fil la firu Herend fri firu Alban ar gart 7 cruth 7 deilb 7 marcachas. Is liach [a guin — H.], is mucc remitéit⁶ mess, [is nóidiu ar aeis, H]. Damna flatha as dech⁷ tanic Herind⁸ insin Nóidiu⁹ Conaire maic Etersceoli 1 Lé fri¹⁰

---

1 ros-cóechastar Eg do coechad doa F do chaechad dó, St.
2 The Irish here is obscure, and probably corrupt For *tricha cét*, cf. § 138
3 Cf § 77 supra
4 ro chich YBL Roichi St Ro ci F.
5 Sic Eg H has Ro chi Fer rogain co mbo fluch a brat ara bélaib
6 riana Eg remetuit F YBL St remituit H
7 is ferr Eg
8 tanic a tir nErenn H. tainic tir nErind YBL tainic tir nErenn Eg
9 maccnáidiu Eg. nuidiu F YBL,
10. fer F YBL.

flaith a ainm. Secht¹ mbliadna fil i[n]na áes. Ni indóig² lim cid trú daig³ na n-ilgne[e] filet forsind fult fil fair, 7 inna ndath [LU. 92ᵇ] n-écsamail docorethar [in folt] fair⁴. IS é a sainteglach som sin, na tri cóicait maccóem fil imbi.

Mairg iuras in n-orgain, for Lomna, cid fóbithin in maic sin!

Ni cumcid⁵, for Ingcel : nela fémmid dofortecat 7 rl. Ocus iarsin cia acca and ?

106 « Easy for me to liken him ! » Fer rogain wept till he shed⁶ his tears of blood over his cheeks. « Alas for him ! », quoth he This child is a « scion of contention » for the men of Erin with the men of Alba for hospitality, and shape, and form and horsemanship. Sad is his slaughter ! 'Tis a « swine that goes before mast », 'tis a babe in age! the best crown-prince that has (ever) come into Erin ! The child of Conaire son of Eterscél, Lé fri flaith is his name. Seven years there are in his age It seems to me very likely that he is miserable because of the many appearances on his hair and the various hues that the hair assumes upon him. This is his special household, the thrice fifty lads that are around him.

« Woe », says Lomna, « to him that shall wreak the Destruction, were it (only) because of that boy! »

« Ye cannot », says Ingcel. « Clouds of weakness are coming on you, etc. And after that whom sawest thou there? »

IMDA NA NDALEMAN.

107. Atcondarc and sessiur arbélaib na himdad⁷ cétna. Monga findbudi foraib bruit úanidi⁸ impu⁹: deilgi créda¹⁰ i

---

1 ocht Eg
2 The facsimile has *inndóig* ni hindoig, Lg Ni hindoigh H ni indoic F
3 dag Eg diag LU YBL diag St
4 daig na n-ilgne docuirither an folt fair H dieg na n-ilgne docuirighthir in folt fair, St diag na n ilgnæ dochum in folt fair YBL F.
5 cumgi H Eg chumcid St cuimeitt F
6 literally « yielded », tarlaic, from to-air-ro-léic
7 na imda Lg na himdha, St na himdae H na himdadh F na nimdad LU
8 huaini aille Eg huainidi YBL uainidi H uainidhiu F
9 impaibh F
10 delga cóemu creduma Eg. delcni credai H. deilge creduma, St

n-aurslocud a mbrat, It é lethgabra¹ amail Chonall Cernach. Focheird cach fer [dib, Eg.] a brat immáraile, 7 is lúathidir rothán mbúaled² : is ing inda-airthet do súil³. Samailte let sin, a Fir rogain.

The Room of the Cupbearers.

107. There I saw six men in front of the same room. Fair yellow manes upon them: green mantles about them: tin brooches at the opening of their mantles. Half-horses (centaurs) are they, like Conall Cernach⁴. Each of them throws his mantle round another and is as swift as a mill-wheel. Thine eye can hardly follow them. Liken thou those, O Fer rogain! »

108. Ni *anse* damsa ón. Sé dálemain ríg Temra⁵ insin. .i. Úan 7 Bróen 7 Banna⁶, Delt 7 Drucht 7 Dathen. Nis-dérband⁷ día ndáil ind reb sin, 7 ní clúi a n-intliucht ocá ndáil. It mathi ind óic fil and. Tothóethsat a tri chumlund⁸ léo. Conráinfet⁹ comgnim fri cach seser¹⁰ isin Brudin, 7 aslúifet airib¹¹, úair¹² is a sídib¹³ dóib. It é dalemain ata¹⁴ dech fil i nHerind insin¹⁵. Mairg iuras in n-orgain fo ndeig sin!

Ni chumcid¹⁶, for Ingcél. Nela 7r. *Ocus* iarsin cia acca and ?

108. « *This is easy for me. Those are the King of Tara's six*

---

1. le*th*gapra H. lethghabar .i. lethech H. 3. 18, p. 532. letgabrai F. lethgleore Eg. Cf. lethgobra supra § 51.
2. mbuaileth YBL. m̄bualeth St. mbuailed H.
3. is ing indarthe*nd* do súil a n-imclóechmód Eg. is ing in doarthet do shuil YBL. is ing inda airteth do (súil) F. Is ing ní daartheth St. is ing in doairthet do hsuil H.
4. the *óenmarcach* of the story of Cúchulainn's death, Rev. Celt., III, 183.
5. ríg Erenn Eg. rig Temrach YBL.
6. Buan 7 Breg 7 Banno, H. Huaim 7 Broen 7 Bandu, St.
7. Nis-tairmmescand Eg. nis derban YBL. St. H.
8. comlín Eg. H. coimlin F. an tri cumlund YBL. a tri chomlin St.
9. conroindfet Eg. *co*nrainfet YBL. *co*nroinnfit H.
10. sesiur YBL. sesir St. F. seissiur Eg. se*cht* H.
11. ragait fein ass, Eg. asluifet toraib, St. asloifit airib H.
12. huaire YBL. St.
13. síd Eg. sidaib YBL. St. F. sidip H.
14. adad YBL. 100ᵇ 13. adda St. ada F.
15. *Ocus* is fat sin dálemain is ferr filett in Herinu Eg. 120ᵃ 2.
16. cumgi H. Eg.

cupbearers, namely Úan and Broen and Banna[1], *Delt and Drucht*[2] *and Dathen That feat does not hinder them from their skinking, and it blunts not their intelligence thereat. Good are the warriors that are there! Thrice their number will fall by them. They will share prowess with any six in the Hostel, and they will escape from their foes, for they are out of the elfmounds. They are the best cupbearers in Erin Woe to him that shall wreak the Destruction (were it only) because of them!* »

« Ye cannot », says Ingcél. « Clouds etc. And after that, whom sawest thou there? »

Imda Tulchinne Druith.

109. Atcondarc and borróclaech arbélaib na imdae[3] cetnae for lár in tige. Athis máili fair. Finnithir canach slébe cach finna asas trí ina chend Unasca[4] óir immá ó[5] Brat breclígda imbi. Nói claidib ina láim[6] 7 nói sceith airgdidi 7 nói n-ubla óir Focheird cech ai díb i n-ardae, 7 ní thuit ni dib for lár, 7 ní bí acht óen dib for a bois, 7 is cumma ocus timthirecht bech[7] il-ló[8] áth cach ae sech araile súas [7 anuas[9].] Intan bá hánem[10] dó atconnarcus[11] ocon chlis[12], 7 amal dorechtachasa[13] sochartatar grith[14] immi co mbátar for lár in tige uile

IS and asbert ind flaith[15] fil isin tig frisin clessamnach. Co-

---

1. 1 e Froth and Rain and Drop
2. 1 e Dew
3. himdad YBL lumda St himdadh F imdad Eg. himdai H.
4. Unascach St F H uanascach H¹
5. huæ YBL St F o H oib H¹ Eg omits
6. lamaib YBL St
7. andar-lat is tímthirecht beich, Eg
8. il-lau YBL St. a lo H 1 loi F
9. sic H
10. hanem H haineam F haincam St n-anem YBL. ham LU
11. Intan ropa anem do, Eg Atconnaresa intan ba n-anem do atchonnar esa, YBL adconnaresa F Atconiresa Eg St atconnaicso H
12. chlius YBL St
13. rodercusa fair Eg dorrecochasa YBL dorrecachasa St dorecachusa H. dorrecacassa F
14. focerd airmgrith YBL.
15. fili Eg flaith YBL.

tráncammar ór' bat m*a*c bec ¹, 7 ni ralá do cless n-airiut² cosin nocht.

Uch, uch, a phopa cháin *Conaire,* [ar sé, —Eg.] is deithber dam : dom-recacha³ súil féig andíaraid, fer co trián⁴ m*ai*cc im[b]lisen foraicce dul nói ndro[n]g⁵. Ní méti dosom a ndéicsin [theg \H.] andíaraid sin. Fichit*ir*⁶ catha de, or se. Rofessar co d*é* brátha⁷ bas n-olc ar dor*us* Bruid*ne*.

The Room of Tulchinne the Juggler.

109. « *There I beheld a great champion, in front of the same room, on the floor of the house. The shame of baldness is on him. White as mountain cotton-grass is each hair that grows through his head. Earrings of gold around his ears. A mantle speckled, coloured, he wore. Nine swords in his hand, and nine silvern shields, and nine apples of gold. He throws each of them upwards, and none of them falls on the ground, and there is only one of them on his palm; each of them rising and falling past another is just like the movement to and fro of bees on a day of beauty. When he was swiftest, I beheld him at the feat, and as I looked, they uttered a cry about him and they were all on the house-floor. Then the Prince who is in the house said to the juggler :* « *We have come together since thou wast a little boy, and till tonight thy juggling never failed thee.* »

« *Alas, alas, fair master Conaire, good cause have I. A keen, angry eye looked at me : a man with the third of a pupil which sees the going of the nine hands. Not much to him is that keen, wrathful sight ! Battles are fought with it* », *saith he.* « *It should be known till doomsday that there is evil in front of the Hostel.* »

---

1. o ropo meice becca sind diblínib Eg. o bim m*a*c YBL. Codorancamar o bi mac, H. Cotrancamar o bi mac, St. F.
2. ni torchair do cless huait, Eg. ni raloi do cles airit, H. ni rala do cles n-airit YBL. ni raba do cless n-airiut F.
3. rom-dèice Eg. romdeici H¹. Domrecacai F. domrecachai H.
4. triun YBL. F. Eg. H¹.
5. atamconairec tria fithissib .ix. ṅdroṅg, Eg. foraice dol nói ndrong, H. foraicce dul noindrong F. St. foraicce dul noi ndrong YBL. atamconnairc tria fithisibh (.i. conair) nói ndroroch (.i. roth), H¹.
6. fichither YBL. ficit*ir* H. Fechait*er* Eg.
7. Rofesaither co dered ṁbratha, Eg. Rofessar co dered bratha, St. rofesar ço deired mbrátha, F.

110. Gabais iarom na claidbiu inna láim[1], 7 na scéith[2] airgdidi 7 na ubla[3] óir, 7 fochartatar[4] grith imbi dorise[5] co mbátár for lár [in] tige uile. Dorat im-moth[6] anisin, 7 ro léic a chles n-úad[7], 7 asbert. A Fir chaille, comérig! ná laig a slige[8], sligairdbi do muic. Fin[n]tai cia fail ar dorus tige do amlius[9] fer mBruidne.

Atá[10] and, or se, Fer Cualngi[11], [Fer le[12],] Fer gar, Fer rógel, Fer rógain. Dlomsat gním nad lobur, logud[13] Conaire[14] o coic maccaib Duind Desa, ó cóic comaltaib[15] carthachaib [Conaire, Eg]

Samailte lat sin, a Fir rogain Cia ro cháchain in láid se?

110. Then he took the swords in his hand, and the silvern shields and the apples of gold; and again they uttered a cry and were all on the floor of the house. That amazed him[16], and he gave over his play and said.

« *O Fer caille, arise! Do not . its slaughter. Sacrifice thy pig! Find out who is in front of the house to injure the men of the Hostel* »

« *There* », *said he*, « *are Fer Cualngi, Fer lé, Fer gar, Fer rogel, Fer rogain. They have announced a deed which is not feeble, the annihilation of Conaire by Donn Désa's five sons, by Conaire's five loving foster brothers.* »

« *Liken thou that, O Fer rogain! Who has chanted that lay?* »

1 Gabais iarum a clesa 1 na claidib Eg
2 sgiatha F
3 hublai YBL hubloi H.
4 focertat Eg
5 arithise YBL afritisi H arithisi F doridise Eg.
6 a mod Eg im-mothar YBL. St a motugud H imon teach F
7 a clesa huad Eg
8 asleig YBL aslig H St F
9 mulius LU amlius Eg YBL aimles H F amlius St
10 Ataat H
11 Cualge YBL Cualngne F
12 sic YBL H F Fer lé St Eg
13 logad F loghudh YBL matad H
14 Dlomsat gnim laiset ar logud Conaire do marbad Eg
15 comdaltaib St F
16. lit put him (dorat, rectius darat) into stupor (moth, Ml. 68ᵇ 9).

111. Ni *anse* limsa a sam*ail*, or Fer rogain. Taulchinne¹ rigdrúth² ríg Temr*ach* : clessamnach *Conaire* insin Fer comaic [LU. 93]³ mór in fer sin. Tothóetsat tri n*onb*uir ina chétchumscli⁴ leis, 7 *conr*ainfe⁵ comgním fri cach n-óen⁶ isin Brudin, 7 immaricfa⁷ elúd do ass cid crechtnaigthe. Cid ni chena ni bu ortai⁸ ind org*uin* cid fobithin ind fir sin.

Céinmair noda-ainse*d*⁹¹ *for* Lomna.

Ni cumcid », for Ingcél¹⁰ [7 iarsin cia accai and ? — F.].

111. « *Easy for me to liken him* », *says Fer rogain.* « *Taulchinne the chief juggler of the King of Tara; he is Conaire's conjurer A man of great might is that man Thrice nine will fall by him in his first encounter, and he will share prowess with every one in the Hostel, and he will chance to escape therefrom though wounded. What then? Even on account of this man (only) the Destruction should not be wrought.* »

« *Long live he who should spare him!* » *says Lomna Drúth.*

« *Ye cannot* », *says Ingcél, etc*

IMDA NA MUCCIDI¹¹.

112. Atc*on*narc triar i n-airthiur in tige, tri dubberrthae foraib : tri forti úanidi impu tri dublenna tairsiu· tri gabulgici uasaib hi tóib fraiged se dubassi dóib ar crund Cia sút, a Fir rogain ?

« Ni *anse*, ol Fer rog*ain* : Tri muccaidi ind ríg sin, Dub 7 Dond 7 Dorcha : tri brathir, tri ma*icc* Maphir Themr*ach*.

---

1. Taulchaine, St YBL Taulchine F. Tuilchinne Eg Taulchaini H
2. rigdruith YBL
3. In this and the next page of LU the writing is in one column
4. *ch*étchumschu St. cetcuinschu F
5. *conr*aindi YBL comrainfe Eg. *conr*oinnfi H
6. fri gach n-aoinfer H
7. immarame 7rl YBL
8. Facs LU mbuorta Nirbo ortæ St nibo ordctai F (the *c* written over the *t*) nibo ortæ YBL. imaricfi 7 rl nibo H, *which ends here*
9. cein nodaainsed LU. cenmair nodnansed YBL monginar nodansed Eg 111ᵇ2. nodnainsed F.
10. add YBL nel*u* 7rl.
11. §§ 112-125 are omitted by YBL. F. St and § 112 is omitted by Eg.

Céinmair nudn-ains*ed*, mairg nodn-géna¹! ar bá mó búaid a n-anacail oldas a ngona.

Ni c*u*mcid, for (Ingcél etc.)

The Room of the Swineherds.

112. « *I beheld a trio in the front of the house : three dark crown-tufts on them : three green frocks around them : three dark mantles over them : three forked ...(?) above them on the side of the wall. Six black greaves they had on the mast². Who are yon, O Fer rogain ?* »

« *Easy to say* », answers Fer rogain: « *the three swineherds of the king, Dub and Donn and Dorcha : three brothers are they, three sons of Mapher of Tara. Long live he who should protect them! woe to him who shall slay them!* » *for greater would be the triumph of protecting them than (the triumph) of slaying them!* »

« *Ye cannot* », says Ingcél, etc.

IMDA NA N-ARAD N-AIREGDA.

113. Atc*o*nnarc triar n-aili ara mbelaib: téora lanna óir for airthiur a cind: teora berrbróca impu de lín glas imdentai di ór: tri cochlini corcrai impu : *tr*i broit chrédumi ina láim. Samail[te] let sin, a Fir r*o*gain.

Ros-fetar, ol se. Cul 7 Frecul 7 Forcul, tri prímaraid ind ríg sin, tri comais, tri maic Sidbi 7 Cuinge. Atbéla fer cech airm leo, 7 conráinfet buáid n-echta.

The Room of the principal Charioteers.

113. « *I beheld another trio in front of them : three plates of gold on their foreheads : three short aprons they wore, of grey linen embroidered with gold : three crimson capes about them : three goads of bronze in their hands. Liken thou that, O Fer rogain!* »

« *I know them* », he answered. « *Cul and Frecul and Forcul, the three charioteers of the King : three of the same age : three sons of Pole and Yoke. A man will perish by each of their weapons, and they will share the triumph of slaughter.* »

---

1. leg. noda-ainsed, mairg noda-génad.
2. Some part of the house or its furniture = craund siuil § 115.

Imda Chuscraid maicc Concobair.

114. Atconnarc imdái n-aili. Ochtur claidbech inti 7 máeth-ocláech eturro. Máel dub fair 7 belra formend leiss Contúaset áes na Brudni uli a condelg Aildem di dáimib hé. Cáimsi imbi 7 brat gelderg Eo áirgit inna brot.

Rofetursa sin, ol Fer rogain, i. Cuscraid Mend Macha macc Conchobair fil hi ngialnai lasin rig. A chometaidi immorro in t-ochtur fil immi i. da Fland, da Chummain, da Áed, da Chrimthan. Conróinfet comgnim fri cech n-óen isin Brudin, 7 immaricfa élod dóib ass fri a ndaltai[1].

The Room of Cuscrad son of Conchobar

114. I beheld another room. Therein were eight swordsmen, and among them a stripling Black hair is on him, and very stammering speech has he. All the folk of the Hostel listen to his counsel. Handsomest of men he is. he wears a shirt and a bright-red mantle, with a brooch of silver therein »

« I know him », says Fer rogain « 'tis Cuscraid Menn of Armagh, Conchobar's son, who is in hostageship with the king And his guards are those eight (swordsmen) around him, namely, two Flanns, two Cummains, two Aeds, two Crimthans. They will share prowess with every one in the Hostel, and they will chance to escape from it with their fosterling »

Imda na Foarad.

115. Atchonnarc nónbur, for craund siuil dóib. Nói cochleni impu co lubun chorcrai 7 land óir for cind cach ae Nói mbruit inna lámaib. [Samalte — Eg 116ᵇ 2].

Ro[s]fetursa sin, ol Fer rogain. Riado, Riamcobur, Riade, Buadon, Búadchar, Buadgnad, Err, Iner[2], Argatlam — nói n-araid foglomma la tri primaradu ind rig. Atbela fer cech-ai dib, 7r.

---

1. For the corresponding passage on Eg 116ᵇ 1 see Appendix § 114 It is followed by a description of Conaire's three wizards.
2 Inerr Eg

The Room of the Under-charioteers.

115. I beheld nine men: on the mast were they. Nine capes they wore, with a purple loop. A plate of gold on the head of each of them. Nine goads in their hands. Liken thou. »

« *I know those* », *quoth Fer rogain :* « *Riado, Riamcobur, Riade, Buadon, Búadchar, Buadgnad, Eirr, Íneirr, Argatlam — nine charioteers in apprenticeship with the three chief charioteers of the king. A man will perish at the hands of each of them, etc.*

IMDA NA SAXANACH.

116. At*connarc* isind leith atuáid din tig n*ó*nbur. N*ó*i monga f*or*baidi f*or*aib. Noi camsi fogarti impu. Noi lennæ córcrai tairsiu ce*n* delgae indib. N*ó*i manaise. *Nói* cromsceith déirg úasaib. [Samalthe, Eg. 117ª 1].

Oswald Rus-fetamar, ol se, .i. Ósalt[1] 7 a da chomalta, Osbrit[2] Lamfota 7 a dá chomalta, Lindas[3] 7 a da chomalta, tri rigdomna do Saxanaib sin file*t* ocond r*í*g. Co*n*rainfet in lucht sin buáid ng[n]íma, 7rl.

The Room of the Englishmen.

116. « *On the northern side of the house I beheld nine men. Nine very yellow manes were on them. Nine linen frocks somewhat short were round them: nine purple plaids over them without brooches therein. Nine broad spears, nine red curved shields above them.* »

« *We know them* », *quoth he.* « *Oswald and his two fosterbrothers, Osbrit Longhand and his two fosterbrothers, Lindas and his two fosterbrothers. Three crown-princes of England who are with the king. That set will share victorious prowess, etc.*

IMDA NA RITERED.

117. At*condarc* triar n-aili. Teóra máela f*or*aib, tri lenti

1. Ozaltt Eg.
2. Ozbritt Eg.
3. Oult Eg.

mpu¹, 7 tri broit hi forcepul. Sraigell il-laim cachae. [Samailie 7rl. Eg.].

Rus-fetursa sin, ol se. Echdruim, [LU. 94] Echriud, Echrúathar, tri marcaig ind rig sin .i. a thrí ritiri. Tri brathir iat, tri maic Argatroin². Mairg iuras in n-orcain cid fodáig in trir sin!

The Room of the Equerries.

117. « I beheld another trio. Three cropt heads of hair on them, three frocks they wore, and three mantles wrapt (around them). A whip in the hand of each. »

« I know those », quoth he (Fer rogain). « Echdruim, Echriud, Echrúathar, the three horsemen of the king, that is, his three equerries. Three brothers are they, three sons of Argatron. Woe to him who shall wreak the Destruction, were it (only) because of that trio.

IMDA NA MBRET[H]EMAN.

118. Atconnarc triar n-aili isind imdai ocaib. Fer cáin ro gab a máelad hi cetad³. Di ocláig leis⁴ co mongaib foraib. Téora lenda cummascdai impu⁵. Eo argit i mbrot caechnai dib. Tri gascid úasaib hi fraig. Samail⁶ let sin, a Fir rogain.

Rus-fetar son, ol se. Fergus Ferde, Fer fordae, 7 Domáine Mossud, tri brithemain ind rig sin. Mairg iuras in n-orcain cid fodeig in trír sin! Atbéla fer cachæ dib.

The Room of the Judges.

118. I beheld another trio in the room by them. A handsome [leg. bald] man who had got his baldness newly. By him were two young men with manes upon them. Three mixed plaids they wore. A pin of silver in the mantle of each of them. Three suits of armour above them on the wall. Liken thou that, O Fer rogain! »

---

1. teora leni hi cestul fri gelcnes dóib Eg.
2. Argatroir Eg.
3. fer moel rogabad [leg. rogab a] moelad hi cétud, Eg. 116ᵇ 2.
4. da óclach leiss Eg.
5. teora caimsi impu co teoraib lannaib cumascdai Eg.
6. Samailte Eg.

8

« *I know those* », *quoth he.* « *Fergus Ferde, Fergus Fordae and Domáine Mossud, those are the king's three judges. Woe to him who shall wreak the Destruction were it only because of that trio! A man will perish by each of them.* »

Imdúi na Crutiri.

119. At*condarc* nónbur n-aile friu anair. Nói monga cráebacha cassa foraib. *Nói* mbroit glassa luascaig impu. *Nói* ndelce óir ina mbrataib. *Nói* failge glano[1] immá láma. Ordnasc óir im ordain cach ae. Auchuimriuch[2] n-óir 'm o[3] chach fir. Muince aircit im brágit cach ae. *Nói* mbuile co n-inchaib órdaib uasib hi fraig ⁊ *nói* flesca findarcit inna lamaib. [Samailte Eg.].

Ro[s]fet*ur*sa sin, ol se. Noi crutiri ind rig insin [7 a *nói* cruite úasaib, Eg.]. Side 7 Dide, Dulothe 7 Deichrinni, Caumul 7 Cellgen, Ól 7 Ólene 7 Olchói[4]. Atbela fer cach ae leo.

The Room of the Harpers.

119. « *To the east of them I beheld another ennead. Nine branchy, curly manes upon them. Nine grey, floating (?) mantles about them: nine pins of gold in their mantles. Nine rings of crystal round their arms. A thumbring of gold round each man's thumb: an ear-tie of gold round each man's ear: a torque of silver round each man's throat. Nine bags with golden faces above them on the wall. Nine rods of white silver in their hands. Liken thou (them).* »

« *I know those* », *quoth he (Fer rogain).* « *They are the king's nine harpers, with their nine harps above them: Side and Dide, Dulothe and Deichrinne, Caumul and Cellgen, Ól and Ólene and Olchói. A man will perish by each of them.* »

Imdai na Clesamnach.

120. At*condarc* triar n-aile isind airidi. Teora caimsi hi

---

1. glan*ide* Eg. 117ª 1.
2. eo comrach Eg.
3. i n-ói Eg.
4. Sígae, Dige, Degrime, Emul, Caumul, Celtgen, Olae, Olchae, Olenae, Eg.

foditib (.i. hi cenglaib) impu. Sciatha cethrocairi ina¹ lámaib co telaib óir foraib 7 ubla airgit, 7 gai bic intlassi leu.

Ros-fetursa, ol se. Cless 7 Clissine 7 Clessamun, tri clessamnaig ind rig sin. Tri comais, tri derbráthir, tri maicc Naffir Rochlis. Atbéla² fer cach ae léo

The Room of the Conjurers.

120. « *I saw another trio on the dais Three bedgowns girt about them. Four-cornered shields in their hands, with bosses of gold upon them. Apples of silver they had, and small inlaid spears* »

« *I know them* », *says Fer rogain* « *Cless and Clissine and Clessamun, the king's three conjurers Three of the same age are they, three brothers, three sons of Naffer Rochless A man will perish by each of them*

IMDAI TRI N-ANMED IND RIG

121 Atcondarc triar n-aili hi comfocraib imdai ind rig fessin. Tri broit gorma impu 7 teóra caimsi co ndergintlaid tairsiu Airocabtha a ngascid úasaib hi fraigid.

Rus-fetursa sin, ol se i. Dris 7 Draigen 7 Aittit, tri anmed³ ind rig, tri maicc Scéith foilt. Atbela fer cach airm léo

The Room of the three Lampooners.

121. « *I beheld another trio hard by the room of the King himself Three blue mantles around them, and three bedgowns with red insertion over them. Their arms had been hung above them on the wall* »

« *I know those* », *quoth he.* « *Dris 7 Draigen 7 Aittit* (« *Thorn and Bramble and Furze* »), *the king's three lampooners, three sons of Sciath foilt*⁴ *A man will perish by each of their weapons* »

IMDAI NA MBADB.

122. Atcondarc triar nocht hi cléthi in tigi A tócsca fola trethu, 7 súanemain a n-airlig ara mbraigti.

1 MS. in ina
2 Atbéba LU
3 leg anmid ? anmeda ?
4 Sciachfolt ?

R*us*-feta*r*sa sin, ol se: t*r*i ernbaid úagboid: triar orgar la cach n-aim insin.

The Room of the Badbs.

122. « I beheld a trio, naked, on the rooftree of the house: their jets of blood (coming) through them, and the ropes[1] of their slaughter on their necks. »

« Those I know », saith he, « three ... of awful boding. Those are the three that are slaughtered at every time. »

IMDA NA FULACHTORI.

123. At*c*ondarc triar oc dénam fulochta i mberrbrócaib intlassib. Fer find líath, 7 di oclaig 'na farrad.

R*us*-fetu*r*sa sin, ol Fer rogain. Tri primfulachtore ind ríg sin .i. in Dagdae 7 a da daltae .i. Séig 7 Segdae da mac Rofir Oenbero. Atbéla fer la cach n-ae díb, 7r.

The room of the Kitcheners.

123. « I beheld a trio cooking, in short inlaid aprons: a fair grey man, and two youths in his company.

« I know those », quoth Fer rogain: « they are the King's three chief kitcheners, namely, the Dagdae and his two fosterlings, Séig and Segdae, the two sons of Rofer Singlespit. A man will perish by each of them », etc.

IMDA NA FILED.

124. At*c*ondarc triar n-aili and. Téora landa óir tar a cend. T*r*i broit bric impu: teora camsi *co n*dergintlaid: teora bretnassa óir inna mbrattaib: teora bunsacha uasaib hi fraig.

Rofetu*r*sa sin, or Fer rogin: tri filid ind rig sin .i. Sui 7 Rodui 7 Fordui: tri comais, t*r*i brathir, t*r*i maic Maphir Rochétail. Atbela fer cech fir dib, 7 *c*ongeba cach dias búaid n-oenfir ctorro. Mairg iura*s* ind orcain! 7r.

---

1. With these ropes C. H. Tawney compared the Homeric πείρατ' ὀλέθρου Il. 6, 143: Od. 22, 41: cf. also the Anglo-saxon Dha feowere fæges rápas, « the four ropes of the doomed man ». Salomon and Saturn, ed. Kemble, p. 164, wridhene wæl-hlencan « twisted chains of slaughter », Elene 47.

124 « *I beheld another trio there. Three plates of gold over their heads. Three speckled mantles about them; three linen shirts with red insertion; three golden brooches in their mantles; three wooden darts above them on the wall.* »

« *Those I know* », says Fer rogain; « *the three poets of that king: Sui and Rodui and Foidui; three of the same age, three brothers; three sons of Maphar of the Mighty Song. A man will perish for each of them, and every pair will keep between them one man's victory. Woe to him who shall wreak the Destruction!* » etc

[LU 95ª] IMDA NA FOSCHOMLTAIDI

125. At*condarc* and dá óclaech ina sessom os cind ind rig. Dá cromsciath 7 da bendchlaidiub mara occo. Lenna derca impu: delci findairgit isna brataib.

Bun 7 Meccun sin, ol se, da chometaid[1] ind rig in sin, da macc Maffir Thuill.

The Room of the Servant-guards.

125 « *There I beheld two warriors standing over the king. Two curved shields they had, and two great pointed swords. Red kilts they wore, and in the mantles pins of white silver.* »

« *Bole and Root are those* », quoth he, « *the king's two guards, two sons of Maffer Toll* »

IMDA NA COMETAIDI IND RIG.

126. At*condarc*[2] nonbór i n-imdae and arbelaib na imdai cetnae. Mongae findbudi foroib. Berrbróca[3] impu, 7 cochléne brecca 7 scéith béimnecha for*a*ib. Claidib[4] dét il-láim cach fir dib, 7 cach fer dotháet isa tech fólóimet*ar*[5] a béim cosna claidbib. Ní lomethar[6] nech dul dond imdae cen airiasacht dóib. Samailte lat sin, a Fir rogain.

1 MS chometaib
2 Here F YBL and Eg recommence
3 Bernbroga YBL
4 claidbi YBL claidib co n-eltaib Eg
5 folaimtis, Eg 120ᵇ 2 foloimmetar St F foloimetar YBL
6. laimather Eg lomethar F lometar YBL lamaither H¹.

Ní ansé damsa ón. Tri Mochmatnig Midi, tri Búageltaig[1] Brég, tri Sostaig[2] Slébe Fuait. Nónbor cométaide ind ríg sin[3]. Toth&etsat nói ndechenbair léo ina cetcumschu, 7rl[4]. Mairg iuras in n-oigain fó ndéig sin!
Ní cumcid for Ingcél. Néla femmid, 7 rl. Ocus iarsin cia acca and?

The Room of the King's Guardsmen.

126. « *I beheld nine men in a room there in front of the same room Fair yellow manes upon them short aprons they wore and spotted capes: they carried smiting shields An ivory-hilted sword in the hand of each of them, and whoever enters the house they essay to smite him with the swords. No one dares to go to the room (of the King) without their consent. Liken thou that, O Fer rogain!* »

« *Easy for me is that Three Mochmatnechs of Meath, three Buagellachs of Bregia, three Sostachs of Sliab Fuait, the nine guardsmen of that King. Nine decads will fall by them in their first conflict, etc Woe to him that shall wreak the Destruction because of them (only)!*

« *Ye cannot* », *says Ingcél.* « *Clouds of weakness etc. And whom sawest thou then?* »

IMDA NIA 7 BRUTHNI .I. DA ROSS MÉSI CONAIRI.

127 Atcondarc imdae n-aile n-and 7 días indi Ité daimdabcha[5] balcremra. Berrbróca[6] impu it é gormdonna[7] ind fir Culmonga cumri foraib, ité auiarda for étun. It lúathidir roth [m]búah[8] cechtar de sech araili, ind-ala hái[9] dond imdai, alaile don temid. Samailte lat sin, a Fir rogain.

---

1 buaideltaig YBL
2 Rostaig St
3 YBL and Eg omit this sentence
4 St and YBL add 7 immiricefa elud F adds 7 immiaricefa elud 7rl.
5 toirnidi Eg 120b 2
6 bernu broci Eg
7 donna gorma Eg gormdonda YBL goimdonnai F.
8 roth mbuaile YBL F Eg roth mbuaile St
9 indara de Eg. indalaih YBL ind ila de St F.

Ni *anse* damsa. Nia[1] 7 Bruthni[2], da[3] foss mése[4] Conaire insin. Is í días as dech fail[5] i n-Herind im less a tigernæ. Iss ed fótera[6] duinni dóib 7 aurarda dia fult, athigid in[7] tened[8] co menic. Ni fil isin bith dias[9] bas[10] ferr ina ndán andáte Tothoétsat tri nónbor léo ina cétcumscli, 7 conrainfet[11] comgnim fri cach, 7 immaricfa elud dóib. *Ocus* iarsin cia acca and?

The Room of Nia and Bruthne, Conaire's two waiters

127 « There I beheld another room, and a pair was in it, and they are « oxtubs », stout and thick Aprons they wore, and the men were dark and brown. They had short backhair on them, but high upon their foreheads They are as swift as a waterwheel, each of them past another, one of them to the (King's) room, the other to the fire. Likest thou those, O Fer rogain ! »

« Easy to me. They are Nia and Bruthne, Conaire's two tableservants. They are the pair that is best in Erin for their lord's advantage What causes brownness to them and height to their hair is their frequent haunting of the fire. In the world is no pair better in their art than they. Thrice nine men will fall by them in their first encounter, and they will share prowess with every one, and they will chance to escape. And after that whom sawest thou? »

IMDA SENCHA 7 DUBTHAIG 7 GOBNEND MAICC LURGNIG.

128. Atcondarc imdae as nesam do[12] Conaire tri primláich inti · it é cétliatha. Teora lenna dubglassa impu. Remithir[13]

---

1 Niadh St
2. Bruitne F, Bruithni St
3 dia Eg
4 du foss messi YBL
5 is iat sin dias is ferr fil, Eg
6 fodera F fodera YBL fotera Eg
7. na YBL
8 aithighit in teinid, F
9 nisfil isin bith dis, YBL nisfil isin bith dis, St Nisfil isin bith diass, F
10 as Eg St
11 comraindfet Eg 7 maidfit 7rl YBL
12 St inserts imndæ F inserts imdai Eg omits do
13. Remir St remir F reimithir Eg

medón fir cach ball dib[1]. Tri claid*ib* duba dimóra léo, sia*thir*[2] claid*eb* ngarmnae cach ae. No didlastáis finnae *for* usciu[3]. Lágen mór il-laim ind fir medónaig, *cóica* semmend trethe[4]. Dagere cuinge sesrige a crand fil indi. Cressaigthe*s* in fer medónach in lágin sin[6], ingi ná tíagat a hu*irc* ecgi[7] essi, 7 benaid ah hurlond[8] fria bais co fá thri. Lónchore mór ara mbélaib[9], méit chore colbthaige[10]. Dublind úathmar and : mesc*thus* béos isin duiblinn isin[11].

Mád chian co tairi a fobdud [LU. 95ᵇ] lassaid for a crand[12]. Indar-lat is derc[13] tentide bís i n-uacht*ur* in tige. Sama*ilte* lat sin, a Fir rogain.

The Room of Sencha and Dubthach and Gobniu son of Lurgnech.

128. « I beheld the room that is next to Conaire. Three chief champions, in their first greyness, are therein. As thick as a man's waist is each of their limbs. They have three black swords, each as long as a weaver's beam. These swords would split a hair on water. A great lance in the hand of the midmost man, with fifty rivets through it. The shaft therein is a good load for the yoke of a plough-team. The midmost man brandishes that lance so that its edge-studs (?) hardly stay therein, and he strikes the haft thrice against his palm. There is a great boiler in front of them, as big as a calf's caldron, wherein is a black and horrible liquid. Moreover he plunges it (the lance) into that black fluid. If its quenching be delayed

1. dia mballaib Eg.
2. sithidir Eg. sithigtir YBL. sithir St. F.
3. notescfaitis finna i n-agid srotha, Eg. no dedhlaistis finda for usciu, YBL. no dailastais finna *for* usce, St. no do ilsatáis F.
4. semand trea YBL seim*menn* credumai F. sema*nn* créduma St.
5. Cressaigis Eg. H¹. Cresaigthi YBL. cresaigthe St. cressaigthiu F.
6. moir sin YBL. St. F. mór sin Eg. mair sin H¹.
7. a huraicdi Eg. 121ᵃ 1. a huire cicgi YBL. a huire ecgi St. a huire eci F. apparently synonymous with *semmend* « rivets ».
8. haurlonn St. haurlond F.
9. ara bélaib Eg.
10. cholbthaigi YBL.
11. mescthar beos comenic in sleg mor isin dublinn sin Eg. mesc*thus* beo*us* isin duiblind sin, YBL. isi dublinn sin, St. isi dublin isin F.
12. Mad chian ctir nadá fothrucud sin dublassoig [leg. dub-lassaid] for a crund, Eg. for a crunn YBL. St.
13. draicc Eg drecc YBL. drech St. F.

it flames on its shaft (and then) thou wouldst suppose that there is a fiery dragon in the top of the house Liken thou that, O Fer rogain! »

129 Ni *anse* Tri láich ata dech gaibthe¹ gaisced i nHerind .i. Sencha macc alaind² Ailella 7 Dub*thach* Dóel Ulad 7 Goibnend macc Lurgnig³ *Ocus* ind Luin Cheltchair ma*i*c Uthidir⁴ forricht⁵ hi cath Maigi T*ui*red, iss í fil il-láim Duib*thig* Dúil⁶ Ulad Is bés di ind reb sin [do dénam, Eg] intan as apaig⁷ fuil námat do thestin⁸ di, is écen corc co neim dia fábdud⁹ intan f*r*isáil*ter* gnim gona duine di¹⁰ Manis-tairi sin¹¹, lassaid ar a durnd, 7 ragaid tria fer a himorchuir no tria chomdid¹² (nó chomsid) ind rigthaige. Mád fúasma¹³ doberthar di mairfid fer cach¹⁴ fúasma¹⁵ ó bethir ocond reib sin di ón t*r*áth co araile, 7 nisn-aidléba¹⁶. *Ocus* mád urchur¹⁷ mairfid nónbor cacha inchair¹⁸, 7 bid rí *no* rígdomna *nó* aire¹⁹ díbe*r*gae in nómad fer

Tong*u* a tonges²⁰ mo thúath, bid sochaide *for*sa ndailfe deoga tonnaid²¹ innocht ar dor*us* na Brud*ne* ind Luin [sin] Celtchair ma*i*c Guth*idir*²² Tong*u* do dia tonges²³ mo th*ú*ath, doto[e]tsat

1 gabthae YBL gaibthiu F (leg gaibte?) ata dech filet doneoch gabas, Eg
2 om St F
3 Luirggnig, St
4. Guithichair St F
5 in Luinb*an* Celtchair ma*i*c Guth*idir* frith Eg ind luin ba Celtchair [with *ud* written over *ac*] ma*i*c Uitheochair forricht, YBL 101ᵃ 34
6 Dail St
7 as n-apaid YBL is apaid F
8 thestin Eg testin YBL thesin LU thesstin St teistin H
9 badad St
10 dia bádud intan is arithi guin duimi di Eg dia badud intan frisailter etc F
11 Mani fagba in gai sin a frithalim ina fobairt neimi Eg 121ᵃ 2
12 coimtig Eg, choimtig YBL comtid St coimtid F
13 fúasnad Eg fuasma YBL fuismad St
14 cacha St cech F
15 fúasnaid Eg fuasma YBL St
16 nisnaidliba St YBL F
17. aurchur St YBL inserts legthar
18 cach urchara, YBL cach aurchora, St cech aurchara F
19 airig St F YBL aerech Eg
20 Tongusa a toing, St Tong a toing mo thuatha YBL
21 tonnaig YBL tondaidh F
22 Cuithechair St Cuithichair F
23 Tong do dia a toing, St F.

chét lasin triar sin ina cet*chumsclui*, 7 *conráinfe*[1] comgnim[2] fri cach triar isin Bru*din* innocht, 7 maid*fid* búaid ríg *nó* airig dibergae, 7 immaricfa el*ud* dóib.

Mairg iuras in n-org*ain*, for Lomna Drúth, cid fóbíthin in triir sin'

Ní cumcid, for Ingcél, 7r. *Ocus* iarsin cia acca and?

129. « *Easy to say Three heroes who are best at grasping weapons in Erin, namely, Sencha the beautiful son of Ailill, and Dubthach Chafer of Ulaid, and Goibnenn son of Luigneach And the Luin of Celtchar son of Uthider, which was found in the battle of Mag Tuired, this is in the hand of Dubthach Chafer of Ulaid. That feat is usual for it when it is ripe to pour forth a foeman's blood A caldron full of poison is needed to quench it when a deed of manslaying is expected Unless this come to the lance, it flames on its haft and will go through its bearer or the master of the palace (wherein it is). If it be a blow that is to be given thereby it will kill a man at every blow, when it is at that feat, from one hour to another, though it may not reach him. And if it be a cast, it will kill nine men at every cast, and one of the nine will be a king or crownprince or chieftain of the reavers*[3].

« *I swear what my tribe swears, there will be a multitude unto whom tonight the Luin of Celtchar will deal drinks of death in*

---

1 *conroindfe* Eg *conrainfed* YBL *conrainfe* St F.
2 caingnim F
3 This and the preceding paragraph suggested the following passage in Ferguson's *Conary*

« In hands of Duftach is the famous *lann*
Of Keltar son of Utechar, which erst
A wizard of the Tuath De Danann brought
To battle at Moy Tury, and there lost
Found after And these motions of the spear
And sudden sallies hard to be restrained
Affect it oft as blood of enemies
Is ripe for spilling, and a cauldron then
Full of witch-brewage needs must be at hand
To quench it, when the homicidal act
Is by its blade expected, quench it not,
It blazes up, even in the holder's hand,
And through the holder and the door-planks through
Flies forth to sate itself in massacre

So the spear of Diomede μα΄νεται ἐν παλάμῃσιν, Il, VIII, 111.

*front of the Hostel. I swear to God what my tribe swears that, in
their first encounter, three hundred will fall by that trio, and they
will share prowess with every three in the Hostel tonight. And they
will boast of victory over a king or chief of the reavers, and the
three will chance to escape.* »

« *Woe* », says Lomna Drúth, « *to him who shall wreak the
Destruction, were it (only) because of that trio!* »

« *Ye cannot* », says Ingcél, etc. « *And after that, whom sawest
thou there?* »

IMDA TRÍ N-AIT[H]ECH FER FALGA.

130. At*condarc* and imdae 7 triar inti. Triar fer fortrén feramail[1] fortamail nacha sella duini tairisethar fri án teóra dre-
cha éitchi. androchta[2]. a*s*a n-imómon imcissin úath. Imda-
tuigethar[3] celt clithargarb finna *con*nách a chuirp imcháit
agrind arruisc[4] roamnais, tría fróech finnu[5] ferb, cen étaige
imtuige co certsála sis. La téora monga echda uathmara ségda[6]
co slissu. laich luind lúatar claid*biu*[7] balcbéimnechu fri bib-
dadu. béim búrit[8] fri téora sústa iarndae[9] *con*a secht slabradaib
tredúalachaib tréchissi, *con*a secht cendphartib iarndaib[10] a[11] cind
cacha slabraidé. trummithir tinni deich [m]brudamna[12] cach
n-ae. Tri dondfir móra. Culmonga duba echda[13] foraib rosegat[14]
a ndí sáil. Dá ndagtrían[15] damseiche[16] [do chriss Eg.] im-me-

1. *om.* YBL. Eg.
2. anrachta YBL. androchta Eg. 112ᵃ 2.
3. Imdotuighedar F. imda guigethar YBL. *ocus* ma tuigethar Eg.
4. imcaither grinn a ruisc Eg. imchanag rind aruisc YBL. 101ᵇ 2. im chath agrind a ruisc, St.
5. finnfad Eg. finna St.
6. slega Eg. segtha YBL. segta St.
7. luatha ar claidbiu Eg. luath ar claidbiu YBL. St. F.
8. beim buirid YBL. beim bruit St. beim buirit F. Burait beim H¹.
9. iarnaidib Eg. iarn*ai*dhi H¹.
10. iárnaidib Eg. iarnduib St.
11. ar Eg. i YBL.
12. degbruithe damna Eg. degbhruite domna H¹. mbruit damnae YBL. deich bruthdamnæ St. deich bruthdamnai, F.
13. culmonga tiuga bah echda YBL.
14. no segat St.
15. Dagdoethan St. Dagduethan F.
16. rosegat aṅ druib damda damsheithi YBL. rosagat a ṅdí sáil fil dá ṅdag-trían damseche Eg.

dón cach ae, 7 it remithir¹ slíastae fir cech dubdrolom² cethairchoir forda-dúna³ ISs ed étach fil impu, celt⁴ asas tréu. Ro cessa trillse⁵ dia cúlmongaib, 7 sithrogait⁶ ía[i]rnd sithremithir⁷ cuing n-imechtair il-láim cach ae⁸, 7 slabrad⁹ iarind¹⁰ a cind cacha longe 7 pistul iairnd [LU. 96ᵃ] a[s] sithremithir¹¹ cuing n-úarmedóin¹² a cind cecha slabraid¹³, 7 atát ina mbruc¹⁴ isin tig, 7 is leór graim a n-imcisin. Ni fil isin tig ná beth ina foimtin¹⁵ Samailte lat sin, a Fir rogain.

The Room of the three Manx Giants

130 There I beheld a room with a trio in it Three men mighty, manly, overbearing, which see no one abiding at their three hideous, crooked aspects. A fearful view because of the terror of them. A . . dress of rough hair covers them, so that their bodies .. of their savage eyes through a ... of cows' hair, without garments enwrapping down to the right heels With three manes, equine, awful, majestic, down to (their) sides Fierce heroes who wield against foemen hardsmiting swords. A blow they give with three iron flails having seven chains triple-twisted, three-edged¹⁶, with seven iron knobs at the end of every chain : each of them as heavy as an ingot of ten smeltings (?). Three big brown men. Dark equine back-manes on them, which reach their two heels. Two good thirds of an oxhide in the girdle round each one's waist, and each quadrangular clasp

---

1 remir, St F YBL
2 ndubdrolam YBL dubdrolam St
3 foadúna YBL foduna F fosdúna Eg
4 gelt Eg
5 tri trillsi Eg
6 isead rogoet, YBL i sithrogait Eg
7 sithremir St YBL
8 7 ba sithremithir cuing n-imectraid in matlorg boi hi laim cach fir, Eg
9 is slabrad YBL
10 iairn YBL irainn Eg iarin St
11 sithremir St F
12 n-airmedoin Eg 112ᵇ 1   medoin F n-uarmedoin St n-uarmedoin YBL
13 cacha slabraid YBL St
14 it iat inna mbrucc YBL itaat inna brucce, St
15 Sic Eg YBL foditin LU Ni fil istig nad bed inna foimtin, St ina foimtin F nad beth inna foimtin YBL nach beith ina foimtin (i ina n-oircill) H
16 cis i facbar H 3, 18, p 627

— 125 —

that closes it as thick as a man's thigh. The raiment that is round them is the dress that grows through them[1]. *Tresses of their back-manes were spread, and a long staff of iron, as long and thick as an outer yoke (was) in each man's hand, and an iron chain out of the end of every club, and at the end of every chain an iron pestle as long and thick as a middle yoke. They stand in their sadness in the house, and enough is the horror of their aspect. There is no one in the house that would not be avoiding them. Liken thou that, O Fer rogain!* »

131. Sochtais Fer *rogain*. IS andsa damsa a samail. Ni fetursa [do feraib Erenn nach[2]] do[3] feraib betha manid hé in tríar aithech ucut ro anacht Cuchulainn hi forbais Fer Fálga[4], 7 ro marbsat cóecait láech oca n-anacol, 7 ní relic[5] Cuculainn ammarbad ar a n-ingantai[6]. At é a n-anmand in trír sin .i. Srubdairi mac Dordbruige[7] 7 Conchend[8] Cind Maige 7 Fiad sceme[9] macc Scipe. [Ros-cendaig Conaire do Coincaulainn ar gnoe. atat ina comair seom iarom — Eg.] Totoethsat tri chét léo ina cétchumscliu, 7 conrainfet[10] comgnim fri cach tríar i mBrudin, 7 día tuidch[is]et[11] foraib immach bid intechta tria criathar n-átha bar mbrúar lasin n-innas dofiurat[12] cusnaib sústaib iarind[13]. Mairg iuras in n-orgain cid fóbithin in trir sin, ar ni hilach[14] im ségond[15] 7 is cend arraic comrac friu.

1. i. e. the hair.
2. Sic Eg. *Om.* YBL.
3. di feraib Her*enn* nach di St. di feraib Eirenn na di feruib betha F.
4. Failge, St. Falgai YBL.
5. nir' leig, Eg. ni ro lic YBL. nir leice St.
6. n-ingantaige Eg. n-ingnathaigi YBL. n-ingnathchi, St. n-ingnaithche F.
7. Dorndbraige Eg. Duirn buidi YBL. Dornnbruige, St. Duirnn bruighe F.
8. Conchend (rucht 7 sciide) Eg. Concenn St. Conchenn F.
9. Fiad scimme Eg. Fiadh sceimhe F.
10. conroindfet Eg.
11. tuidchisead YBL. tuidchiset St. tuidcisett F.
12. dofiursatt F.
13. dia tisat foraib himach ragtháit tria chriathar n-átha for mbruirech minaigthe dogénat da bar corpaib immangébat dúib na sústa iarnaidhe, Eg. 121b 1—121b 2. So H[1]. with trifling variations.
14. sic YBL. Eg. armlach LU. facs.
15. segon St. F. soegond YBL. ségonn Eg.

Ní cumcid, for Ingcél. Nela fémmid dofortecat. Ocus iarsin cia acca and ?

131. Fer rogain was silent. « Hard for me to liken them. I know none (such) of the world's men unless they be yon trio of giants to whom Cúchulainn gave quarter at the beleaguerment of the Men of Falga, and when they were getting quarter they killed fifty warriors. But Cúchulainn would not let them be slain, because of their wondrousness These are the names of the three. Srubdaire son of Dordbruige, and Conchenn of Cenn marge, and Fiad sceme son of Scipe Conaire bought them from Cúchulainn for .., so they are along with him. Three hundred will fall by them in their first encounter, and they will surpass in prowess every three in the Hostel, and if they come forth upon you, the fragments of you will be fit to go through the sieve of a cornkiln, from the way in which they will destroy you with the flails of iron Woe to him that shall wreak the Destruction, though it were (only) on account of those three ! For to combat against them is not a « paean round a sluggard(?) » and is « a head of ... »

« Ye cannot », says Ingcél. « Clouds of weakness are coming to you etc. And after that, whom sawest thou there? »

Imda Da Dergae

132. Atcondarc imda n-aile and, 7 óenfer inte¹, 7 dá gilla arabélaib 7 di moing foraib, indala haí² is dub, alaile³ is find. Folt derg forsind láech 7 abrait deirg lais⁴ Da ngrúad chorcorda lais. Rosc roglas rocháin occa⁵ 7 brat úanidi immi. Léne gelchulpatach co nderginntlaid⁶ imbi 7 claideb co n-imdurnd⁷ dét⁸ ina laim, 7 airic an echtain⁹ cacha imdae isin tig

er findet das Befriedigen

---

1 indi, F Eg 112ᵇ 2 indti YBL
2 indala næ St indala noi F indara mong Eg
3 araili Eg araili YBL
4 da brai duba laiss, Eg brit derg lais, St abrat dere lais F
5 ina chind Eg
6 ndergindliudh Eg ndergindiud St. F ndergindled YBL
7 imdénum Eg
8 dét gen sg of a neuter dét, Thurneysen, KZ 37, 424
9 tairice frithalaim Eg. aricc arechtain YBL

di lind 7 bíud, ossé cossalach oc timthirecht in tslóig uli Samailte lat sin, a Fir rogain. »

The Room of Dá Derga.

132. « There I beheld another room, with one man therein and in front of him two servants with two manes upon them, one of the two dark, the other fair. Red hair on the warrior, and red eyebrows. Two ruddy cheeks he had, and an eye very blue and beautiful He wore a green cloak and a shirt with a white hood and a red insertion. In his hand was a sword with a hilt of ivory, and he supplies attendance of every room in the house with ale and food, and he quick-footed[1] in serving the whole host Liken thou that, O Fer rogain ? »

133. Rofetursa[2] inna firu[3] sin. Da Derga insain : is láis doronad in Bruden, 7 ó gabais[4] trebad ní ro[5] dúnait a doirse riam o dorigned, acht leth dia mbí in gáeth[6] is fris bís in chomla, 7 o gabais trebad ní tuccad[7] a chairi do thenid[8], acht no bíd oc bruith bid do feraib Herend Ocus in dias fil ara bélaib, dá dalta dosom in dá macc sin .i. dá macc ríg Lagen i Muredach 7 Corpri. Ocus totoethsat tri deichenbair[9] lasin tiar sin ar dorus a tigi[10], 7 maidfid búaid ríg [nó rigdamna — YBL] nó airig dibergae, 7 immaricfa elud dóib ass iarsuidi[u].

Céin mair noda-ainsed[11] for Lomna « Bá ferr búaid a n-anacail oldás búaid a ngona. Bátár anachtai[12] cid fóbíthin ind fir sin Bá túalaing a chomairgi in fer sin, for Lomna Drúth

---

1 incessant, O'Curry, M and C , III, 149 Coss-alach seems a compd of coss « foot » and alach, dat f Alich, Trip Life 340 cogn with Lat alacer
2 7 Rofetarsa in fer YBL Ni ansa Rofetarsa St Ni ansa Rofetursa F.
3. Rosfetarsa Eg
4. rogab Eg
5 Here ends St
6 acht in dorus o mbíd in goeth, Eg
7 tudchaid YBL tucad Eg
8. di thenid YBL
9 dofoethsat tri .x
10 an tigi YBL bruidni Eg
11 nodoansed LU cenmair noda-ainsed YBL 101b 49 Mairg turas in c. f i Eg
12 anachtae LU Ocus ba coir a n-anachul uili, Eg 112b 2 Ba hangta (.i. ba doilig) H¹.

Ní cumcid, for Ingcél. Néla¹ [rl.] *Ocus* iarsin *cia acca and?*

133. « *I know those men. That one is Dá Derga. 'Tis by him that the Hostel was built, and since it was built its doors have never been shut save on the side to which the wind comes — the valve is closed against it — and since he began housekeeping his caldron was never taken from the fire, but it has been boiling food for the men of Erin. The pair before him, those two youths, are his fosterlings, two sons of the king of Leinster, namely Muredach and Corpre. Three decads will fall by that trio in front of their house and they will boast of victory over a king or a chief of the reavers. After this they will chance to escape from it.*

« *Long live he who should protect them !* » *says Lomna.* « *Better were triumph of saving them than triumph of slaying them! They should be spared were it (only) on account of that man. 'Twere meet to give that man quarter* », *says Lomna Drúth.*

« *Ye cannot* », *says Ingcél.* « *Clouds etc And after that whom sawest thou there?* »

IMDA NA TRI NIAD A SIDIB.

134 Atcondarc and imdai 7 triar indi. Tri bruit dergae impu 7 teora léne² derga impu, 7 tri fuilt derga foraib. Derga uli *cona* fiaclaib³. Tri scéith derga úasaib Tri gái⁴ derga mallamaib Tri eich derga ina srianaib doib ar dorus Brudne⁵. Sam*aille lat sin, a Fir rogain*

Ni *anse.* Tri ma[id]⁶ dorónsat [LU. 96ᵇ] gói i sidib. Is i digal doratad foraib la ríg side, a n-orgain co fá thri la rig Temrach⁷. IS é rí dedenach lasa n-orgiter, la *Conaire* macc n-Eterscéli Aslúifet airib ind⁸ fir sin Do chomallad a n-orgni dodeochatár, sech ni genaiter ni génat nech. *Ocus* iarsin *cia acca and?*

---

1. Nellai feimid 7rl St
2. lente Eg
3 derga a fiacla Eg
4 slega Eg
5 ina srianaib leo ar dorus in tigi, YBL. ina srianaib doib for dorus tiche F
6 mid YBL 102ᵃ 5 Niaid F nnd Eg
7 n-Erenn Eg
8 na Eg ind YBL.